Cremains
of the Day

Misty
Simon

KENSINGTON BOOKS
http://www.kensingtonbooks.com

KENSINGTON BOOKS are published by

Kensington Publishing Corp.
119 West 40th Street
New York, NY 10018

Copyright © 2017 by Misty Simon

All Kensington titles, imprints and distributed lines are available at special quantity discounts for bulk purchases for sales promotion, premiums, fund-raising, educational or institutional use. Special book excerpts or customized printings can also be created to fit specific needs. For details, write or phone the office of the Kensington Special Sales Manager: Kensington Publishing Corp., 119 West 40th Street, New York, NY, 10018. Attn. Special Sales Department. Phone: 1-800-221-2647.

Kensington and the K logo Reg. U.S. Pat. & TM Off.

ISBN-13: 978-1-4967-1221-9
ISBN-10: 1-4967-1221-8
First Kensington Mass Market Edition: November 2017

eISBN-13: 978-1-4967-1222-6
eISBN-10: 1-4967-1222-6
First Kensington Electronic Edition: November 2017

10 9 8 7 6 5 4 3 2 1

Printed in the United States of America

Cremains
of the Day

To Daniel and Noelle,
who make it possible for me to write
and who encourage me endlessly.

Acknowledgments

A huge thank-you to my MTW girls, my Boot Squad and CPRW. I wouldn't be here without you. To the Klezwoods for providing music that got the fingers tapping away on the keyboard—your band is awesome! And to my beta reader, Tanya Agler, you rock! It takes a tribe to make a story come together and I have the best one out there. Thank you all!

Chapter 1

Why in the hell was it that no one seemed to be able to aim properly when it came to peeing in a toilet? I blew my hair out of my eyes as I cursed at whoever had the accuracy of a blind elephant. Anyone else might only give this a passing thought, but it was a significant question to me, since I was the one on my knees trying to clean around the bowl at my last house of the day.

"Tallulah, dear, are you almost done in there? I have the party guests coming at six and I'd like to be able to give them a clean house." Darla Hackersham hovered like a vulture waiting for me to keel over at the door of the downstairs powder room in her palatial house. I hated that she called me by my given name; I much preferred Tallie, but it was low on the fighting-over list.

"Almost done, Darla." Looking at the Swatch watch on my wrist, one of the few things I'd kept after the divorce, I stifled a groan. "It's not yet four. This is the last room I have to do. We should be good to go."

"Oh, thank heavens. I don't know what I'd do if anyone showed up with you here cleaning my toilets." She tittered; there really wasn't another word for it. To be honest, I wanted to gag her with my toilet brush, but figured the white handle sticking out of her mouth probably wouldn't go well with the black pearls she always wore.

Still, it was an appealing thought, and one I would never have had a year ago when we were still air-kissing buddies.

"All done," I said, rising from my knees by using my rubber-gloved hands to push on my thighs. Just shy of five-and-a-half feet in my sneakers, I was a far cry from the nearly five-nine I'd claimed back when my feet were never covered in anything but designer shoes with pointy toes and real leather.

"Oh, good! And just in time. Your check will be in the mail."

As Darla turned to walk away, I cleared my throat. Why did we always have to do this? "Ah, no, Darla, it won't, because you've had the bill for a month already. We agreed you'd pay me when I left today." I absolutely hated this part, except that I knew all about Darla's check in the mail. Somehow, it always got lost. It wasn't to the point where I'd start charging up front, yet, but it was a close thing.

For one, the socialite was one of the first people to take me up on my cleaning services shortly after my swan dive from grace. And for two, Darla had connections I couldn't afford to lose. Slowly but surely, I was putting money in my savings. When the dust had settled after my divorce, I was left with almost nothing. At the time I just wanted out, so I let his lawyer talk me into taking far less than half of our worth. But now I wanted security, and Darla's fat check was one step closer to freedom.

"Oh, dear . . . , I don't have my checkbook with me." Darla fluttered her hands at her throat as if nervous, but there was a sly glint in her eyes. She must have forgotten I knew all her habits and all of her dirty corners.

"It's right in the neat little drawer on the left-hand side of your desk."

Darla's eyes narrowed.

"The one in your private office," I added, just in case Darla had "forgotten."

She made a very inelegant snort while her fluttering hand briefly became a fist. I, however, wasn't backing down and could very easily mess up the house in record time. In fact, I still had a bucket of dirty water with bleach at my feet and wasn't afraid to use it. Nudging it with the toe of my old sneaker, I pointedly looked down at the brownish water, daring Darla to fight over the check. She stalked off toward the office without another word. Smart girl.

I used to be Darla. It was no coincidence I couldn't stand her now.

Smiling to myself, I rinsed out my rag, then wiped a tiny smudge off the frame of the gilt-edged mirror in the powder room off the kitchen. Darla had come to me when she and her husband had inherited more money from another dead relative and wanted the perfect showpiece of a house. Of course, now Darla only wanted me to clean all those fabulous new rooms. I could kick myself for telling her to add on. I didn't love cleaning, believe me. Then again, I didn't need to, as long as it paid the bills.

I looked at my watch again, timing Darling Darla. If she went more than five minutes without coming back, the dirty water was going to take a trip down the hall. If it happened to slosh a bit on the trip—well, that wasn't a crying shame.

At exactly five minutes, I lifted the bucket in a loose hand and set it to swinging in time with my steps. Not a drop came out, since I really didn't want to have to clean it all up again. Not to mention it would only prolong my time here and give Darla an excuse to not pay at all.

Raised voices, and something shattering halfway down the hall, sped up my steps. Setting down the bucket, I hustled along the antique runner done in reds and golds to match the wainscoting. When I reached the door to Darla's private office, it was closed and locked. Tugging on the door did nothing, but I still tried. The yelling escalated and I was able to distinguish only that there were two voices, nothing more. The words from the male voice were harsh, but in an accent or dialect I couldn't understand. For all I knew it might have been a different language. It was so garbled, it was hard to tell. What I did know was that Darren, Darla's husband, only spoke perfect Yankee English. I put my shoulder to the door and my mind to the task of breaking the sucker down if I had to.

Unfortunately, just as I was about to give it my all, the door opened in my hand, sending me face-first into the Aubusson rug that covered the gleaming wood floors. Rug burns were the least of my worries when a highly polished black and white shoe came straight at my face. Scrambling out of the way as quickly as I could, I narrowly missed being trampled as the shoe and its match went strolling out the door. Where was Darla?

Of course, I shouldn't have worried. The socialite was sitting as prim and proper as could be, writing out a check, which she then ripped out of the book. I, on the other hand, was fighting hard to not shake on the soft carpet. "Thank you for taking care of the house today, Tallulah. This is payment in full. Now, if you'll make sure to move your car, I really should go up and get dressed. I want to be ready when my guests arrive. Janet and Bob will probably be here first, and you know how they like to catch you off guard if they can. It's like a game to her, one I'm going to make sure I beat her at this time."

Placing the check on the floor next to my burning cheek, Darla strolled out of the room as if nothing had happened. How could she be so calm after that storm of yelling? I wasn't and the yelling hadn't even been directed at me. She left the door open behind her, a blatant invitation to leave.

I'm not ashamed to admit I took the invitation. Whatever Darla had going on was absolutely none of my business, even if I was burning with curiosity right along with my rug burn. Who was the person with the shiny shoes? What had he been yelling? Did Darla really think I hadn't heard anything and could just treat me as if I was invisible?

The answer to the first was unclear, but the answer to the second was never more apparent: I was the hired help, and the hired help did not get involved in the master or mistress of the house's business.

Well, at least the check was for the full amount, I thought as I glanced at it out of the corner of my eye. Now it was just a matter of getting my body up off the floor and cashing this baby before Darla had a chance to put a hold on it.

Scrambling to my feet, I scooped up the check. The bank was my next stop. Then I was going to get a coffee and a shower before heading to my second job, the one that paid the majority of the bills—and the one that created the majority of my problems.

After depositing the check at the bank ATM— I didn't trust Darla as far as I could throw her, which wasn't far at all, but I couldn't take the time to drive an hour to their bank to actually cash it—I stopped by the Bean There, Done That for a tall cup of something hot and severely caffeinated. I couldn't shake the feeling that something bad was going on within the walls of Darla's house. But it wasn't any of my business. Caffeine would definitely help me shake it off.

On a contact high from the delicious aroma of roasting beans and chocolate you could smell from the street, I floated through the door of the small redbrick building on the corner of Locust and Main. I could shut out everything wrong in my world when I stood in this place and inhaled as if I were back in second grade with the rubber cement.

Milk was steamed, orders were called out, money changed hands, and so did enormous amounts of pie and sticky buns. This was the ultimate small business run by a woman who knew what she was doing and how to do it all with a smile, a bounce of her short crop of dark curls, and olive skin. Of course, I might have been a little biased since the owner also happened to be my best friend, Gina Laudermilch. Gina had taken an old apothecary shop and turned it into the place to be for breakfast, lunch or dinner. She had live music on the weekends and book or poetry readings throughout the week. Because there were only seven booths and four two-seater tables, the place was always packed. Someday, I wanted to own the storefront next door and open a teahouse and herbal shop, but that was forever from now with the way my finances were going.

"Tallie Graver! Sit, sit, hon, and I'll bring you coffee." I'd taken my maiden name back and still wasn't used to hearing it. Graver, not a bad last name, but coming from a family of funeral directors made me a sure target in elementary school. And that was Gina's mom, Shirley, with her slight accent left over from the old country. Or so she said. As far as I could tell, the woman had lived in the United States her whole life, and the accent reminded me of the South more than some

European country. But I could have been wrong. Which wouldn't have been anything new.

"Can I have a cruller too?" I yelled to Gina. Her mom would never be able to hear over the steaming milk machine. The woman was notoriously semi-deaf, especially when you were saying something she didn't particularly want to hear.

Gina nodded and put a cruller on one of her bright purple plates in front of me. The scent of still-warm glaze rose up to greet my nose. Doughnuts, the nectar of the gods.

I dug right in, mindful of the time, but not what this sugary sweet was going to do to my hips. As long as I fit into my standard black skirt and one of my pastel blouses, I would be just fine. Shirley put a chocolate whoopie-pie latte down in front of me just as I swallowed my first bite of the cruller. The service was almost as good as the doughnut.

Shirley planted herself in the chair across from me with her elbows anchored on the table. She didn't resemble Gina in the least. With frosted blond hair and skin as white as a piece of chalk, the matriarch of the Laudermilch family wore enough makeup to keep any makeup-counter attendant in commissions for a lifetime. "So, I heard through the grapevine that you're doing the Fletcher funeral tonight. Gina's doing the catering, you understand. You're gonna come and help her, right?"

She wasn't going to leave until I answered her, and I couldn't answer her before I finished my sip of coffee. "Mmm-hmm." I scalded my tongue, but it didn't stop me from taking another sip. "I'll be over following the viewing to help her set up for after the funeral. Did you need something or were you just checking?"

"Oh, I don't need nothing, honey. My stories are on tonight, and I don't want to miss them. You know how I like to watch my stories."

"Sure do." Everything in life was scheduled around her stories. The local gossip and television were the two loves of Shirley's life, right after her daughter. Gina had tried to teach her again and again how to use a DVR, but she never seemed to learn. As for the local gossip, there was no help for that. Gina was well on her way to following in her mom's steps, but I loved her like the sister I'd never had anyway.

"Fine, then. I guess I'll take Gina up on her offer to miss tonight's job after all. You take care of you, Tallie. I don't want to hear about no trouble tonight. Got it? Gina has to be able to count on her friends. We don't want a repeat of your last snafu. You understand?"

"I do."

"And get some cream for that patch on your face. You want to look pretty when you're serving food, not like you just went a round or two with a cheese grater."

I put a hand to my cheek and groaned. The rug burn I thought wouldn't show was showing. I'd have to see how bad it was.

It was like having a second mother. But I just smiled and nodded as Shirley creaked to her feet and left the table to go behind the counter again. I caught Gina's eyes and rolled my own. Gina returned the gesture, making a motion like she was brushing lint off her shoulder. Yeah, I'd brush it off, since the only time I hadn't come through for Gina was about twelve years ago when we were fifteen, but Mama Shirley couldn't seem to let it go.

Severely caffeinated from the sweetness and caffeine of the whoopie-pie latte and stuffed with homemade cruller, I dropped off my plate at the counter and waved on my way out. With that, I trotted across the road to the brick monstrosity standing next to the local fire station where I had essentially grown up.

It wasn't a house, but a business with a discreet plaque letting everyone know it was first opened in 1910. My family had been running the business since then. It was a point of pride for my father, but a bone of contention between us. My one brother had chosen yard maintenance along with general handyman work and the other was a funeral director like my dad, destined someday to take over the family business. Which had left me free to marry Waldo and make babies, according to my mother. Except now the marriage was over, my mother had no grandbabies, and my father was hinting very heavily that I should come work full-time for him and my brother. Which was not going to happen if I could in any way avoid it.

He kept promising me a raise if I'd step up to full-time, but I was having none of it. With my wages here, my wallet was tight, but I had wanted to keep out from under my parents' rule. So, I'd made the tough decision to take on cleaning my former friends' houses to supplement my income.

As I walked into the brick tunnel covering the

driveway, I counted the days until I could be done with the cleaning jobs and concentrate solely on filling out reams of paperwork to run my own business. Too many at this point to be happy, but it was better than nothing.

And, despite the fact I'd once gotten trapped in a coffin in the basement, I didn't mind living with the other, better memories to be had at the family business.

At least my dad had let me rent the small apartment above the parlor. Long ago, my grandfather had lived up there with his whole family. When my parents had married, my mother had nixed that idea before it even entered my father's mind. Living above dead people wasn't my dream come true, either. However, I couldn't ask for better or quieter neighbors.

I strolled by one of the two hearses my father had on hand as I got myself into funeral mode. The behemoth cars were all black with silver scrollwork, very tasteful and beautiful in their own way, but they weren't for everyone. As lovely as they were, it had been traumatizing to have to take my driver's test in one of the big boats. Most likely, the Department of Motor Vehicles employee at Penn DOT had been scarred for life too, since shortly after the momentous event he became a clown in the circus that had come through the next town over.

I barely made it through the door before I was hit by the whirlwind that was my mother.

"Hi, baby! How was your day? The bathroom's all ready for you, sweetheart. I know how hard it is to clean all those floors. I don't understand why you do that when you could just as easily have taken a loan from me. You shouldn't have dishwater hands when you used to direct the help."

Karen Graver was in fine form today as she rambled on, trailing along behind as I went through the side door and straight to the office and bath in the back of the building. She must have been waiting at the door, which wasn't unusual even if it was unnecessary.

It was the same litany every time: Why didn't I let her help financially? Why did I have to make things so much harder for myself? Why was I a working stiff instead of sitting in the lap of luxury? Why hadn't I provided her with at least one grandbaby to dote on since my brothers were probably never going to settle down?

The first two were easy enough. My dad would not look kindly on me taking money from my mom. Especially since my mom wouldn't tell him until some argument came up and she threw it in his face. It was bad enough I lived above the parlor. Even though I insisted on paying rent, my mom never actually cashed the checks. I did not want to be tied to her apron strings, not even with a piece of thread. Living on their dime and taking their money would have made it a rope of steel wire.

The third? That was a question I could and couldn't answer. I wasn't in the lap of luxury because my ex-husband had fought me at every turn for every dime until I just wanted out and took almost nothing with me. He'd gotten the house, most of its contents, and the mortgage.

We hadn't had savings, even though he was an investor, because he had done his best to prove that the rest of the cash had gone to living the life he was accustomed to. I hadn't realized how outside our means we had been living until the divorce was finalized. But now it was over. I could concentrate on going back to the basics, and he could hang himself with all his debt if he wanted.

And the last? Waldo had been a terrible husband. No one could convince me he would have rocked the whole dad thing.

My mother continued to talk while I showered. I could have run upstairs and used my own bathroom; however, I was on a tight schedule. I pushed her out of the room, but the woman carried on the conversation through the door as if we were standing right next to each other. I only hoped no one was in the building except the two of us. What had happened was common knowledge, but the talk about me had died down about a week ago. Thanks went to Muriel Galdon, who was seen streaking down Main Street in nothing but her eighty-year-old birthday suit. I didn't want to be in the spotlight again.

Finally, when I stepped out of the shower into a fluffy towel, I realized she would happily flap her jaws for the entire time I was going to be here. Whipping open the door, I looked her in the eye and said, "Don't you think we ought to get to work so that the funeral will be one Dad can be proud of? You know how he is about his three I's of a funeral."

Karen flitted around for a second, a butterfly with nowhere to land. Her hair was the same honey blond it had been since I could remember: Clairol number 102. The clothes and the scent of gardenias were all the same too. I loved her more than anything in the world, but she needed to find somewhere to land before I dove right off my rocker.

"Yes, Daddy has a list of things. It's a mile long and has everything but the kitchen sink on it."

I hated when she called my dad that. Even I didn't anymore, not since I was eight. He was just Dad to me. His name was Bud to the rest of the world. I would be okay with Bud or even "your dad," but "Daddy" made me cringe. She patted her pants for a second until she got an *aha* look on her face and reached into the front of her blouse to pull a folded piece of paper from her bra. I mentally rolled my eyes, since actually rolling them would only set her off on the lecture circuit. Ah, family dynamics. I understood them better than most.

"Why don't you take the list then and get to work on your stuff?" I asked. "I'll get to mine, and we'll both be done in plenty of time."

"All righty, Miss Mighty. See you on the flip-side."

Was it any wonder I constantly wanted to roll my eyes?

"The flipside it is." I saluted my mom and, after getting dressed, went to my own tasks, which never changed. I didn't need a list to tell me the flowers needed spritzing with an atomizer to make them look fresher; the ones that had died or were brown at all pulled out. The keepsake programs needed fanning out in a tasteful display. Tissues from the closet needed to be pulled out and set strategically around the room and the front foyer, for those who did not think to bring any of their own or had gone through all of the ones they had brought. A light floral spray was applied to the air, unless someone specifically let the staff know they had those who were allergic to such things.

The list went on and on. My dad printed one out for every funeral and made me go down it with a red pen, initialing all the things I knew by heart.

In the end, I pulled it together in record time except for one missing funeral spray of flowers that should have been delivered earlier today. I couldn't find it anywhere, but the time came when I couldn't stay on hold for another minute and still get the rest of my list done. The flowers would have to stay lost until after the funeral, when I could call Monty again and bitch him out for the lack of a delivery.

Running a hand down the black knee-length skirt my father demanded I wear, I then smoothed the waist of the sea green–scooped neck blouse I had on. No wrinkles were allowed here at the Graver Funeral Home. It was rule number four behind the three I's of funeral directing: Indulge, Inter, and Inspire. My father lived by those words. Indulge the deceased's family, inter the body, and inspire all attendees to want to use us for their future funeral needs. The outfit was part of the third I as well as its own rule. Not exactly my idea of nice clothes, but it did lend a similarity to the staff, since we all wore the same thing with different-color blouses of the same cut.

Finally things were set, and thank goodness or I never would have heard the end of it. I was standing ready at the front door when the grieving family came rushing in.

Betty Fletcher's husband was the man in the casket, and she came in last with a tissue tucked into the sleeve of her lacy white shirt with its big bow at the collar. It was a look from the seventies and so was her hair. She'd been stuck there since . . . well, since the seventies. She'd never moved past her own thirties despite the fact she was as out of date as chunky milk.

"Betty, I'm so sorry for your loss." I took the other woman's cold hands and put on a sincere expression. It wasn't much of a stretch. I would sincerely miss Mr. Fletcher. He had been the one to teach me how to ride a bike for the first time, and he was always good for a hard candy in the breast pocket of his short-sleeved dress shirt, no matter what time of year it was. Just thinking about it made me smile.

The rat-a-tat-tat of my black pumps was muffled when we moved from the plank flooring of the foyer onto the plush, rose carpeting of the viewing room.

This was the most important part: I had checked in on Mr. Fletcher shortly after he'd been brought in. Despite my father trying to get me involved in every aspect, I had nothing to do with preparing the body, dressing it, doing the makeup, or making sure the jaw remained closed. But I had wanted to spend a quiet moment with him before the family got here. He had looked so at peace as I'd said my personal good-bye. And I would say another one now, apparently. I didn't have much choice. Mrs. Fletcher was dragging me down the aisle between a hundred chairs like I was a barge being tugged along behind her chugging tug-boat.

Even though I had checked in with him earlier, it could still be hard to see someone who had been so full of life the week before now lying on a white-satin background in his best clothes. The rose-colored cosmetic lights in the ceiling gave him some color in his lifeless face. Yes, he looked peaceful, but he shouldn't be peaceful. He should be up, offering me candy.

As part of the staff here at Graver's, I would not cry, so I cleared my throat, patted Mrs. Fletcher's hand, and backed away with some mumbled excuse about tissues.

The first I in funeral directing: Indulge the client, not yourself.

Escaping to the foyer, I composed myself again with deep breaths and a few head rolls. I could do this. I would do this until I could pay my own way.

I nodded to my brother Jeremy as I walked out the doors to make sure the memory book was straight and take a second for another deep breath.

Catering after the funeral was not really my forte, either, but at least during this job I got to hang with Gina.

And here, in the fire station next to Graver's, we were having a grand old time. The stories were fairly flying around the big hall in front of the garage where they kept the engines. Gina had gone for simple and very Pennsylvanian for the former fire chief and all-around good guy. We had pork and sauerkraut, pigs in a blanket, chicken with gravy on waffles, chicken corn soup, and lots and lots of bread. Dessert was Mr. Fletcher's favorite thing in the world, whoopie pies.

Mr. Fletcher had retired over twenty years ago as fire chief, but the old guys sitting in the back corner with their chairs in a circle and their canes resting on the backs, talked as if it were just yesterday the man had run into a burning building to save someone. That someone had turned out to be a former girlfriend, who promptly kissed him. They fell back in love that day and were married for fifty-six years. And she had told him up until the last fire he'd run that he best not save any of his other former girlfriends, because she was not going to be left for some fire tramp.

Mrs. Fletcher heard the story being told and joined them to put her own embellishments on the tale. One man with a walker, but looking spry enough to be sixty, rose from his chair and held it for her to sit down.

At that moment, Gina waved for me to come over to the kitchen on the left-hand side of the hall. She wasn't subtle about it, either, and if I didn't hustle, she would start yelling at any moment. I hustled to her side because several police officers had just walked in to say good-bye to the deceased. Since they traveled in packs, I was pretty sure my least favorite person, Chief of Police Burton, wouldn't be far behind, and I wanted to avoid him at all costs if possible.

"We need more sauerkraut. Can you hold down the fort, keep the sausages going until I get back? I have another tub back at the shop, but I don't have anyone I can send to go get it."

She was already untying her apron when I said, "I can go get it. There's no need for you to leave when you're the one with the cooking smarts. Just give me the keys and I'll be right back."

I was so thankful she didn't hesitate to dip her hand into her pocket for the keys. As kids, we'd been inseparable. Once Waldo came along, I'd been stupid enough to drop all my friends who didn't fit in with my new status.

Waldo, whose real name was Walden Phillips III, absolutely hated that I called him Waldo. It made my day every time.

Anyway, once I'd moved out of Waldo's house, I'd started working on reestablishing those relationships I had let slip when I was Mrs. Phillips III. There was no denying I had been a stuck-up bitch during those years. Gina hadn't been in the mood to deal with me at first. Yet, when I had called and eaten crow for the second time, it had been as if no time had passed, leaving me extremely thankful Gina hadn't made me eat crow a third time. I didn't blame her for giving me a hard time at first, because I had a lot of mistakes to make up for.

I put my hand out and Gina held the keys for just a second longer than she had to.

The moment was here and gone within the space of two heartbeats. I counted them as I held my breath. Gina handed over the keys with a smile and a nod. "It's in the refrigerator in the back next to the walk-in freezer. You shouldn't have any trouble finding it: Follow your nose."

"Be right back, then." Now I was the one who removed my apron, grabbed my coat from its hanger, and strode out into the chilly night. The temperature had dropped since the gravesite part of the ceremony, while the wind had picked up. It was almost cold for a September night. Dipping my face into the collar of my jacket, I picked up the pace to trot along the sidewalk. Fortunately, Bean There, Done That was not far away, only catty-corner across Main Street. I jaywalked, I admitted it, but nearly anyone who would have thought to arrest me for breaking the law was back at the fire hall, so I wasn't too worried.

Shoving my hands deeper into my pockets, I took the final few steps to the front door. Something did not feel right about the place, but I shook it off as residual funeral pall. I made a mental plan for which light switch I would reach for and how I'd get back to the refrigerator. Although I knew the layout pretty well from the many times I had helped Gina close down for the night, I didn't want to wander around in the dark.

Unlocking the front door with fumbling hands, I pushed through with my shoulder. Blessed warmth enveloped me. Standing in the darkened doorway for a couple of seconds, I let the warmth infiltrate my every pore, or at least the ones it could reach with my jacket on. I reached to the right and flipped the switch to turn on the overhead lights. And screamed.

Chapter 2

"What in the heck are you doing here?" I nearly jumped out of my skin once I recognized Gina's cousin, Katie Mitchner. Even with the other woman facing away from me, there was no mistaking the bright red hair or the tattoo winding around from the side of her neck, then down her arm to take on the look of a sleeve.

She was draped across the wooden café table with her hair swept to the side and her head on her arm as if she was taking a rest. Her wrists and hands disappeared over the side of the small wood table. When she didn't stir at the sound of my voice, I spoke again, louder this time. "Hey, Katie! Wakey, wakey, eggs and bakey!"

Still nothing.

I walked around the table to get a good look at the other woman's face. Maybe Katie was drunk again and had come here to pass out. I couldn't imagine Gina had let her cousin in and then let her stay when the shop was closed for the funeral, but stranger things had happened.

Four steps took me in front of Katie, where I got that good look, and took two stumbling steps back, crashing into the table behind me. I should call the police. Right now.

I had my phone in my hand to do just that when Katie's eyes popped open and she started yelling behind the tape over her mouth.

Okay, first I would find out what she was doing in here, then I would call the police.

Katie's eyes widened and the garbled words increased in volume as I grabbed the edge of the silver duct tape covering her mouth.

"Sorry," I said before I yanked, thankful Katie was awake and alive enough to scream bloody murder.

While she took great big, gulping breaths, I patted her back and said all those nonsensical things people were supposed to say when someone has been traumatized. Unfortunately, while I had plenty of experience dealing with the bereaved, I had almost no experience with the traumatized still-living. I couldn't pat Katie's hand and give her a tissue and offer her solace for her grief. Unless she wanted to mourn the unfortunate caterpillar of hair I'd pulled off her upper lip.

Instead, I fumbled around and finally said, "I hope it didn't hurt too much."

"Christ Almighty, Tallie, it hurt like a bitch. I guess I won't have to go to Andrea's shop this week for my lip wax appointment."

She was joking, which had to be a good thing, I thought, until I saw the way Katie's arms shook on the table. "I should call the police."

"No!" she yelled, then seemed to pull herself back under control. "I mean, not yet. I just need a minute before people come storming in here."

I thought that was an odd response, but she was an odd person, and since all the cops I knew were over at the fire station, I figured I could indulge her request if only to get some more info for Gina. "Do want me to call Gina over? She's just across the street." I even pointed out the front window as if Katie had no idea where the firehouse was.

I might get family dynamics, but human interaction wasn't necessarily one of my strong points.

Katie shook her head, holding up her hands. They were bound too. Yikes.

"Can you just get these off me and maybe not take any more hair this time? Free lip wax I can live with, but bare arms not so much."

Quickly working the end of the yellow rope holding Katie's wrists together, I kept a close eye on not stripping the fine hairs from the other woman's forearms. The knots weren't hard to get at, which made my job that much easier. I stepped back as Katie stood and shook out her hands.

"Wow, my arms are tingling."

I hadn't thought the knots were tight enough to actually cut off the circulation, but what did I know? I had no idea how long she had been sitting there, passed out. But maybe I should find out along with whether someone had taken anything from Gina's shop while I gave Katie a couple minutes to compose herself. Gina was not going to be a happy camper, no matter how this all worked out.

"What happened?" I asked. As I waited for an answer, I began prowling around the shop, making sure the coffee maker and the milk steamer were all in their correct places. I didn't have a key to the register, but knew Gina cleaned it out every day after closing the shop. Somewhere she had a safe. I didn't know where that was and didn't need to know. The only thing I saw out of place were some napkins strewn across the wood counter Gina stood behind six days a week. That wasn't enough to spark my curiosity.

Using the back of her wrist, Katie swiped her big hair off her forehead, then looked at me from the corner of her eye. "Obviously, I was tied up and left for dead."

Katie had always been the lead in any drama put on the stage or acted out in real life. I tried to shove down my skepticism. There was no refuting that Katie had been tied up. I would just leave the "left for dead" part alone.

"Okay, but who tied you up and how did you and they get in here?" The logical question seemed to stump her for a second. Perhaps I was being too harsh. Katie could be dealing with shock and I just couldn't see the outward signs due to her bravado.

"I don't know who tied me up. I was in the back alley on my way in for a few things Gina had asked me to pick up earlier, when all of the sudden I see this guy lying at my feet about a yard away from the door. I bent down to see if he was just sleeping off a drunk when another guy looms out of the darkness and shoves me into the store. He tied me up and told me to shut up when I told him I wouldn't say anything if he'd just walk away without hurting me. And then he duct-taped my mouth shut and left out the back door."

Since my cellphone was still in my hand, I bent to unlock it before Katie drew her next breath. A body in the alley and a tied-up woman in the café was not good, no matter how it happened. I should have called the police the first time I'd mentioned it instead of letting Katie talk me into waiting. Due to my anxiety over the whole situation, I fumbled the six simple numbers of my password three times. Sure, I'd been running on adrenaline and afraid Katie wasn't breathing, but that was not going to be a good enough excuse to keep Chief of Police Burton from railing at me for my failure to do the right thing the first time.

"I think you're going to want to check out the guy in the back alley before you call anything in," Katie said, interrupting my attempt to dial.

I paused to peer at her in disbelief. She had been tied up and "left for dead" in her own words, and there could be a body out in the back alley. What more could she possibly want to talk about before I got the authorities involved? "Why would I want to do that?"

"Because I'm pretty sure your ex-husband is lying out there dead."

What? I couldn't have heard her right. Waldo would never come to this part of town and certainly not to the alley. As far as the *dead* part—he might not be the best of people, but I couldn't imagine anyone would actually take the time and energy to kill him. What the hell could he have done to deserve to die out there?

I was not proud of that last thought. But there had been a lot going on in our marriage I had not known about. Perhaps this was just one more thing I should have been prepared for when the preacher had said *for better or worse*. Waldo's worse gave a whole other meaning to the phrase.

"Wait," I said, not wanting to go off half-cocked or call in some vague, possible crime based solely on a "pretty sure" from the town's drama queen. "Are you not sure if it's Waldo, or not sure if he's dead?"

"Both. Either." She shrugged.

I dialed the next four numbers for my password and got it right on my fourth try. After hitting speed dial number six, I kept the phone to my ear as I headed for the back of the store and the door out to the alley. I wouldn't touch anything, I promised myself. I shouldn't have touched Katie at all to begin with and would probably get my ass figuratively handed to me for that once the police got here. Not to mention, I had seen enough crime-scene investigation television to know not to incriminate myself. But I had to make sure it really was Waldo out there, or make sure it wasn't. If it wasn't, I was going to bean Katie on the head and maybe stick some duct tape to her eyebrows. See how she liked that impromptu wax for giving me heart palpitations.

Using one of the messy napkins from the counter, I turned the knob on the back door and pushed slowly. I didn't know where exactly the body was located. I certainly didn't want to smash whoever the poor sucker was in the head with the door. He might not be dead at all, but regardless, I was not going to add insult to injury.

"Police station, what can I do for you?"

I stopped in the open doorway and gave Suzy at the police station the lowdown of what had happened, or what I had been told happened. Suzy told me to stay on the phone. I heard a beep and took the phone away from my face long enough to see who on earth was calling. Great. Gina. She was probably wondering where in the hell her sauerkraut was.

"Suzy, I have to answer this call. I'll get right back to you."

"Chief's not going to like it."

"Tell Burton it couldn't be avoided."

I clicked over and didn't get a chance to open my mouth before Gina said, "Sauerkraut, Tallie. I have about twenty-five people wanting more sauerkraut with their sausages and you know how I don't like to disappoint customers."

"Yes, well . . . Gina. We have a bit of a crisis over here and quite honestly, sauerkraut is about the last thing on my mind at this point. I think Waldo might be dead out in your back alley and your cousin was recently tied up and duct-taped inside your café. You might want to send someone else over for the food while I wait here for the police."

Gina had been squawking nonsensically the whole time I had been talking, but once I took a breath she jammed herself into the conversation.

"What in the hell is going on?"

"I think I just explained it pretty succinctly." In my edginess over the whole situation I adopted formality to keep myself from the shakes. "I'm waiting for the police and you need to send some-one else for the sauerkraut. I have to go now so I can call Suzy at the police station back. Talk to you soon." I hung up because another call was beeping in my ear again. I almost never used this thing and now all of a sudden I was as busy as a New York City switchboard operator from the 1940s.

It looked like I wouldn't have to call Suzy back. Suzy was calling me.

"You haven't gone out back yet, have you?" Suzy asked in lieu of a greeting.

I had my foot raised to cross the threshold and kept it hesitating there while I said nothing. Should I stay or should I go now? Old song, but very pertinent question. I decided to step out in-stead of back in. If Waldo was out there, I wanted to see it with my own eyes, not just go on Katie's sketchy information.

"Chief is coming down right now. He was out on another call, but he's about two minutes away. You do not want to be caught in that alley, honey."

"Then I won't get caught." I hung up on her before more warnings could be issued. I had about a minute to scope things out. The limited time could go very fast.

Leaving the door opened behind me, I stepped out into the alley, then cursed the tall floodlight for being blown. The town was supposed to take care of these kinds of things, but they didn't always worry so much when it was downtown with other lights in the vicinity. Of course, the pool of darkness was exactly where I could see a faint outline of something lying on the ground.

Did I really want to see Waldo dead? I mean, I didn't like him and near the end of the divorce I'd had a few inappropriate thoughts about wanting to see him thrown off a bridge. But that had just been frustration and hatred for the way he'd treated me. I wouldn't have really ever wanted to see anything like that. This was different, though. If he was really dead out back, I didn't think I wanted to see him like that. I had a hard enough time with cleaned-up corpses in the funeral home who looked like they were only sleeping.

Couldn't I just wait for the police to come and have them tell me themselves what had happened?

But Waldo and I had been married for six years, and I wanted to know if it really was him out back of the shop he would never have stepped one expensively-shod foot into.

Thankfully, Gina kept a small flashlight on the keychain for the shop. With trepidation and shaking fingers, I pressed the button, then had a hard time keeping the light on. It flickered over the scene before me like a weird rave strobe.

Yep, it was definitely Waldo. His hair was standing up from his forehead in a way that would have appalled him and had him scurrying to the bathroom for another dose of gel. I acknowledged that was a totally inappropriate thought when I could be staring at my dead ex-husband, but I also knew I was just trying to deal with the shock. Other than being crumpled against the wall, nothing else looked out of place. His suit was perfectly straight on his tall frame. His tie was not even askew.

And as much as I had ignored orders to stay out of here, I certainly wasn't going to touch him and disturb the scene when it was obvious something foul-playish had happened.

I was about to step back into Bean There when flashing blue and red lights streaked the alley wall. It cast the whole place in an eerie light, a surreal light where I would have sworn I saw Waldo's chest jerk. Foul-playish or not, if Waldo was breathing then I was not going to leave him out here.

Running back out into the alley, I put my hand on his throat and came up with a pulse. "Hurry!" I yelled down the alley. "He's still breathing and I have no idea where he's hurt!"

In the end, Gina got her sauerkraut and a bunch of other stuff she carried from the refrigerator of Bean There herself. She set up a food operation at the fire station and fed people for the several hours it took to "canvas the scene," as Burton said. A lot of the funeral-goers were on various law-enforcement teams in the area, and they all trooped over in their Sunday best to see if they could help. Burton liked his fresh coffee as much as the next person and was trying to get things taken care of quickly so Gina could open in the morning for her regulars. The fact that Gina's mom was his cousin probably didn't hurt, either.

I stayed back to fill coffee cups that were then

gripped tightly in busy hands and dish up more bowls of chicken corn soup than I thought we had people. My mom brought over the slow cooker and started up her famous chili, while several other women also brought theirs with a variety of things just warmed from their freezers.

"Emergency rations," Erma Kettleman said as she staked out one corner of the folding table to set up ham-and-bean soup and a basket of fresh-made bread. A lot of the town had wandered down this way once they heard the sirens going and saw the flashing blue and red lights. They weren't necessarily nosy . . . No, that's not true: They were very nosy and not ashamed of it.

"I heard tell that's your husband out there." Lonny Jenkins was not my favorite person in town and had made that distinction for me when we were in seventh grade and he asked me to the winter formal just to win a bet for ten bucks. He lost when I said no, but still.

"Ex-husband," I said and turned my back to talk to Gina. "Make sure you pick up the donation jar and empty it. We don't want anyone to accidentally walk off with any of the money." I faced Lonny again and gave him my biggest, fakest smile. "Did you need something else?"

He frowned. "Just a sausage."

"Coming up. Make sure you leave something in the donation jar."

It was about nine when Chief of Police James Burton came through the big front double doors of the firehouse. He tried to make a beeline for me, yet kept getting waylaid. I wondered if this was divine intervention for me to have time to sneak out the back. The thought died quickly because he was in front of me before I could make a run for it.

"Need to talk to you, girl. Take off the apron and meet me in that blue salon thing your dad has on the first floor." His silvering hair fairly bristled on his head, and his mustache vibrated with his intensity. Just under six feet tall and fit, he was a few years past fifty, and thought I was a nuisance to society at large.

I did not want to meet him in the blue salon, even though it was one of our prettiest. But Burton had already walked away, back through the throng of people trying to get some juicy piece of gossip no one else had so they would seem in the know.

I had a feeling I was about to get more of an earful than I had ever hoped for.

I took off the apron with a sigh.

"It's going to be okay," Gina said, resting a hand on my shoulder. "I know you didn't love Waldo anymore, but it still has to be weird to find him in an alley all unconscious and stuff."

"You're telling me."

"Just go see what Burton wants, honey; don't sweat it. I'll corral everyone out of here. I'm about out of food, anyway. I have no idea what I'm going to serve at the Bean tomorrow. Did we empty out the fridge?"

"Not entirely." I placed the stained apron on the foldout table and looked longingly at all the cleanup that had to be done. I could stay and ignore Burton's summons. Of course, it wouldn't get me anywhere but yelled at, no matter how tempting. However, I'd rather be covered in the smell of sauerkraut pots than face the truth of what had happened this evening. Finding Waldo in that alley might be something I could never forget.

And tomorrow I might be reminded endlessly of the encounter because I had houses to clean and was almost positive my various employers were going to have a ton of questions. It was one of their own who had been jumped, or mugged, or something.

They'd be curious. And despite the fact that I was back on the wrong side of the tracks, they'd try to pump me for information. Not to mention, he'd been in a dark alley by himself, presumably. It was not going to be a happy day. Oh, man. Darla was first up on my list of people to clean for after her party this evening. Questions would be inevitable.

My uncle Sherman, resident giant at six-foot-six and the current head of the fire department, came over as I was walking around the corner of the table heading to the funeral home.

"Don't keep Burton waiting, Tallie. The guy's a son of a bitch, but hopefully he'll know what he's doing this time. As much as I dislike Waldo, I hope he pulls through, though I wouldn't mind if he was maimed." He rested a beefy hand on my shoulder.

The attitude reminded me there was bad blood between the two heads of our emergency-services departments. I knew why Burton didn't like me, but had no idea what the deal was with Uncle

Sherman. Good God, was this day never ever going to end?

"That's not funny, Sherman." Although better maimed than dead.

As I walked out the front doors of the firehouse, I made the right turn on the relatively quiet sidewalk to see what the chief of police wanted. None of it was going to be to my liking. Waldo and I had been lawfully divorced for two months, but officially separated for about six months before that. I had no idea why he had been out in the alley, and none as to why Katie had been tied up in the store. It was too much to think it was a coincidence, but I was having a hard time thinking of Katie and Waldo being together. Unless, of course, he was back on the "wrong side of the tracks" again, as his mother had said when he started dating me.

With my head down, I stared at the familiar cracks in the sidewalk while I dragged my feet over the ten yards separating me from the front door of the funeral parlor. And because I was doing everything I could to drag out the time before I had to meet Burton, I did not see anyone on the sidewalk with me until I nearly toppled a guy standing on the stairs of Graver's.

He had dark hair and wore a light coat in nondescript dark blue. From the stitching on the jacket, I knew he was from the flower shop, but only Dobbins ever delivered to us, and this was certainly not a smiley twenty-year-old kid. This one was all man. He was scowling and had fierce dark eyebrows to match his dark hair. I couldn't see much more with the streetlight shedding light the wrong way, and I refused to admit I wanted to be able to see more. Regardless of the rest, he had a huge spray of funeral flowers in his hands. Quite honestly, I was a little skeptical of this whole night, so call me rude when I immediately took him to task for not having the spray here five hours ago.

"Those were supposed to be here this afternoon. And where's my usual guy, Dobbins? Dobbins is the only one who ever brings our deliveries, because my father likes that they don't have to be rearranged when they get here." I had my hands on my hips and my feet spread apart in classic offensive posture without a single conscious directive from my brain. Part of me realized I was transferring my anger and anxiety onto the nearest source, but I couldn't bring myself to care.

"I got lost." The guy shrugged. "Dobbins has the week off." His voice was gruff and yet smooth at the same time. I felt a nether part or two tingle and told them to calm the hell down at this totally and completely inappropriate time. Too much had happened in the last several hours for any kind of tingling to happen.

"How on earth did you get lost coming two blocks over and one block down? This is not a big town. It can't take more than twenty minutes to wander aimlessly over the entire place, especially in a car."

His gaze zeroed in on me. Though I had wanted to know what the whole of his face looked like a moment ago, when he focused on me, I would have chosen to go on ignorant forever. He was beautiful, and not in a fake, movie-star way, but a rugged, manly way. My heart beat a little faster. I told the damn thing to stop that right this very instant.

"I need to deliver these immediately for the funeral."

"Nice way to avoid the question and the accusation. If those are the flowers I was missing for the funeral this afternoon, then you are way late and about twenty dollars too short. Monty is not going to be happy with you when you get back to the flower shop. I can tell you that. And you're way too early for the next funeral."

"What do you mean, the next funeral?"

His gaze went from intense to laser-strength. I found I did not like being on the receiving end of that look. I backed up a step and went around him to get the upper hand on the steps to the front door. I wasn't a shorty, and I wasn't little in the same reference, but this guy towered over me.

"Well?"

Oh, he actually wanted an answer? "I don't know. Whatever funeral is next on the books." The information seemed to make him stand taller and take even more of an interest in me, though I hadn't thought it was possible.

He broke eye contact for a moment to look back over his shoulder. I took the opportunity to hustle up the rest of the stairs and jerk the door open. I heard him shout something, but ignored him in favor of locking the door behind me, then immediately going to find Burton. I'd rather deal with a reprimand for not listening to the chief of police's commands about going into the crime scene than deal with whatever that had been out on the front stoop. I really hoped Dobbins would be back for the next delivery. The thought of dealing with that guy ever again didn't sit well with me.

"It's about time you got here," Burton said, coming out of the salon to the right and scaring the bejesus out of me.

I wasn't normally a skittish or easily frazzled person. But this whole night had me seriously on edge. Waldo's robbery, or beating, or whatever had happened to him, was affecting me more than I had thought. "I got stopped by some incredibly late flower guy on my way in. Sorry. You want some coffee? I think I'm going to make tea to settle myself down."

"None for me. I'm just going to go check out this guy who accosted you. No delivery guy's going to be out this late unless he's got pizza in his hand."

I let Burton tramp after the guy who reminded me of a bad dream gone good and went in search of something stronger than herbal tea. I was only able to come up with English Breakfast. With the pot on the small stove in the kitchen, I leaned back against the counter and listened for any evidence of a scuffle out on the front steps. It would have served the overbearing guy right to come up against the chief of police in our town. We might have been small, but Burton took his job—and his crew cut—very seriously.

Burton returned as the kettle shrilled, poking his head into the kitchen and giving me the all-clear signal. "Nothing shady out on the street, girl."

I breathed a sigh of relief, even if it was short-lived. "Why don't we sit in here? I really don't want to go back into the salon if I don't have to."

"You're in the salon all the time. What's the difference tonight?"

I did not want to tell him the difference was my ex-husband could have possibly been laid out there if things had gone differently. I couldn't think straight with that in my head. But I didn't go there. Instead I gave Burton a weak smile and a quick, "Please."

"Fine, but this is still an official inquiry."

"Sounds ominous." I took a sip of perfectly doctored tea—lots of cream and more sugar than my mother would have been happy with—and tried to quell the shaking in my hands. My adrenaline was fading from the last few hours since finding Katie and Waldo. I had seen shock before when I'd shown Waldo my monthly bills for new shoes, but had rarely experienced it firsthand. Now was a different story altogether as the adrenaline wore off and the reality set in.

"Look, you need to sit down. I need to get your story while it's still fresh in your mind. I would have done this at the scene of the crime, but things got crazy and you fled back to the food." Burton had been the chief of police for years. I did not like being in the same room with him due to mishaps when I was a missus. Burton had had to deal with me and Waldo numerous times over the years. I sent him away when he'd come to the door with another noise-violation call, told him to run along when he tried to give me a parking ticket, and various other things I'd rather not think of ever again. His radar was definitely one I had wanted to avoid when I left Waldo and now I was right in his direct line of sight. Sitting with him now made me feel like I was going to the pokey at any minute, even though I'd done nothing wrong. Except step out into the alley when I knew I shouldn't have.

I gulped the tea this time and felt it slide down to warm my throat. I could do this. I'd done a number of hard things in my life. This was the least of them. He was just looking for information. It could have been worse in some big community where I probably would have been the number-one suspect as the angry, duped ex. "I'm not a suspect?" I asked.

"I'm certainly not ruling it out, girl. There's unaccounted-for time and I know for a fact you stepped out into that alley after specifically being told not to. We've got a lot of folks who say you were over at the firehouse making chow, and then you talked to Gina. She sent you over for more kraut and then Katie says you walked in right after she'd been tied to the chair. I can't imagine how you'd have had enough time to do all that and still come around to . . ." He looked at his notepad. ". . . Rip tape off Katie's lip faster than she could scream *ow*. But I'll do my own investigation, if you please. Some people will say anything to protect someone they like."

A slight smile crept across my lips. Katie had screamed a hell of a lot more than *ow*. But the disapproving look from Burton put the kibosh on that pretty quickly. I cleared my throat. "Sorry."

"This here is a serious matter, and we need to treat it with respect. I know that ex of yours was a horse's patootie, but we have a serious issue on our hands, and I don't know what, why, or how yet."

"You don't know how?"

"Nope. We sent him on to the hospital to get some answers. As of right now, I don't see any definite reason that would have put him on the ground like that. He's a little banged up and his hair wasn't up to its usual standards, but nothing else seems to be disturbed. He even has all his change and money, ID and credit cards. Nothing was taken and I don't get it. Why was he out there in the alley, anyway, and how on earth did he turn up unconscious? You put him there?"

"Of course not." Shaken that he would even consider that, I gulped again, this time with no tea to soothe my dry throat.

"We'll see. We shall see." He licked his thumb and turned the page on his notebook. "Now, do you have any idea if he had any kind of diseases or medical problems? What about enemies?"

"Medical problems were nil. He was as healthy as the horse he was the patootie of." That got a chuckle, but it sounded like it was given grudgingly. Especially when he cleared his throat and scowled at me. "I don't know about enemies, though. I wasn't aware of what he was even doing all those years and had no idea about his business dealings or business partners. I just spent his money and led my vapid, stupid life until I couldn't stand it anymore."

Burton patted my leg in a familiar gesture. A

lot of people had done the same over the last three months, but I always felt like behind the concerned gesture was a sneer because I had thought I was so high and mighty.

Burton, though, left no room for misunderstanding. "You were stupid, no doubt about that. And you'd be stupid to hide something from me now. I'm keeping my eye on you."

My cousin, Matt, who incidentally said he loved me but also had enjoyed watching my swan dive, came busting into the kitchen from the front of the building and skidded to a stop on the polished linoleum. He caught himself on the back of my chair, barely stopping in time to stay out of the cabinets behind me.

"Just got the call from the doctor over the radio. Stun-gunned in the balls, boss." He looked as horrified as I felt. He ducked his head and tugged on his hat when he finally looked up with a sheepish blush on his face. "Oh, sorry, Tallie."

"It's okay. I wasn't using them anymore anyway."

Chapter 3

"Tallulah Beverly!" Burton said with a straight face before he started to cough to cover his laugh.

"All right, so that wasn't the most decorous thing to say, but does that mean he's not going to die?" I admit to wishing death on him when I was in the midst of our marriage, but in reality it would be horrible for anyone to die so young.

"Yes," Matt cut in. "They said he's going to be fine, only not . . . um . . . up to snuff for a little while."

"That was terrible," I said with my own snicker. Waldo had gotten into more trouble with his pecker than anyone I knew, so I didn't feel bad for thinking of him laid up but not able to get it up.

"Okay, children, let's get back down to business." Burton waved Matt away. My cousin gave me a discreet wave, then headed out the door, though he didn't actually leave. I caught him out of the corner of my eye, standing right outside the door. To keep me in or other people out?

Would the chief of police definitely think I was involved now? I would have thought hitting someone in the balls with a stun gun must take some serious hate. I didn't know anyone who hated anyone with that kind of passion. Certainly not me.

"So does this keep me on your suspect list or take me off?" I asked him.

He tapped his pen to his chin. "It moves you up from a *maybe* to a top suspect, Tallie. Don't think you're going to weasel out of this if you did it. Don't leave town, got it? Either you come clean now or you let me do some serious digging and we'll see where we end up. I don't know if you had time to run around and shock a guy in the manhood, but I'm not ruling you out until I know for sure you didn't do it. I need more than your say."

"No innocent until proven guilty?" I tapped my fingers on the side of my mug to keep my nerves at bay.

"Not at this point. You keep your nose clean and we'll do our investigating. I tried talking to Walden before he went to the hospital, but he refused to name anyone. Says he couldn't see who hit him." He scratched his chin. "First I have to find out what kind of jolt he got to the gonads and if it was prolonged."

I swallowed a groan as Burton crossed his legs and Matt dropped his hands to cover his own crotch in a moment of stunned silence for the poor guy. God, no one deserved that. Even if Waldo had called me a ball-buster at the end of our marriage, I still would have never wished that on anyone.

Burton and Matt left shortly after, allowing me to sit with my rapidly cooling tea, think, and take a few breaths.

I thumped my head on the table, then rose up when I heard the front door open and close and my mother's voice call for me. I couldn't face her right now.

Sneaking up the back stairs as quietly as I could, I locked myself into my apartment three stories above the dead. After flipping on the lights, I called Gina.

"Is there a bunch more cleanup to do?" I asked as soon as she answered.

"No, it's pretty much all done. I grabbed Lonny and a few other guys to help all the women get the things put away, then sent everyone home. Your uncle Sherman said the firemen would clean up the floors for us since we fed them. I'm going home now to drop into bed. Are you okay?"

"I guess so." Not really, but I had a lot to process through my poor little brain before I talked it out with my best friend.

"Was it a nasty scene?"

"No, it looked like he had taken a nap in the wrong place at the wrong time. That's all."

"What I want to know is what in the hell was he doing in the back of my building, and what was Katie doing in it?"

"The police would like to know that too. Burton said he hasn't got a place to start at this point. But he seems pretty convinced I probably did it."

"What? That's crap! There's no way you would have had enough time and I would know if you had a stun gun." She paused. "You don't, do you?"

"No, I don't." And thank God for that. I had thought about buying one once and was never so thankful for skipping that particular purchase. "How do you know about the stun gun? I just heard about it myself."

"My mom interrupted her own stories to tell me she heard it from Cherise, who heard it from Mabel, who heard it from Suzy at the station. You know how these things go."

Of course I did. I had been the topic of the grapevine often enough to know how fast it traveled and how widespread it was.

"I also heard they don't have much to go on. I can understand that," Gina said. "Every time I got close to Katie and asked a question about what she was doing in my shop, she'd get hysterical. Then I'd get the beady eye for disturbing poor, traumatized Katie. But she didn't look traumatized to me except for the bright red lip you gave her."

"I have a feeling when she looks at it in the morning, she is not going to be a happy camper."

"But at least she'll be hair-free and not tied up on a chair." Gina snorted. "I'd like to tie her up to a chair myself at this point. She refused to go to the hospital when they took Waldo. Apparently she's just fine, unless I ask her a question. No matter how many times or ways I said anything about being in the Bean, she refuses to tell me how she got in the shop. I never gave her a key and

Burton said it didn't look like anyone had forced their way in."

"Does she just ignore you?" I couldn't imagine Gina wasn't trying to be her most persuasive, and few people got past Gina's most persuasive.

"She won't give me a straight answer. Any time I get close to one she starts wailing like I'm asking her to cut her own arm off."

"Maybe it brings it all back for her." Even though I was trying to give her cousin the benefit of the doubt, Gina was having none of that.

She snorted, again. "You always were nicer than I was. She knows how pissed I am about her being in there when she shouldn't have been, and she doesn't want my wrath. Though if she thinks I'm not going to chew her a new one for breaking in, she's got a version of reality that doesn't exist here in our world."

"Maybe she has a key you don't know about. You should get the locks changed."

"One step ahead of you, babe. Lou's already over there taking care of it. Let's see her try to get in again. I might just have to get my own stun gun."

"Gina," I whispered, horrified and yet fighting not to laugh. "You can't even joke about that right now. You do not want to get dragged in for questioning."

"Eh, let them try. On that note, I'd better go. Four a.m. is going to come awfully early to this girl. Especially since I have to be up to make enough breakfast pastries to replace everything I put out tonight, instead of getting up and working my butt off with that cute trainer they have on cable first thing in the morning."

"I could come over and—"

"Uh-uh. You remember what happened when we were nine and I let you use my Easy-Bake Oven? There's a reason you had a cook at your big fancy house on the hill with Waldo. I'll be fine on my own. I have some raw dough for most of it tucked into the freezer at home. I'll pull it out before I go to bed so it's ready in the morning. Now I'm going to say good night. I hope you sleep okay. Call me when you get up in the morning."

"Will do."

"And make sure to let me know when you decide to go out with Darla's pool boy. Did he ask you out again when you were there today?"

"Ugh. Absolutely not. I avoid him like the plague. He's okay-looking, but I'm not ready and I don't want to have anything to do with anything associated with Darla."

"Come on, now. That's not a valid reason for avoiding the guy."

"I've already told you no way. I have enough on my normal plate without dating someone who owes their paycheck to Darla."

"Come on, Tallie. He's not all bad."

"I'm not discussing this. I will have to use all my mental energy to avoid the trap that is Waldo. You know he's going to be pissed about not having use of his—uhm—equipment. He hasn't yet completely gotten the memo that I left. I have a feeling I'll be getting a call sometime soon to come help him out in his convalescence."

"Keep calling him Waldo and he'll never even consider asking you to help."

"That's my plan."

"You should have never married him."

"Preaching to the choir, sister. I was young and I thought I was in love. He whisked me off my feet with promises and gifts and more promises. I wanted out from under the way my parents expected me to join the funeral home. It was like the perfect storm of stupidity and shallowness."

"Yeah, well. At least it's over now."

"There is that." And maybe he wouldn't call.

We hung up and I sank back onto the wine-colored couch I had brought from the exercise room in my big former mansion. It was one of the few pieces Waldo had allowed me to walk away with. I'd been tempted to take more. We'd had so much he probably wouldn't have noticed, but I was more honest than that. Plus, if I'd gotten caught, it wouldn't have been worth the headache.

I didn't hear anyone coming up the stairs, so I took a chance and jumped into the shower for the third time today. I did not want to go to bed just yet, not with images of Waldo in disarray on the alley ground still swirling around in my head.

What had happened? As much as I should be concerned for Waldo—and I was, in a way like one human being for another—I figured whatever had happened, he had gotten himself into it. Who knew what pies his hand was submerged in? But it did worry me that someone out there was stun gun–happy and not afraid to use it. Plus, the whole tying up and taping Katie. It had to be the same person. But who? And why?

Freshly washed and ready for some shut-eye, I grabbed peanut butter crackers to quell the rumbling in my belly. In the flurry of making food for the emergency responders and the police, I hadn't actually eaten anything, just kept dishing it out. In fact, I realized I hadn't eaten since the cruller after cleaning Darla's house. That was never a good thing.

With my belly finally full, I pulled the Murphy bed out of the wall before turning off every light. Tomorrow I would clean a couple of houses, beg off from others, and then go to Sherman to see if he knew anything about the who and why. The fire chief might not be buddy-buddy with the chief of police, but they did communicate.

Mr. Fleefers, my faithless but cuddly cat, strolled in from wherever he'd been and bounced up on the bed. "Half the time I have no idea where you are. I know we have a large space to roam, but thanks for deciding to grace me with your royal presence."

There were some advantages to being related to Sherman, I thought as I petted the cat, who was settling in and soothing my thoughts with his purring. I wasn't above using those advantages. If Sherman wouldn't talk, then I could always go after my cousin Matt. Most likely I should leave well enough alone, but I couldn't seem to let the thought go that Waldo and Katie being there at the same time, even though on opposite sides of the door, had to be more than a coincidence. Not that it was my business anymore who he slept with but, really? Katie?

Maybe I would also put a call into Monty to find

out a little more about this new flower-delivery guy. Not because I wanted to know him any better. Just because I liked to know who I was dealing with and it was best to be prepared for when my dad had a fit about the floral arrangements being delivered in less than a stellar state.

It was a big wish list of questions. Drifting off to sleep, I decided I'd tackle them one at a time.

The next morning the sun was peeking through the blinds on my third-floor window way before I was ready to get out of bed. But then I remembered I had to clean Darla's house. If I could get there early enough, I shouldn't have to speak to her at all. Having cashed her check yesterday afternoon, I wouldn't be due another payment for two weeks.

The drive to the Hackershams' house at 7:30 was uneventful. I parked around back because Darla enjoyed making me do it. And because the woman took great glee in making me use the servants' entrance.

I honestly didn't give a damn. When I was in the midst of the high life I had thought it was fabulous—don't get me wrong, I loved all my shoes and clothes and unlimited spending account and not worrying about actually budgeting for anything—but it got wearying toward the end. Plus, Waldo was no real prize when it came down to it. Outside, he was a delicious specimen of male but inside, not so much.

I hadn't left him when I found out he was cheating (courtesy of the lovely Darla), but I had made him leave our bedroom and never darken my doorway again. Not that he'd darkened it often. In fact, it had been over two years since we'd had sex—since I'd had sex.

Then, I found out about the skimming he'd been doing from some of his smaller accounts. His job as an investment banker gave him access to millions, money people entrusted to him for their retirement. And he was misusing the money and abusing their trust. That I couldn't abide. So I took my Lexus and hightailed it out of there after reporting him to the authorities. My understanding was that he had an answer for everything. I didn't believe him. They shouldn't have, either, though at that point it was no longer my problem. Of course, then I found out about the sheer number of women he'd bedded and that was just about the Clorox in my coffee.

I knocked once on the back door and was admitted immediately by Letty, the live-in maid. I was tempted to ask her if she'd seen the guy with the fancy black and white shoes yesterday, but we didn't ever talk much other than to exchange hellos, and then I immediately got to work. Part of me thought Darla just enjoyed me cleaning her house. I mean, why did she need me and a live-in maid? But her checks were good and I wasn't complaining.

They'd had some huge party last night. Glasses and garbage, misplaced pillows, and drunkenly leaning chairs were a testament to the fact that no one had made any effort at all to clean up after themselves. I was not surprised, but after last night's events, I really did not want to be here.

Darla wouldn't be awake until sometime after ten. I could run the vacuum cleaner and probably sing at the top of my lungs and not wake her up from her Valium-and-vodka–induced sleep. Darla also had a white-noise machine and a sleeping mask. I was safe. And if I could be quick, I'd be out of here with plenty of time to avoid the mistress of the house.

Starting with the kitchen, I cleaned counters and dishes, which left me too much time to think. I had no intention of trying to help figure out what had happened to Waldo. Or why he'd been in the alley and Katie in the Bean. Moving on, though, there was a very busy little part of my brain working while I scrubbed the same damned toilet that yet again could not enjoy a well-aimed stream. If I were Darla I might think about painting a freaking bull's-eye in the bowl, but that was just me.

The doorbell rang several times, interrupting my toilet musings. I continued to wipe down the counter as I listened for Letty to answer. By the time the person at the door leaned on the doorbell, I had had enough and yanked open the door myself.

On the stoop stood the now-infamous flower guy.

"You again?"

He cleared his throat. "Right. Max." And he pointed at the name embroidered on his chest.

We stared at each other for a moment until I raised one of my eyebrows. "Was there a reason you're here, *Max*?" I couldn't miss the huge spray of flowers in his arms, but I wasn't going to let him off the hook so easily. I still had a feeling there was something more going on there than the surface showed.

"Right! Here's a delivery for Darla Hackersham." He thrust the flowers at me. Without any other choice, I took them. I had no money in my pockets for a tip, and Letty was apparently in the back, probably watching one of her daytime talk shows.

"Well, thanks." I stepped back and shut the door in his face.

The card in the dozen roses was not in an envelope. It was easy enough to see Mr. Wagner, another man in the upper crust of our little burg, had sent them. I took a moment to smile because I used to get flowers from him too. He was one of the few people I actually missed from my former life.

Placing the bouquet on the piecrust table outside the living room, I figured someone would see them there, then got back down to the hard work.

The living room, formal dining room, music room, and library were all full of champagne glasses, ashtrays, and general messiness. Four garbage bags and three rounds of dishes later, I went to scope out the office and the sitting room. As far as I knew, no one should have been in there. Darla made a point to keep her parties tightly contained even if she didn't clean.

I made a cursory pass over each room and found them to be just as I had left them yesterday afternoon. As I neared her office, I tried not to think about the man with the shoes that had almost connected with my face. Even though I still knew the majority of movers and shakers in Darla and Waldo's circle, I had no idea who he was. The voice wasn't familiar at all. Very few new people were ever allowed into the circle.

But as far as I knew, I had never seen the guy and I couldn't place the voice. Who had he been? Why had he been here and what was with the yelling? Not that it was any of my business. Darla had her own things going on, and I was just the house cleaner; nothing more, nothing less.

Done with all my tasks, I called out a good-bye to Letty, then made a beeline for my car. I was riding very close to the 10:00 mark and not interested in rehashing what had happened with Waldo last night. I was surprised Darla hadn't set her alarm clock to grill me about the whole sordid thing.

But I wasn't looking that particular gift horse in the mouth.

I hauled tail away from the house with my thoughts still whirling. I had about a half an hour before the next house and wanted a caffeine fix. I could go to the apartment above the dead, but knew I had nothing more exciting than store-bought coffee to feed my need.

So I went to Gina's and headed right for the counter. I got a drink, then turned to find there wasn't a single spot to sit since it was almost ten in the morning. Not wanting to answer all the questions being called out across the shop anyway, I played the friend card and went into the back. Here Gina had a break room with some terrifically comfortable chairs she'd found at a garage sale.

"What are you doing back here?" Gina asked

three minutes after I sat myself down at the small table in the Bean's back room. I'd thought I'd have a moment to savor my drink before going on to the next house. Apparently, Gina had other ideas.

"Just taking a moment to breathe before I get back to business. My phone has been ringing off my hip, and everyone keeps trying to flag me down to hear what I saw. I have about fourteen people who've called Waldo a bastard and five who think he was a saint for putting up with me for so many years. I just wanted a few quiet minutes."

"Yeah, well, I don't think you're going to get them here. Burton's been looking for you and some guy came in saying he had a flower delivery for you. I could've sworn I'd seen him before, but couldn't place him. He said this was the address he'd been given to deliver to. What's up with that?"

I had a quick vision of the dark, manly man from last night and this morning at Darla's, then resolutely shook it off. Surely there were other delivery places in town. Besides, who on earth would be sending me flowers?

"Did he leave the arrangement?"

"No, he said he'd be back after three. So you might want to be here when he does show, because I really want to know who on earth is sending you flowers."

If it was Max who was looking for me, why hadn't he just given them to me at Darla's? "You don't have to make it sound so unthinkable that I could get flowers."

"From who? You haven't dated anyone since you moved out of Waldo's. No matter who I try to suggest. You don't even look at guys as anything more than a necessary tool to do whatever job you need done."

"Yes, thank you. I know."

"Oh, don't go getting your panties all in a wad. I'm just saying I don't know who would be sending you flowers right now, and it's way too early for a widow's bouquet."

"Good Lord, Gina. I won't be getting any widow's spray. Waldo is not going to die. He only got stun-gunned. Other than that, he's healthy, according to the doctors at the hospital. I guess I'll be here at three, then, won't I?"

"And so will I. But first you'd better go find Burton and see what he wants. He might just put an APB out on you if you don't show up soon."

"Right. The first first, though, is that I'm going to finish my latte." I eyed Gina and tried to convey I'd really like to do that on my own, in peace and quiet.

She got the hint. With a smile, she left the room and went back out front to help her customers. I could hear the murmur of conversation out there and figured most of it would be about Waldo's attack. While I didn't know everyone in town, it was still on the smallish size. Since nothing else was currently going on, the attack would be major gossip, especially because it wasn't a cut-and-dried case. I didn't know how many details others were aware of, but I wasn't going to be the one running around telling people Waldo had been hit in the only place he valued more than his wallet.

Once I finished my latte, I would go back out into the world, looking for Burton. Might as well get it all over with so I could go on to the next house.

Rising from the chair, I heard a crinkle of paper. My list of houses for the day was in my back pocket and must have fallen out. I shoved it back in my pocket as I headed out the door. Mama Shirley was on her way back here, and I didn't want to get caught in another motherly conversation at the moment.

As I ducked out the back of the store, I couldn't help but stare at the spot where Waldo had been last night. A couple of pieces of fluttering crime-scene tape still decorated the alley, but for the most part it was clear. Burton and the police must have come back this morning and finished up whatever they couldn't do last night in the dark.

Waldo's hair had stood up from his head like the plumage of a bird. I never would have thought he'd been jolted in the man bits, but it was not like it would have been my go-to thought. Who would do something like that?

My phone went off in my pocket as soon as I exited the alley and turned the corner onto Main Street. Who could possibly want what from me now?

"What's up, Letty?" I said after I glanced at the display screen.

"Hey, Tallie. You left your vacuum here. I didn't know if you'd need it wherever you're going next."

Damn. I would definitely need it. A lot of my clients had those whole-house vacuum cleaners. I didn't trust those little buggers to actually get things done, or at least not correctly.

After doing some mental calculating of my time, I realized I'd better haul ass if I wanted to make it to my next house on time. How could I be so stupid as to leave my tools at my last job? "I'll be over in a few. Thanks."

"It'll be in the living room then. I have to go out to do some shopping. You know where the key is."

"Yeah, see you." I booked it to the car. This was going to be a long day and it had only recently gotten started.

Hopefully, I'd be in and out of there before Darla noticed I had even been there the first time. My phone had been burning up with calls all morning. Most of them I didn't know, and the ones I would have expected never called. Fine by me. If the old guard wanted information, they could get it elsewhere.

With Letty gone shopping, I bent into the little patch of mulch on the left side of the back porch, dug out a ridiculous ceramic lotus flower, and cracked it open to reveal the spare key. I really hoped luck would stay on my side so I could be in and out of the house without running into Darla.

I had at least a slim chance since it was only a little after ten.

Because Darla knew Burton personally, I figured she would be all atwitter about Waldo being buzzed in the balls. I did not want to have that conversation with her. I had seen Darla eyeing my husband more than once when we were still married. Personally, I thought Darla had only told me about the cheating because Waldo wouldn't sleep with her. But that was just a theory.

Closing the door softly behind me, I made tracks through the kitchen, snagging a cookie from the jar on the way. I hadn't had breakfast yet and that latte was not helping my stomach feel full. As I munched, I walked softly into the living room. Someone must have seen the flowers on the table from earlier because the bouquet was no longer there.

And then there was my high-end vacuum cleaner. I hadn't gone with the cheapy brand. In anticipation of lots of vacuuming, I'd bought a good one, then offered people my services. Eighteen clients later, this vacuum was my best friend and stalwart companion.

A whirring noise started behind me, which had me jerking my head to the left. The whole-house vacuum cleaner seemed to be attacking the wall. This was why I didn't like those buggers. They got stuck on weird things, and it just creeped me out to have a machine roving the floor without any supervision. I turned it off and scooted it to the threshold of the hardwood floor with my toe. Letty could put it away when she got back. She most likely was the one who started it, though I didn't get why when I'd just cleaned.

After wrapping the cord around the length of my vacuum, I got behind it, lowered the arm, and began scooting my way across the floor, humming. Today would not be the long day I had thought it would be. The trouble was past, Waldo would recover, and whatever had been going on with him would not touch me. I wouldn't let it. He'd ruined enough of my life. I wasn't going to let him do it any longer.

I got halfway to the kitchen when all that coffee hit my bladder like a tidal wave. It was one I'd cleaned, so I figured no one else had used it in the hour I'd been gone. I decided to detour, since as of yet there had not been a single sign of Darla. I could chance it for another two minutes.

Trooping down the hall, I walked past the door to the library, another that gave a different entrance to the kitchen, and a closet for various linens for the dining-room table and extra candles. I knew what was in there because I'd had to set up more parties in the last six months than I had attended in the six years before I'd split from Waldo. Darren's firm must have really taken off at some point for them to be able to afford all the things they now had and all the entertaining they now did. When they inherited and remodeled, Darla had told me they used most of what they'd been given. From all the new stuff and entertaining, I figured business must be booming, or they'd inherited again. I wasn't on the inside anymore, so I wouldn't know.

I made my pit stop, then left while making sure

everything was where it should be. I was good to go. On my way to get my hands on my vacuum again, I passed the closet for a second time. I was three strides beyond the door when I realized something looked out of place.

Why was the door open? Maybe that was where the house vacuum was kept and the door had been left ajar for it to put itself to bed after it was done.

But what I had seen out of place suddenly registered, and I gasped. It had been a foot. A foot had been sticking out of the closet, shod in an expensive high-heeled shoe. I was almost more frightened to find an entire body attached to the foot, but I had to go look. God help me.

Chapter 4

Maybe I was hallucinating. I had to have been, because there couldn't possibly be a foot sticking out of the closet on the main floor. Darla could tie one on with the best of them, but she'd never been so drunk she'd fallen into a closet. Darren wouldn't have let her. It could potentially ruin his reputation, and reputation was very important to Darren. So if she wasn't drunk, then what did that leave me? My mind flashed to Waldo in the alley. Could she be hurt?

I was afraid to turn back around to see if what I thought I saw was real. But I couldn't walk out of the house without knowing Darla was at least going to recover. I didn't particularly like the woman, but I did have standards.

Turning around slowly, I kept my eyes closed for a moment just to center myself. I would open them and there would be nothing out of the ordinary. She would be drunk and Darren had just gone to bed too early to realize she hadn't come upstairs. And since I was the help, me seeing her drunk in a closet wouldn't wreak any havoc on his reputation. I was just seeing bad things in unlikely places because of what had happened to Waldo. That was all there was to it.

When I opened my eyes, though, there was definitely a foot sticking out of the closet. I'd know those silver heels anywhere. Darla had made a point to show them to me last week while I wore grubby sneakers. She had sneered when she said she knew I couldn't possibly afford them.

I took a deep breath and yanked open the door, immediately stopping in my tracks.

Darla wasn't just hurt. She was definitely dead. There was no way the woman was going to start breathing like Waldo had last night. She had a big butcher knife sticking out of her chest.

My stomach rolled, bile flew fast and furious into my throat, and I was pretty sure I stopped breathing because my head went light.

Gasping for air, I checked for a pulse, just in case. When I didn't find one in her neck or either wrist, I jerked away from the body. My God, this was much, much worse than Waldo being stun-gunned in the privates. Darla was dead. And Darla being dead was very, very bad. It wasn't as if she could have fallen on that knife all by herself. My brain was racing as fast as it could, trying to figure out if somehow I had missed the foot and the closet when I was here earlier. But I'd vacuumed right around this spot. No way would I have missed it.

Which meant Darla must have been killed in the last hour or so. Had it been after Letty left? That would have narrowed the window even further.

Regardless of what had happened, I had to call the police. Now.

Darren would not fire me for reporting his wife dead. Would he?

Of course he wouldn't. I probably should have called the police first, but I really had thought she had just gotten too drunk. It never had occurred to me she would be dead. Hurt maybe, but definitely not dead.

I was going to be sick.

I held it in, barely. My brain locked in on the caution I was given last night to not contaminate the scene and I was pretty sure puke would be rated as a contaminant. This was serious and I was right in the middle of it *again*.

The thought of having to report another incident after facing the chief of police last night and being told not to leave town was fresh in my mind too. There was no way Burton would think I had any reason to kill Darla. But I didn't think he would have believed I had it in me to stun-gun my ex-husband either and yet, I'd been told I was a suspect. Hyperventilating now would not make things better, so I tried some deep breathing as I turned from the body to look at anything else. Once I focused on the far wall, I felt a little more in control. So instead of freaking out as I so desperately wanted to, I simply called Uncle Sherman.

"Darla Hackersham is dead. What should I do?" I said without waiting for him to say hello. Turning back to stare down at Darla, I tried to see if there was anything else around her to tell who the killer might be. Nothing.

I turned away again because people who were laid out on nice silver slabs and waiting for the last makeup job of their lives were one thing. This was something completely different. Between Waldo, the guy with the shiny shoes, Katie's bad knot job, and now Darla, I was pretty sure I was reaching maximum capacity for out-of-the-norm experiences.

Give me a toilet with a poor aimer any day over this craziness.

The line crackled as he sighed. "What have you gotten yourself into now, girl? Where are you?"

I gave him Darla's address while I tried not to turn around to look at her again. My brain just was not processing that Darla would not be trying to slip out of her bill anymore or hosting parties where no one could seem to aim at the hole in the toilet.

"I'll call Burton and be right there. For God's sake, don't touch anything." He clicked off and I couldn't keep myself from turning again. With my phone in hand, I really looked at all of Darla as I hadn't before when I was too focused on the shoes and the big butcher knife. She was dressed to the nines: Black pencil-thin skirt, a button-down blouse with swirls of red and blue, silver and purple, and those shoes. My eyes went to her throat, looking for her signature black pearls. Where the hell were they? She'd had them on yesterday and as far as I knew she never took them off.

Now that the closet door was all the way open and I knew Darla was in there, the smell of dead body was all but overwhelming, if only in my mind. Most likely there really wasn't a smell, and I was just projecting. She hadn't been dead long enough to smell. But in the window right across the way there was a new, beautiful arrangement of fresh flowers. I stuck my nose in them to keep the phantom smell of decay at bay and immediately got what amounted to a paper cut on my nose.

Snaking my hand into the arrangement of roses and lilies in pale and dark pink, I came out with a rectangle of thick paper with the distinctive logo of Monty's floral shop. Before I could read it, Sherman came banging on the door, yelling he was with the police. At that moment, it occurred to me I might not be the only one in the house. If Darla's killer was still here, I did not want to be alone. I whipped open the door fast enough for Sherman to almost fall in.

"What took you so long?" He trooped in with Matt and Burton following him. Actually, Burton was jockeying for point position, but Sherman just used one meaty hand to keep him behind him.

I pointed to the closet and didn't say another word.

"Why am I not surprised at all to find you here?" Burton said as he walked past me.

I was escorted to Darla's study where I'd sustained my rug burns the day before. Roaming the room did nothing for the feeling of being caged. I just wanted to get back to cleaning houses and get out of here, leave this all behind.

I couldn't shake the image of how terrible Darla had looked with that knife in her chest.

Normally, when the funeral home got bodies they were cleaned and sterile, not freshly killed. I shuddered as I stepped up to look through the back window. The room overlooked the pool house and apartment Darla had commissioned about five years ago. Two months ago she'd installed a pool boy for the pool house. I hadn't seen much of him except in the garden a time or two. He had tried to talk me into a date the second time, and I'd stayed away from him after that. I was most definitely not in the market for anyone so shortly after finally getting out from under Waldo. I would have probably liked some companionship and I missed the sex, but was not interested in the man who walked around with a toothpick in his mouth and perpetually looked like he'd just rolled out of bed and into his *Magnum P.I.* Bermuda shorts.

I stood there for a moment or two until I realized the bottom of my sock was getting wet through the hole in my sneaker. Putting my hand down on the floor, I found it damp. Where had the water come from?

And then I saw the window was cracked and remembered there had been a storm earlier that morning. I'd have to bring it up to Darren so he could arrange to have the carpets cleaned and the window fixed if necessary. If I ever talked to him again. Who knew what he would do once he found out his wife, the runner of his house and life, was dead.

That thought was not one I wanted floating in my head, so I redirected myself. I could call my dad and tell him we had a new customer, but that would be crass and jumping to conclusions. In reality, I just wanted to leave. Except that Burton had made sure to say I needed to hang around for questions.

After another five minutes staring at the walls, I went looking for him. I needed to get out of here right now. So many emotions were bombarding me that I couldn't think straight. I needed the routine of cleaning, the normality of rubber gloves and the familiar smell of cleaning products. Darla was gone and there was nothing I could do about it. I might not have been friends with her anymore, but having her life snuffed out and finding her like that, was too much to comprehend. So I focused on the fact that there were houses to clean. I found Burton hunched over the body. His broad shoulders blocked out the full length of Darla, but I averted my eyes anyway.

"Hey, can I talk to you, please?"

"Give me a minute here, Tallie. I'm in the middle of something."

"Okay, then, I'm going to go. I have houses to clean and things to do. Can you just ask me your questions later?" I sounded a bit whiny, but didn't care. I'd rather be anywhere other than here.

"Don't go blabbing to everyone about all this until I know what I'm dealing with. And do not leave town. This is more than stunning your ex-husband in the gonads."

My God. He could not think I had killed Darla. For what? Why? I had no reason to cause her harm, no matter how often I might complain about her. I opened my mouth to say something, but nothing came out. I snapped my jaw shut when Burton pointed his pen at me.

"I highly suggest you think about where you've been all morning and when you last saw this woman. I know you cleaned for her, but how much did you hate it? How awful was she to you on a daily basis? Think about that before you say one word." He turned back to the body.

"Fine." My shoulders slumped. I knew Burton didn't like me, but he couldn't really think I would murder someone in cold blood. Could he? I gulped. "I'll—um—be on my cell if and when you need me. And don't forget the Hackershams had a live-in maid and a pool boy. You might want to check them out, though Letty said she was going shopping before I came back here. Also don't forget to ask me about the guy with the shiny shoes." He totally could have killed her! If I only knew who he was, I'd hand him and his designer footwear over on a silver platter that I spit-shined myself.

"Look at you, already coming up with other people to pass the blame onto." He shook his head as he eyed me from his position on the floor. "Oh, I'm going to need you, all right. I'm going to need you to talk. A lot. So keep that cell phone on and be ready. And no blabbing."

"Got it." I did everything I could to keep the tremor out of my voice, but I didn't think I suc-ceeded.

I ran out the front door of Darla's house before he could change his mind. Pulling into Gina's lot, I figured the news of Darla's death and my role in finding her had not yet hit downtown. On the way, I'd used said cell phone to postpone my next house for a few days, citing a headache. No one should be looking for me for another hour or so. That meant I could drink some cappuccino and get myself under control. I wasn't going to be the one to tell anyone about this new twist at this point. Especially since I appeared to be suspect number one. Again. My stomach rolled. The least I could do was follow Burton's orders and Burton had ordered, so I was going to obey. Though I might be tempted, I was very close to a line I didn't want to cross with him.

Fortunately, the news hadn't hit, so I walked into the Bean without getting a second glance from anyone. For the last few months, I'd tried to fade into the background and do my thing after making such a spectacle of myself when I'd been Mrs. Walden Phillips III. I didn't want the attention, now.

As soon as Gina saw me she whisked me into the back room. Her grip on my arm was far stronger than it needed to be, since I was moving right along without any hesitation. Did her grapevine extend even to the extent that she knew about the murder already?

"That guy with the flowers is sitting out there waiting for you. I wanted to grab you first."

"But it's not three yet." In truth, I had forgotten all about that in light of what had happened a few hours ago. Who was this guy? And who the hell was sending me flowers? To Gina's shop, no less. I had an apartment right across the street, for heaven's sake.

I turned to march back the way we had come.

Gina tightened her grip on my arm, effectively stopping me in mid-turn. "I think I know him, but I'm not sure. You're going to want to be careful."

Gina was not one to panic unnecessarily.

"What do you mean?"

"I don't know. He just doesn't seem like the type to be delivering flowers, and he had no idea what I was talking about when I mentioned the beautiful baby's breath in the arrangement."

"Just because he delivers them doesn't mean he'd know all their names." Though that was weak. I couldn't think of a single person who wasn't at least aware of what baby's breath was. It was a standard.

"You know how I am with this kind of thing. He's giving me a bad vibe. I'm just saying."

"Then should I sneak out the back? I don't have to get the flowers today. You can direct him across the street and tell him I told you he can drop them there." A thought occurred to me. "Ugh, that will thrill my mom, though, especially depending on who they're from." I had to think. "You know what? I'm just going to go get them and be done with him."

"If you're sure."

"He delivers flowers, and I kind of, sort of, met him the other night outside the parlor. Then again at Darla's this morning when he delivered flowers to her. Plus, I'll be surrounded by a bunch of people. It's not going to be a problem."

But he looked different seated in the coffee shop. He still had that brooding thing going on and the shirt with *Max* on the pocket. However, there was something about him that struck a chord in me, like an old familiar song I hadn't heard in years but could still sing the chorus of.

"You're looking for me?" I said, stalking up to his table and towering over him as best I could. The plan had been to not give him room to rise from his chair and therefore keep the upper hand. But he nixed that plan, and seriously violated my personal space all at the same time, as he rose to over six feet in front of me, backing me up a step with his movement.

"Tallulah, you don't remember me, do you?"

I swallowed at the way he said my name. No one but Darla called me that, not even my mother. "Of course, I do. You're the guy who delivered flowers yesterday evening and then this morning at Darla's."

"But not before that?"

"No." Was he a stalker?

"Think back."

"Look, Max, I don't know how far I'd have to think back, but honestly I don't have time to play guessing games with . . ." And then it hit me so hard I wasn't sure why I wasn't toppled onto my butt. "Max Bennett? Are you that Max?"

A grin broke out on his face that was reminiscent of the one he'd had when we made a bike run for the candy store years ago. Fifteen years ago to precise, when I was eleven and he was just about to turn fifteen. I'd been the tagalong as he and my brother, Jeremy, were best friends that summer before he moved to Washington, D.C. Holy wow! Had he grown up or what? But what was he doing here?

"It's been a while." The smile stayed in place,

then widened a little to include a dimple low in his left cheek.

Yeah, he'd grown up all right and in the best possible way. I ran my tongue over my lower lip to check for drool and was thankful to find none. I was also embarrassed to find his eyes watching the movement.

"Wow, so you're back and delivering flowers?" I tried hard not to put any judgment into my words. Who was I to talk when I used to have a staff of four and now *was* the staff?

"Just for a bit until I figure things out."

"Boy, do I get that. Well, it was nice seeing you, but you'd better give me my bouquet and be on your way. Monty does not like lingering delivery-men."

"Actually, I was wondering if there was somewhere private we could talk."

I hesitated in taking a step back from the intensity in his gaze. I might have known him fifteen years ago, and he was sexy as sin, but I'd had one of those already and look where that got me. Not to mention that people changed in fifteen years. Delicious or not, I wasn't taking any chances with the weird stuff going on around here. "I can't. Maybe we could have coffee some time, though."

"I . . ." He started, then trailed off.

When I looked behind me, I saw Gina's mom, Shirley, standing behind my left shoulder with a rolling pin in her hand. The expression on her face was one I wouldn't want to see in a dark alley, and the answer as to what had stopped him. I didn't know anyone who continued to speak after being given that look.

"Look, Max, for now, just hand over the flowers, and we can talk another time."

He did not look happy in the least. Smart boy, though, because he also didn't try to balk at my very pointed suggestion. He left the flowers with the small white envelope tucked into the blooms. It squatted on the small café table where the delicate scent of violets reached my nose. I loved violets. Now, who would send me this arrangement? I considered opening the card then and there, but whereas I hadn't gotten a second glance upon entering, I was now the main attraction.

I hustled into the back before anyone could ask questions. I took the card out of the bouquet after catching another whiff of the violets. Lifting the flap of the envelope, I tried to think of who on earth would send me flowers and came up with no one. That was a little bit sad.

The card was simply signed *Darla*.

Reeling back with anger and fear, I ran through the front of the Bean. I had to find Max to ask him what in the hell this was and if he really thought it was funny. It sure as hell wasn't to me.

He was nowhere to be seen. Frustration built as I realized I had no idea if he had walked or drove a delivery van. Either one could have had him disappearing down one of the many small side streets.

I whipped out my cell phone as I stood on the sidewalk. A few button presses later, I put a call into Monty, my favorite florist and one of the few people who I had known as Mrs. Phillips III that I still wanted to know as just plain Tallie.

"It's a great day at Floral Fancies," Monty answered with a smile in his voice. The man was perpetually happy. I wished I knew his secret. But I was about to wipe that smile right off his face.

"It's not going to be so great anymore unless you tell me who in the world ordered a bouquet of flowers for me sent from Darla."

"Tallie, hon. What are you talking about? I can't believe that bitch would send you anything but a phony check."

"Well, your delivery guy Max just delivered a bunch of violets with my name on them and a card with your sunshine all over it. They were signed from Darla."

"Max? I don't remember sending him out with anything since this morning with flowers from Darla. She'd better pay her bill soon or I'm going to start holding the flowers hostage until she does."

"Monty . . ." Now was not the time to tell him she was dead. I wasn't allowed to say anything and truthfully I was trying to avoid that thought and the mental image that flew into my head as soon as I heard or saw her name.

"I know I shouldn't speak ill of one of my best customers, but the woman still owes me almost a thousand dollars for flowers over the last two weeks. I sent her an invoice and called her, but she hung up on me this morning."

Not so happy, now, was he? "Well, if you see Max, send him back my way because I want to know where these flowers came from."

"You're not alone. I had a delivery for him that I just texted him about. He hasn't answered yet, so I'll have Greg take it out. You know Greg? Maybe I'll ask him if he had something to do with that bouquet from Darla, but I doubt it."

Yeah, I knew Greg. He was a big, hulking man who had been a big, hulking boy in junior high. But he was as gentle as a dragonfly and his hand-writing was atrocious, not at all like the fine scrawl I was looking at now.

"Did you have any orders for me at all? Maybe the wrong card got put on them? When did you call her this morning?" I slipped the question in and hoped he would answer it without wanting to know why I wanted to know.

I waited impatiently while he flipped through orders. Monty was old-fashioned and still refused to go the way of the computer. Everything was done in triplicate. I knew because I had worked for him one summer when I was a teenager—the year I absolutely refused to have anything to do with the funeral home. It was a long time ago and a different time, but even now I refused to let my dad make me be anything more than a glorified trash-can emptier.

"Nope, no orders. I can't think of the last time I had an order in your name. I called the house about ten, but Darla hung up without saying anything."

"Okay." I hung up with him and started pacing the sidewalk. Monty had no idea if it had actually been Darla who'd picked up the phone and then hung up. It could have been her killer, and I had no way of proving anything.

On the other hand, apparently Gina had been right and no one had sent me flowers. Monty's pointed reminder hit a mark, though. I hadn't been with anyone in years who would send me flowers. *Nice reminder and thank you very much, Monty.* Still, where had the bouquet come from, and why would Max drop it off to me after he'd just winked at me with the dimple and jogged my memory as to who he was? Did he have something to do with what had happened to Waldo and Darla? Not that it couldn't have been someone else entirely, but he was the only shady person I could find right now, and it might just make sense.

Did he have handwriting like this? Although in looking at the handwriting again, it sure did resemble the way Darla made her D's. I rarely looked at the signature on my checks, so I wasn't positive it was exactly the same. As long as they cashed, I couldn't care less how Darla signed things. But maybe I would have to see about getting my hands on something Darla had written on. Not that I could waltz into Darren's home and grab a letter from her desk, but there might be other possibilities.

In the meantime, I wanted to know where Max was, who had really killed Darla, and I still had three more houses to clean today.

I hadn't been the one to say anything and no one asked me questions, but at the three other houses I cleaned, the main topic of conversation was Darla's death and Waldo's crotch-stunning. I whisked through them as fast as possible, mentally promising I'd do a more thorough job next time. The women at each house had been clustered with other friends, talking around me and over me to each other as I washed floors and vacuumed steps. And in the whole thing there was nothing new. Apparently, worrying that I would be asked questions endlessly was not an issue. I was the help and beneath them. I didn't even correct them when they repeated something that wasn't true. Let them drown in their own gossip and incorrect information. I had more important things to worry about.

At about four, I did leave a message with Suzy at the police station to let Burton know I had gotten a weird flower delivery. Suzy simply laughed, telling me I was low on the list of priorities. Well, at least I had tried.

After that, I went up to my apartment and jumped on my trusty computer. I might not know exactly where Max Bennett was at this precise moment, but I could try to see where he'd been before and why he was delivering flowers in a town he hadn't been back to in years. No funerals were scheduled for today and I didn't have any more trash cans to empty, so I dove into my search like I was on the hunt for a cheesesteak.

I put his name into a search engine and came up with tons of Max Bennetts, including a musician and an actor. I scrolled past the many links to movie databases and music interviews, accomplishments and Grammy nominations. Three pages later, I wondered if there was a way to narrow my search. I wasn't tech savvy at all, since for years I'd been more concerned with making sure my underwear matched my shoes and clothes.

I had no idea if his name was just Max or if it was Maxwell. The fastest thing to do would have been to call my brother and ask him for background. I should have known the simplest thing is almost never the thing that works for me.

"Hey, Tallie, I hear you've been getting yourself into some trouble. I bet you wouldn't be in this predicament if you'd just come work for Dad the way he asked you to."

And there went the eye rolling again. I was going to give myself a headache if I didn't get that under control.

"Yeah, thanks. Not happening. Anyway, I was just thinking about your old friend Max."

"The one you had a crush on and followed around like a puppy?"

I didn't remember it that way. "I did not," I said indignantly. "I tagged along with both of you because I wanted to hang with the older kids, not because I had a crush."

"Interesting." The laughter in his voice did nothing for my disposition.

"Don't mock me."

"Oh, I'm not. You had big googly eyes for the guy whether you want to admit it or not." He laughed, not realizing that had he been standing next to me I would have socked him in the arm.

"It wasn't like that."

"Fine, but I find it telling that you just happened to be thinking about him today out of the blue.

"I'd love to keep teasing you since it's like the

old days, but I have to go. I'm getting a call for a pickup. Talk to you later."

He hung up before I could ask my question another way. I should have just mentioned that I'd seen Max and was wondering if Jeremy knew he was in town and how long he'd been here.

My next line of action could have been to call my mother, but if I thought my conversation with Jeremy hadn't gone well, I could be absolutely certain my mom would not let me off the hook if she thought I was interested in anyone male.

Back to the search engine for me, then. And I came up with almost nothing. No social-media posts, no blogs, no websites with his name attached that weren't the musician or the actor. Frustration built, but I tried to tamp it down— especially since that was the moment Burton finally called to have me come down to the station.

Suzy nodded at me when I entered the police station. I'd been here before for many field trips when I was a kid, but hadn't stepped foot inside since. While I was married, I got plenty of tickets for parking and quite a few noise-violation citations, but Waldo always took care of those and would grease palms to keep us out of trouble. It wasn't a mystery as to why Burton was not fond of me. Money had thwarted him time and again and now he was probably relishing the fact that I had no more protection. I just hoped he wasn't so vindictive about my stupidity in my early twenties that he'd ignore all other evidence in favor of making me the prime suspect.

I was escorted into a room in the back with low-grade carpeting and two uncomfortable chairs. I knew because I tried out both.

I sat, twiddling my thumbs, bouncing my hands off my knees and switching positions for at least twenty minutes, before Burton made an appearance. He stared at me from the moment he walked in, his eyes narrowed and his buzz cut nearly bristling with indignation.

I wished I had thought to bring a lawyer.

"Now, we're going to have a nice little talk, Tallulah, and you're going to answer my questions or I'm going to find a way to lock you up overnight. In fact, I might think of a way to do that anyway."

"I'll answer anything you ask, but if I don't know the answer then that's the answer you'll get."

"Just make sure it's the truth," he said gruffly.

"I've never lied to . . ."

I trailed off because his eyes narrowed to the point that I wasn't quite sure how he was even able to see.

"Don't start. Just answer the questions and we'll be done."

I crossed my arms tightly over my chest. I would answer only what he asked and would not share another thing. If he wasn't going to trust me, then oversharing was not going to help.

"What happened at Darla's today?"

A nicely vague question with so many answers. I gave him the rundown from my first arrival to my final departure, including the call from Letty and the flower delivery. I also tried to tell him about the shiny-shoes guy, but he brushed it off.

"I don't want speculation. I need facts." He scribbled a couple things down on a notepad and I wished that he had done better with penmanship in school so that I could read what the hell it said. That was not to be, though, because he cupped his arm around the top of the notepad like he thought I was trying to cheat on a school test.

At that point, I sat back in my chair and started thinking of a battle plan. I won't say I met the challenge, but when he finally let me go—after walking me past the holding cells where I would *not* be spending the night—I knew I had to begin my own search for what had happened at Darla's. Either that or I might very well be sleeping somewhere not as quiet, and certainly not as comfortable, as above the dead.

Shaken, I avoided anyone at the funeral home as I ducked upstairs. I needed a plan, but had no idea where to even start. If I could find the killer first, then I might be able to point Burton in the right direction.

First I needed a mindless break from the last twenty-four hours. Had it really only been last night that I'd found Waldo in the alley?

The evening stretched out before me. Maybe I'd watch a movie to remove my brain from the situation enough to have some fresh ideas pop in. I was not afraid to admit I was at a loss.

I thought about calling Gina to see if she wanted to do dinner, but quite honestly, I was tired from the day and, amid everything else, still trying to figure out who would send me a bunch of violets pretending they were from Darla. It creeped me out, truth be told. Before I'd come upstairs, I'd thrown them in the garbage can out back.

I'd made my last phone call, a message for my mom to let her know I was at home, when the phone started ringing in my hand. Call after call had tumbled through the phone throughout the day and I shuffled all of them to voicemail. It was going to be filled soon. While earlier the rich women at the houses gossiped to each other and ignored me like the paint on the walls, by now others had heard I was the connection to finding each victim. Apparently, they wanted to be my best friend to get the scoop before someone else.

I thunked my head on the phone until a particular ring assigned to Waldo the Wonder Ass came through. I definitely was not going to answer that one. After a few seconds, the phone pinged, letting me know he had left a message. The tone sounded ominous in my living room.

Deciding I'd better get it over with, I started checking the other messages to clear things out when I came to his. Thankfully, no one had said anything about me being the killer, so maybe Burton either wasn't sharing that tidbit, or wasn't as married to the thought as he'd led me to believe. I was about to hit the limit of the people I knew, much less the people who had my cell-phone number, when Waldo's voice filled my ear.

"Tallie, I need you to pick me up from the hospital, and for God's sake, bring me some clothes." The call ended and I stared at the phone as the instructions rolled through to delete the message.

Hell yeah, I was deleting that message, and I was not going to pick up Waldo. He had family around here. Or he had some bimbo of the week who could help. He was no longer my responsibility. I had the papers to prove it.

Still, I knew Waldo. If I didn't call to let him know I wasn't picking him up, he'd call over and over again until I answered. As if to prove me right, the phone rang in my hand with the ring that signaled him. Again, I thought about letting it go to voicemail. I sighed. Since I was still sitting here and still peeved and scared enough about all of this, I answered. There was no better armor than anger to get me through any confrontation with Waldo.

"What?"

"Is that any way to greet your husband?"

"It's the perfect way to greet my ex-husband. Before you ask, I'm not picking you up. Surely you have your mom or a friend or girlfriend who can do it."

There was dead silence on the other end of the phone.

"No one?" I asked incredulously.

"No one I'd call."

Grumpy Waldo was not something new and, as ever, I refused to deal with it. "Well, you'll need to find someone. I have to go now. Don't call again." I clicked off before he could say anything else. Our marriage had not been all roses, certainly, but our divorce had been a compost pile so far.

The phone rang again. I was a half-breath away from yelling for Waldo to leave me alone when I recognized the number. What on earth was Darren doing calling me?

"Hello?"

"Tallie, this is Darren Hackersham," he said in his best business voice. I'd heard him slur with whiskey with the best of them. I was surprised he wasn't drunk now with having just lost his wife.

"Darren, I'm so sorry for your loss."

"Yes, thank you." Impatience sizzled along the phone line, taking me aback. He continued as if his whole world had not been rocked. Then again, maybe it hadn't. "Tallie, I would like you to come over tomorrow and clean again. I know you were here this morning, but I'd like everything neat as a pin after the police had to move things around in their search for evidence. I will, of course, pay you extra for fitting me into your schedule. I also have a proposition for you. It concerns Darla."

"Okay." I drew the word out. Didn't he care at all that Darla had been found dead less than twelve hours ago? Although, perhaps this was the way he was keeping himself together and I could always use the extra money. "What time would you like me there?"

"Any time tomorrow will be fine. I'll be working at home in the mornings for right now in deference to the recent tragedy, but I'll go into the office during the afternoon. Please be prompt." Then he hung up, obviously sure I'd say yes.

Well, that was interesting. Darren and I had never been best buddies when I was with Waldo. In fact, Waldo had made a point to not invite him to several parties. Darren had taken that out on me since he couldn't risk his reputation by taking it to the mat with Waldo. I wondered what that proposition might be, hoping it wasn't something I was going to have to slap him over.

The damned phone rang again. I was about to shut the thing off before I threw it across the room.

"Seriously, Waldo, I am not picking you up," I said when I saw who it was.

"Tallie, I appreciate the position you feel you're in, but he really can't be released from the hospital until someone comes to get him. It's five-thirty and I need him out of here before the night people start coming in."

My mother's third cousin, Vera, who was a charge nurse at the hospital, was calling from Waldo's cell phone—who, incidentally, I could hear ranting in the background.

"Why does it have to be me?" I whined.

"To be frank with you, honey, you're listed as next of kin on his records. We've tried several other people who can't come get him. Now, he needs to be picked up today. We don't have cause to keep him and we need to boost him out. I have people waiting for beds, and all he does is bitch."

This, of course, did not surprise me at all. When did Waldo *not* bitch? I didn't want to be the one to pick him up, though. Yet, I couldn't think of anyone who would. Although maybe I could ask Uncle Sherman. The man had a soft spot for me, even if he intensely disliked Waldo. I mentioned the possibility and Vera laughed. Yeah, I didn't think so.

"Fine, I'll come get him. I'll be there in twenty minutes."

The movie was out of the question, so I put away the remote control before dragging myself off the couch. This was not quite the way I had thought of spending my evening, obviously. Then again, the man had been stun-gunned in the nether parts. Maybe he'd be docile.

Knowing Waldo was a creature of habit, I ran over to his house, let myself in with his garden key, and grabbed him a pair of pants, a button-down shirt, and socks. I hesitated to open his underwear drawers. I really didn't want to be in there. But he would be a pain in my rear end if he didn't have clean underwear. Sometimes it was easier to give in than fight over these types of things.

I put his not-so-secret key back into his back-yard bird feeder, then made my way over to the hospital. By the time I got there, it had been twenty-five minutes since I'd talked to Vera. You'd have thought it was seven days later.

"What took you so long?" he demanded as soon as I walked in the door.

Instead of answering and engaging him, I threw his bag of clothes onto the hospital bed, then walked back out looking for Vera.

Vera raised an eyebrow at me in my jeans and T-shirt that had seen better days. "You know your mother would have your head if she saw you out and about like that."

"Since she's not here, I don't think that's going to be a problem." I smiled at her and she winked. "Now, I can just leave His Highness at home by himself, right? I did not sign on for more than chauffeur service."

"Yes, he can be alone despite the fact he's trying to play the sympathy card to anyone who will listen—which is exactly no one."

"All right, I just wanted to make sure, because he's not above lying to make sure he gets what he wants. I think I can resist punching him for the ten minutes it will take for us to get to his house."

"If you do punch him, just make it somewhere he doesn't have to come back to us for."

"Will do." I saluted her, figuring I'd given Waldo enough time to get dressed.

I did, however, knock on the door to make sure he was decent before I opened it. I had seen plenty of him when we were married and didn't need another view.

"Let's get out of here," he said when I opened the door to see him fully dressed and his hair back to its normal slickness.

"After you."

I trailed along behind him to the car, in case he fell or fainted. He'd very vocally denied a ride in the wheelchair.

I beeped the alarm of the car off as he neared it. I'd told him what aisle we were in before we'd cleared the front door. It was easier to let him think he was in control. He got into the passenger side gingerly. I got into the driver's seat and started the car.

What followed was ten minutes (make that seven, since I hauled tail) of absolute silence. He didn't once try to talk to me. In fact, he kept his face turned toward the window and his hands in his lap.

Fine by me.

Pulling into the driveway of the house I used to think was my pride and joy, I broke the silence. "Do you need help into the house?"

"No." He still hadn't looked at me. I didn't know whether to be grateful or offended.

"Fine. I hope you feel better."

"I'll feel better after this whole thing is finished." I didn't know what that meant, but knew better than to ask. I didn't want to know.

"Well, see you later." That was a lame thing to say. What else was appropriate, though?

"Not if I can help it."

All righty, then.

I watched him walk stiffly up to the front door and unlock it. There was something off with him, but I didn't know what. Ever since we'd separated he'd been high-handed, rude, and full of himself. Now he seemed deflated. But you know what? It wasn't my business and I was not going to get involved.

I backed out of the driveway with little to no direction. I'd go home and do a budget, maybe. Or it wasn't too late to start that movie. This was no more than a blip out of my life and he'd be fine.

When his ringtone sounded on my phone in the passenger seat, I groaned. I'd thought I'd gotten away far too fast and too easily.

"Yes?"

"I forgot a prescription I was supposed to have filled before I came home. Can you go get it?"

The fact that he asked instead of demanded was strange enough, but the tone of his voice was also softer. This was shades of the Waldo I had met and loved all of those years ago. My skin crawled.

"Yeah, I didn't even make it down the street yet."

"Then go now. I'm not going to be able to survive without this medication. Don't do anything else but fill it and come right back."

That was more like the Waldo I had left.

"Whatever. I'll be back there as soon as I can."

"It only makes you sound ignorant to say *whatever*. Since you're already on your way and I want the medication as quickly as possible, you may as well just pay for it."

What kind of odds did I have that he'd ever pay me back? Yeah, pretty much none. Waldo didn't even lie about a check in the mail, he just didn't give me anything, not even an excuse.

I sighed. He had great insurance, so it probably wouldn't cost me a fortune.

As I headed over to the pharmacy, I deliberately took my time. I might be ignorant, but I didn't have to be on his time schedule. Once there, I strolled through several aisles just to waste some more time. Looking at a magazine, I wondered what on earth the new heartthrob of the teenybopper set saw in him. I checked out the prophylactics aisle, though I had no use for them, and neither would Waldo for a while. I smelled some shampoo and considered dyeing my hair. By that time, my name had been called for prescription pickup, but I stopped in my tracks when I saw a familiar dark head over the tops of the short aisles.

The infamous Max was coming in. What were the chances he had followed me? I couldn't decide whether I should jump out and scare the heck out of him or run the other way. In the end, I ducked down behind the condoms, hoping he wasn't brave enough to look for me there, if he was even looking for me.

I totally was missing an opportunity to ask him what the heck was up with that bouquet from Darla. However, I was also missing out on possibly being stalked, which, since he was extremely good looking, could have been okay, but not after that delivery.

He looked around, going down the aisle next to me. I snuck into the next aisle, this one filled with baby paraphernalia. Perhaps the store had set this up deliberately. *Here's what happens if you didn't first shop in aisle 6A.*

I picked the perfect time to spring up. He'd rounded the corner and I stepped right into his space, causing him to jump back.

"What are you doing here, Max? Do you need something to cover the goods for a fantastic Friday night?" I gestured to the next aisle, then watched him blush.

"No. I was looking for you." He regained his composure and closed the distance between us, talking in a low voice. "You're in danger, Tallie."

"Yeah, from you," I retorted, jabbing him in the shoulder with my finger. "You're the only one who's following me around. The only one who delivered a bunch of flowers from a dead woman.

Whatever you think you want, or whatever you think I have, I don't. Now leave. I talked with Monty. He said he never gave you a delivery for me and certainly not one from Darla."

His eyes got hard at that last statement, and I was glad we were in the middle of the pharmacy. If he tried to lay one finger on me, I would scream bloody murder. Even the bored girl behind the front counter wouldn't be able to ignore me.

"If you had listened to me when I dropped those flowers off, I wouldn't have had to stalk you."

I made some ridiculous noise between a snort and a scoff. "Whatever."

"It's true. I had hoped to talk to you then, but you blew me off, making a spectacle out of us both. I couldn't exactly have a private conversation in the middle of Bean There, Done That after you demanded I get out."

"So if you listened to me then, why aren't you listening to me now? Did I not say it slowly enough? Get. Out."

"No, I'm not leaving until you talk to me." He shoved his hands into his pockets and widened his stance.

"And I'm not talking to you until hell freezes over, or you come up with a better reason than wanting to talk to me after freaking me out with a bouquet of flowers from a dead woman. Does Jeremy even know you're in town?"

He ran a rough hand over the top of his dark hair. There was a twinge in some parts of me I shouldn't mention in polite company, but I very fiercely squelched it. I was not one of those women who got all riled by a powerful man. I would not start today. I liked mine docile and agreeable.

He lifted a hand, probably aiming to grab my arm, and I literally growled at him. He raised both hands as if in surrender.

"What can I say to make you talk to me?"

I didn't waste any time thinking up a more polite answer to that ridiculous question. "Nothing."

"How about that if you don't start talking, not only is the IRS going to come after you with a vengeance, but that Darla's death might have had something to do with your ex-husband, which could bleed over onto you?"

Chapter 5

"What?" I said right as the overhead speaker squawked my name again. I turned to him and looked him dead in the eye. "You do not go anywhere. I will be right back."

I wouldn't have said he smiled at me, but a side of his mouth quirked up as he crossed his arms, then leaned against the display of pacifiers. "I'll be right here waiting."

After running to get Waldo's meds, I hightailed it back to the aisle where I'd left Max. Would he still be there? I wouldn't have been surprised if he'd jetted out, but there he was with his severe face on.

Where were we going to have this conversation we were supposedly going to have? All I knew was he had better come up with some damn good answers with those questions he'd just put into my head.

I wouldn't say I was out of breath when I got back to him, but I wasn't exactly floating like a butterfly, either.

"We can't go to my house," I said without preamble. "I don't trust you."

"I don't think you want to come to where I'm staying."

"You got that right, buster. We'll go to the funeral home." I left a brief message for Waldo, letting him know he was going to have to just bite the bullet a little bit longer and to deal with it. Hey, if I was paying for it all, then we were working on my timetable. And if he had something to do with Darla's murder, then I would brave taking the meds to his mom's and asking her to take them to him. Or maybe I'd send Max in with them and see how that worked out.

First I had to find out what Max knew and whether or not he was bullshitting me.

I let myself into the side door of the funeral home as the moon rose higher in the sky, knowing today was my father's day to have dinner with his friends at the VFW, Jeremy was out on the call for a body before a date, and my mother would be playing bunco, then going to Zumba for the evening. I wasn't telling Max that, though.

Leaving the door slightly ajar, in case I had to make a run for it, I led Max into the small kitchenette where I had sat with Burton last night. God, was that really just last night? How the time does fly when you're surrounded by intrigue and a dead body thrown in for good measure.

I didn't offer Max anything to drink or eat and that, along with the slightly ajar door, seemed to amuse him.

"You know, if I really wanted to take you out, I could have already done it."

"You could try, but you'd have failed. I'm on my guard at all times," I blustered.

He was out of his chair with his hand resting around my throat before I could draw another breath. I kneed him in the nuts because he might be fast, but I was a dirty player.

I made myself a cup of tea while he regained his breath in the chair at the table. I even hummed along to myself to cover the sound of him coughing.

"Are you ready to talk yet?" I asked as I sat down opposite him, blowing across the top of my cup to cool it down—and to get the scent to waft across the table to him. Who knew if he liked tea or if he'd gag? Regardless, I was doing my best to hide the fact my knees were knocking hard enough to rattle the table if I had been taller.

He swallowed manly-like and cleared his throat for a second. The first sound out of his mouth sounded like a mouse squeak, so he tried again. "You pack quite a punch."

"No, you'd know if I had punched you. That was a knee to the groin."

"Yes, thanks for that."

"You're welcome." I blew on the tea again, blowing on my palms at the same time. Terror gripped me that I was about to drop the mug and shatter more than just the ceramic when I showed how nervous I was. "Now, you said you had information. Spill. And it had better be worth enduring you following me into the protection aisle."

"Can I at least have a glass of water?"

"Oh, I guess." I grabbed a cup, filled it, then set it down about a foot from him on the table, making sure to keep out of arm's length of him. I wasn't stupid. Fifteen years ago had no bearing on right now. Wait until I told Jeremy his old friend was a loon.

Max had the gall to laugh. "You know, I'm not here to take you down, or out, or whatever your fervent imagination is whirling with. If you can believe it, I'm actually here to help you."

I snorted. "Last I'd seen you were delivering flowers late, being a general nuisance, and stalking me in the pharmacy. And if you remember, you just tried to attack me. How is that supposed to help me?"

"Look, I'm going to start at the beginning. Try to hold yourself in check while I tell the story, then I'll answer your questions when I'm done. Deal?"

"No, that's not a deal. I reserve the right to interrupt you at any time with pithy comments and scathing abuse." Sometimes, I got ballsy when I was scared; what more can I say?

This time his laugh was nicer and put me at least a little more at ease. "Duly noted. And for the record, I'm sorry for scaring you. That wasn't my intention. I've obviously been going about this all wrong and shouldn't have come in like a stalker. I was actually trying to protect you and I messed that up."

"I'm not going to argue with you on that one. I don't know what you think you're protecting me from, but following me around and generally making me feel unsafe is not the way to go."

He sat back in his chair, folded his hands over his flat stomach, and looked down at his lap. His head came up and his eyes zeroed in on me. "First off, what I'm about to tell you does not leave this room—not to Gina, not to your nosy mother, and not to your Uncle Sherman, not even your brothers."

"You know the players in my life. You have to remember how nosy they are, so I make no guarantees."

"Comments to a minimum, remember?"

"Yeah, that's not going to happen. So instead of starting your story with a warning, let's start with how the heck you know all that, and what it means to you. Where did you get all this info?"

It was a legitimate question, but he pinched the bridge of his nose and blew out a breath. "I'm an officer of the law."

Shock hit me low in the gut. "Shouldn't you be talking to Burton, then? I didn't hire anyone to follow me around, and I can't believe I warrant the attention of an outside law-enforcement agency. I haven't even gotten a speeding ticket in ten years." Well, not one that actually showed up on my record. I hadn't been the best of people when I'd been Mrs. Phillips III.

His neck flushed a little, making me wonder about his claim. Especially when his eyes darted away for a moment as he took a quick swallow of the water.

"What law are you an officer of, anyway?"

He just stared. Was he trying to bluff? I should've probably warned him I could bluff with the best of them, and therefore spot a bluffer a mile away. I'd have no problem when said bluffer was sitting across the table from me trying to still the drum of his fingertips on the old, scarred wooden table.

"What law? And I want to see your badge." I thought of offering him a few choices when he just continued to sit there, but I didn't want him latching onto something I said and running with it.

Silence was not a problem for me. I'd learned well from my dealing with my exuberant mother.

He pinched the bridge of his nose again and blew out another breath. "Fine. I'm an officer of the tax law."

I didn't even try to help it, I burst out laughing. "Seriously?" I asked when I had composed myself while he looked pained. "You are an officer of the tax law. Does that make you a Tax Ninja? A Supreme Bean Counter? The Taxinator?" I could have gone on, but he slammed his hand down on the table. I jumped, at the last second gripping my chair so I didn't fly out of it.

"This is not a joke, Tallulah. You're in danger and you are also under investigation by the tax bureau. You might not take me seriously, but you should. Something is going on here. I intend to get to the bottom of it. I'm an investigator of the tax law you're mocking. There were rumors something big was happening in this town, so I took it upon myself to look it up. And when I saw it was you, and possibly your family, I took the assignment to come and help. I fought for it when they wanted to send someone else so that I could try to protect you and, by extension, your family."

"And I'm supposed to believe this why? Just

because you say it? Do they often send guys in to investigate and have them pretend to deliver flowers? Follow the person around and try to make them feel unsafe? What, you think I'm going to fall into your arms and tell you all because you're this big, strong man?"

"You're right and I already admitted I was wrong. Honestly, I was going to try to do this without making contact with any of you at all, but it got out of hand."

"Pretty quickly, I'd say, if you've only been here for a day and your whole plan is shot to hell."

"This is not how I normally do my job. I was supposed to come in, gather information about your bank records, then take it back to my superiors so we could begin an investigation into tax evasion and embezzlement. But when I saw you and heard about how you're trying to rebuild your life, I decided to also find information that would keep you out of it."

Scooting back in my chair, I sobered right up.

"Please listen to me." He blew out a breath. "I have to make progress soon, before something even worse happens. I don't want you to be afraid of me, but you should be afraid. Your ex-husband hasn't paid business or personal taxes in years and years. He stashed that money somewhere along with a whole lot more, and they want to know where it is. Darla Hackersham was connected in some way. Now she's dead and Walden Phillips the Third is the walking wounded. My guess is someone is trying to get to that money before anyone else does. I want to know who is it and where it is. I wasn't going to ask before, but since this is so much bigger than what I thought I was signing on for at first, I'd really like you to help me since following you around and trying to ferret out the information is not working."

"But—but—but—" It was all I could get out of the enormous tornado of confusion going on in my head. Dorothy's ride to Oz had nothing on me.

"Look, let me lay it out. If you have questions afterward, then by all means ask them. But this game-playing is not getting me anywhere. And I have to get somewhere before Walden takes it upon himself to either get killed too, or someone finds that money. Now, are you ready to listen?"

"Yes," I squeaked, wrapping my hands around my mug and wishing it had some hard Irish cream in it.

"Now, when Walden didn't pay his taxes, he was still making enough to pay for your lifestyle without breaking a sweat. That money is not in his bank account, neither is it invested in stocks. It was a ton of money, far more than he claimed. The tax bureau was given information he was somehow in league with Darla and Darla had information regarding the whereabouts of the money. I came down here to find out if there was a way to get that information. But when I dropped off the flowers to her yesterday, her maid was there, and I had no time to try to get anything out of Darla. Then she was dead. I had thought about talking to you, but you didn't fall for the delivery-guy thing at all."

"Of course not."

He groaned. "I wasn't that bad, was I?" He shook his head, but continued. "I guess I was, but

I watched an unidentified man drop those flowers off at the back door of this place today and took them before you could get them. I was trying to bring them to you because I had steamed open the envelope of the card and knew whose signature that was. I wanted to talk to you, but obviously I went about it the wrong way. I've never been undercover before, and that's not an excuse, just a roundabout apology. Here's a more direct one: I'm sorry. I didn't know how else to approach you. Especially because I know Monty had not gotten a call for those flowers."

"How do you know that?" I whispered. My mind was trying to grasp so many things at once that I grabbed the only thing I could hold on to.

"I went through his receipts and I've been watching you."

"You what?" I was frantically trying to think if I had done anything financially inappropriate. I couldn't come up with anything, but that didn't mean I hadn't done it. "Wait, before you answer that, why are you involved in all this? You say you got the assignment, but why? And why isn't it a bigger team? For the kind of money you're talking about, it seems like it would be a whole slew of people looking into this and seizing records, not trying to ferret them out under the radar."

"Jeremy was my best friend. And I remembered liking you more than you like me right now. I didn't want you to get caught up in the mess if I could help it. Beyond that, unless the total is in the billions, I'm good enough for the first round of data collection. It's only when we get permission to open a true investigation that the teams get bigger."

"Huh." Not too intelligent, but it was the best I could do under the circumstances. I was half afraid I was having some kind of nightmare I wasn't able to wake up from. Either that, or I was going to hurl my tea at him and take off at a dead run. That business of Waldo's was in my name, if I remembered correctly, and had been for years. Even though we were divorced, would that mean I was still going to be responsible for all those taxes? The embezzling, even though I had nothing to show for it? Maybe instead of hurling my tea at Tax Max, I'd just hurl.

"I don't have a card to give you, as I'm supposed to be here only to gather evidence undercover, but you were getting way too inquisitive, and I can't have you blowing my cover. Plus, I could use your help. We can get this solved together."

I tried breathing through my nose to calm the urge to vomit. "Do you think the IRS will give me a tax break if I can come up with the money from Waldo?"

This time he laughed and I didn't find it derisive or threatening: A step in the right direction. "Yeah, I don't know about that. I guess it doesn't hurt to ask."

I relaxed a little. It didn't sound like they were after me specifically, so that was good. "Let me just state this for the record. I have no idea where that money is and no idea where it might be. I didn't even know Waldo had it. I certainly didn't know Darla and he were involved, though it doesn't surprise me at all." I believed in not speaking ill of the dead, but that woman was a hussy.

"They don't think you do. I looked into it before I took it upon myself to come up here. I talked to the guy in the office who started the inquiry and begged a chance to come straighten things out before we officially come in." He stopped and clamped his jaw closed. Took a breath and continued. "You've lived pretty frugally since moving out of Walden's home. They haven't had any luck finding that money, though, and so I came down here to sniff it out before someone else does. I haven't been here long. Normally I'd have more time, but Darla's murder might have stepped up my timetable a little more than I'm comfortable with."

"Do you really think someone murdered her for Waldo's money?" That sounded strange even to me. "Why wouldn't that just go after Waldo?" And why had Max clamped his jaw shut? Was it the begging part? I knew he was a tax consultant and with everything going on I had assumed he was here as a tax consultant, like a freelance investigator or something. But maybe there was more to this story than I knew. I didn't think he was going to hurt me at this point, but I wasn't totally convinced he was being aboveboard with me, either.

"You'd be surprised at what people will do when money is involved, even small amounts. And believe me, this is no small amount."

"That dirty, rat-fink bastard!" I wanted to ask Max more about his role here, but it had just occurred to me that Waldo had a bunch of money lying around somewhere while I was busting my hump to clean ex-friends' houses and dividing myself between what I wanted to do and what I had to do to make ends meet and gather a nest egg. I should keep his damned pain pills and not give them to him. In fact, I should go over there and threaten to shove them all down his throat if he didn't tell me where this treasure trove was hiding.

"You'll want to let go of that thought, whatever it is," Max said, breaking my mad.

"I do not need you reading my mind."

He smiled, all his pearly whites showing. "It's not the mind I'm reading, but your body language. Depending on how much we can find, there might be some left over after paying everything back and the fines. It should most likely at least get rid of your portion that's owed, but we have to get it first."

So I might owe something. I'd have to start searching out more cleaning jobs. That did nothing to brighten my mood. "Oh, I have an idea how I can get it for you." Waldo hadn't called me a ballbuster for nothing.

"I'm sure you do, but it needs to be throttled back."

"Are you sure?" I wouldn't say my wariness of him had dissipated altogether, but I was getting a much better vibe off him after hearing why he was here. Caution could stay, but the hostility I had been feeling was drifting away.

He laughed. "Yeah, you kind of scared me there

with your ferociousness, so I think we need to throttle it back."

"Oh, fine." I still could dream about it, though.

He stared into my eyes, making me squiggle in my chair. "Look, the problem here is I had no easy entrance to anyone, certainly not any of the wealthy people. I have no reason to contact Mr. Phillips, and he's not going to open his home to me. He's definitely not going to trust me with anything more than that phony smile."

So I wasn't the only one who could see past the Waldo he showed to everyone else. He wasn't going to get off easily when his clients found out about his tax evasion and definitely not if he'd been embezzling. I had thought he was doing just that before I left, but couldn't find any proof. If Max could get the proof, all those rich people were going to hang him, and then they'd see what he was really like.

"What do you want me to do?" Squiggling in the chair became bouncing with urgency to get started. Now.

"Stop being so eager, for one thing."

Okay, now he was going from funny to chastising. I really did not like chastising. "Do you not understand what this could mean for me?" I asked, knocking my knuckles on the table. "If I can get Waldo to hand over this money, or even take it from him, then I won't have horrendous taxes to pay. I'm struggling as it is, and I can't imagine what the total amount is. No matter what it is, I won't be able to afford it." I was dangerously close to tears with this new, mammoth wrinkle. "If Waldo gives it up then I can continue with my life as it should have been years ago before I even married the stupid man." I had a feeling I was pretty much yelling by the end of the monologue, but didn't much care. Max, for his part, didn't act like he'd even heard any change in my voice.

"I get what you're saying. I know it's tempting, but let's inject a little logic into this."

No conversation starting with *let's be logical* ever went my way. "Fine, logic me to death." Flopping back in my chair, I crossed my arms.

"I'm trying to keep you from death. For one thing, if Darla had pressed Mr. Phillips for the location of the money, or more money, and now she's dead—it's very possible he's the reason she's dead."

"But he was in the hospital this morning when I found Darla dead." I could spout my own logic when I had to.

"True, but that doesn't mean he hadn't found someone else to do the dirty work for him. I can't imagine Mr. Phillips getting his hands dirty."

"You've got that right. And you can drop the *mister*. I call him Waldo because it irritates him, just follow suit," I said.

He ignored my comment. "So until we can be assured where the money is, you might be putting yourself in harm's way by confronting him. What if he's not so against taking you out?"

I hadn't thought of that and Max knew it. "I can't imagine Waldo would kill me," I said with a bit of hesitation in my voice. I heard it and hated it.

"You barely took any of the money he admitted he had and that led the IRS to investigate him, leading to him being on a train to getting slammed for tax evasion for starters and hopefully embezzlement for the win. When he finds out, do you really think he'd hesitate if he saw a chance? He could blame it on whoever killed Darla and get away with it along with possibly leaving the country. You want that because you're impatient?"

Well, when he put it like that I felt like an idiot. "Sorry."

"Yeah, so am I. I'd love to be able to nail him and would if I really was a ninja bean counter, but that's not the way we're going to have to approach this. We have to go in methodical and get all our ducks in a row. According to my supervisor, there's information he had shared the whereabouts of the money with Darla. That might be what got her killed."

I was good with methodical when it involved cleaning, but this was obviously not the same. In fact, it might never be the same again if what he said was true.

"What do you want me to do?" If he said go about my normal business and leave Waldo alone, I was going to scream.

He raised an eyebrow, and I figured he got the message from the frown lines on my forehead far more than anything I could have said.

He blew out a breath that sounded just like

exasperation. "Okay. You have a prescription to deliver to him, right?"

"Yes."

"So do that and see if you can get anything out of him when you're over there. *Subtle* is your new middle name. Don't press and don't say anything directly about the money or the tax thing. Maybe you can ask if he'd heard about Darla, since he was in the hospital. Make sure to say something about how horrible it was. Watch for his reaction. You get checks from Darla, right?"

"I did, yes." And that was one more thing I would have to worry about now. Was Darren going to keep me on, or just make Letty do more work? "Why?"

"Does the writing on the card from the flowers look like hers?"

I thought hard about it, but honestly couldn't swear by it. I had a contract I'd signed with Darla in my apartment and that was it. While I didn't mind making Waldo wait longer, I didn't want Max up in my apartment. Shaking my head made him frown.

"Can I ask Waldo what happened out in the alley? I'm sure I can antagonize him into telling me." I warmed to that idea. Tallulah Graver, Amateur Sleuth. "Should I wear a wiretap in case he decides to confess all to me?"

This time his laugh was much bigger and far more appealing, crinkling up his eyes and showing off his pearly-white teeth as well as the dimple in his left cheek. There was the boy who would always buy me a Tootsie Roll even if my brother wouldn't.

"No, no wiretap. I think we'll go in low-key. I'll follow you in my car and park down the street. I doubt he's going to try anything as long as you don't do something overt, but I'd feel safer being near you."

"It's obvious you don't know me."

"I know you well enough to know you can do this. Just go in and give him the meds, engage in some conversation with him, and feel him out for what he knows about Darla. He hasn't answered any questions for the police about what happened in the alley. He swears he never saw anyone and must have been dragged into the alley, because there was no way he would have been back there."

"I can do that." And I had just the way to accomplish it, though it was going to cost swallowing some of my pride.

I fully expected to be harangued as soon as I knocked on Waldo's door, and I wasn't disappointed.

"What did you do? Stop to get a manicure and pedicure?"

I couldn't recall the last time I had either, but the goal here was to not piss him off further. I was trying really, really hard to remember that.

"They had to look for the medication. I nearly had to go to another pharmacy because they couldn't find it." I almost said I was sorry, but as much as I didn't want to pounce on him for information, I also didn't think it would be a good idea to start acting all acquiescent and out of character from the way we normally interacted with each other. He'd be as skeptical of me being nice as I would be if he suddenly handed me a check for a year's worth of bills.

"Fine, I suppose that's okay, then."

"Well, thank you, Your Highness." Typical us. We hadn't had a decent conversation without sniping in several years.

"Well, you can leave now, unless you want to clean my house or make me dinner," he said snidely.

No *thank you*, no *I appreciate it*. Nothing. The jerk.

Though, his offering to let me clean his house was just the opening I had been waiting for. "I am not going to clean your house, you big jerk. I can't imagine you don't have some bimbo to help you out around here. In fact, where's the bimbo who could have brought you home?"

His eyes narrowed as he glared at me. Good. Perhaps that would keep him from thinking too much about why I was holding the bag of clothes from the hospital and heading toward the laundry room.

"I'm just going to throw these on the floor in the laundry room, then I'll get out of your hair."

I stomped off to hide the sound of the brown paper bag crinkling. Someone from the hospital had put the clothes into the bag and handed them to me when I'd picked him up. I'd placed them inside the front door when I'd dropped him off, but after talking to Max I could have kicked myself. I had access to the clothes he had supposedly been dragged in. It had been dark in the alley when I'd seen him last night, but I didn't remember any kind of drag marks. Then again, they could have been on his butt. And that was exactly what I was checking for.

Nothing. I found nothing and that just raised my already high level of suspicion. Why wouldn't he answer the cops about the alleyway unless it was either illegal or embarrassing? Either way, Waldo was not going to tell me, so I decided to get my other question answered instead.

"Hey!" I yelled from the laundry room off the kitchen. "Did you hear about Darla?"

He didn't answer. I knew it was because he hated yelling in the house. He'd installed intercoms for that very reason. In return, I'd avoided the things like the plague.

I fished in his pockets like the old days, and nearly crowed when I encountered crinkly paper. As quietly as I could, I pulled the paper from his pants. Not surprisingly, there was a phone number on the back of a restaurant receipt. Despite the fact I detested him, he was attractive in a pretty-boy, polished way. His dark hair didn't have a single strand of gray in it and his deep blue eyes contrasted with his hair, making them mesmerizing. He had impeccable manners when he wanted to and charm that could make a tree want to peel off its own bark. He was a trim man, well-kept, and actually pretty delicious if you didn't look below the surface. Most people didn't. They saw the packaging but not the rotten sandwich inside the box.

There were more times than I wanted to think about when we'd been at dinner and he'd been given completely inappropriate invitations. But then we'd laugh about it later. I'd had no idea he'd actually been taking quite a few of the proposers up on their offerings until right before I left.

I shook my head. That was in the past and had nothing to do with today. Today, I turned the receipt over and read he'd had dinner with some-one on Wednesday night that he'd paid for. Steaks and salads with the dressing on the side. But what caught my eye was that the second steak eater had ordered theirs well-done enough to probably make the chef want to substitute a piece of shoe leather instead. And a baked potato with blue-cheese dressing. There was only one person I knew who ate their baked potato with blue cheese.

And she was dead.

Chapter 6

I hightailed it out of my former house as fast as I could without arousing suspicion. Of course, that wasn't too hard since Waldo was already engrossed in calling everyone he knew. His voice trailed me out the door as he lamented about how much pain he was in and how he'd appreciate it if they'd bring him food and take care of things—out of the goodness of their hearts, of course. He wasn't going to pay anyone to clean his house or mow his lawn. Not if he could help it.

There could be any number of reasons Darla and Waldo had been at dinner two days before her death. Any number of reasons, but none I could come up with. As much as Darla had wanted my husband, as far as I could tell they had never actually slept together. I wasn't sure why, since he'd pretty much slept with anything that didn't run away, but he'd disdained Darla, starting about two years ago. I had no idea why it had happened, or how, but suddenly Waldo had been looking down his nose at Darla and refusing her dinner invitations. He only allowed us to accept if it came directly from Darren. Even then, Waldo had been careful to stay away from Darla at a party. It was a flip I had noticed but not commented on. Before it had been Darren he snubbed, but whatever happened two years ago had made Waldo change his mind and snub Darla while cozying up to Darren. Well, as much as the snobby Waldo cozied up to anyone who didn't leave their number on the back of a receipt.

So why on earth would he and Darla have had dinner? And when exactly was Waldo stun-gunned? I knew from listening to the homeowners' gossip, as if the help didn't have ears, that he'd been seen at Darla's party. In fact, he'd been thought to still be there when the attack happened. After a quick call to my cousin, Matt confirmed Waldo had been seen at the party twenty minutes before the attack. So exactly when had he left and why?

Unfortunately, those were questions no one seemed to have answers for. This dinner receipt only intensified my curiosity. Zooming home was probably not my best idea, but I didn't have another one.

I zipped into my parking spot at the funeral home and was halfway up the steps when someone grabbed my arm. I turned with a yell and the start of a well-aimed kick when I realized it was Max who had ahold of me.

"You scared the crap out of me!" I did not drop my foot just yet.

"And you tore out of that house like a bat out of hell, if we're trading clichés." He raised an eyebrow at me. "I could have sworn you were going to come back out and talk with me to discuss what you were able to find out at your ex-husband's house."

A door opened downstairs, and I put my finger to my lips to shush him as I dropped my foot to the carpet. I motioned with my head for him to follow me, then shook off the tingles his hand made race up and down my arm. Now was certainly not the time to remember I was a woman and he a man.

I shooed him in front of me, then hustled up to the third-floor landing, just as my mom called from below.

"I have a few things to do upstairs, Mom!" I yelled down. "I'll call you when I'm done."

Not that I could keep my mom away for an indefinite amount of time. Nor was I doing anything I shouldn't. But since Max was the first man to come to my apartment since I'd moved in, I didn't want the added questions of who he was and what he was doing there. I still didn't know if he'd even told Jeremy he was here. I hadn't made the time to ask, with all the information coming at me.

Unlocking the door, I motioned Max to walk in ahead of me. Had I cleaned up this morning before I'd left? At this point I couldn't do anything about it. He'd either deal with the mess or run screaming. Either would be fine with me.

Although the running might have been better. The receipt was positively burning a hole in my pocket. But I didn't know yet if I trusted Max enough to show it to him.

He took a seat on the couch, sprawling in a way

that I'd have no choice but to touch some part of him if I sat there too. Instead, I grabbed a chair from the kitchen and sat in the middle of the living area.

A chuckle was his only reaction. It was enough that I wanted to move my chair further away, like into the hallway. One phone call from me and Max would be run out of town. Just one. As tempting as that was, this tax cheating, and even more worrying, the embezzling, would certainly bite me in the butt if I didn't find out where the money was. And if I didn't find out where the money was, I was going to do something much worse than just shock Waldo in the man parts. I'd rip the damn thing off with a hot pair of tongs.

"So, what made you run out of the house?" Max focused all his considerable energy on me, making a tingle hit me low in the gut.

Yeah, not happening.

I cleared my throat. "First I want to know if Jeremy knows you're here."

He cleared his throat. "I hadn't wanted to tell him until I knew more about the situation, so the answer is no."

"Why all the secrecy?"

"Well, Tallie, this isn't exactly the kind of news you can go around yelling until you have proof. I thought it would be better to wait until I had something." He shook his head. "Your brother and I have kept in contact, but I've never dropped by. I thought I'd be able to stay out of sight. But Darla's death is a game-changer."

"I guess that makes sense," I conceded. Although it still left me with reservations and questions.

"I'm not sure I should share anything with you until I know what exactly you plan to do when you find the money. Am I going to be dragged into this screaming and kicking?"

"I'll be honest with you. Probably. If the business made the money while you were still married, then the potential is there for you to also be liable. I'm not going to lie, if that's what you expected."

I didn't know what to expect. Knowing I might get a whopper of a tax bill, however, and possibly be tied to embezzlement, made me want to run for my small bathroom and retch. How could Waldo do this to me?

I scoffed at myself. It wasn't as if it was the only thing he'd ever done, even if it was the worst.

"And there's no way for me to protect myself?"

"You can swear you had no idea and they will take it into consideration for the embezzlement. The taxes are a different matter. The business is in your name and the fine for those is a whopper. The best thing you can do is find the money to take a dent out of what's going to be owed in the long run."

"Well, shit."

"No truer words."

I glanced over at him to see if he was being real with me or pulling me along. Was he really an investigator, or had he caught wind of the money somehow and wanted me to find it, then he'd take it from me? And I couldn't shake the fact that he had been at almost every incident since this had all started. He could have easily stunned Waldo, then grabbed his big funeral arrangement and met me at the door of the funeral parlor claiming he'd gotten lost in a town he had lived in until he was fifteen.

But then I shook my head. Why would he go to such elaborate lengths? Not only that, but I had heard Jeremy talk about him over the years in passing. He definitely had some sort of high-paying job having to do with taxes. I just had never known the specifics or cared enough to ask.

Wouldn't my mother have a field day if I set my sights on another high-dollar beau?

That too was off the table. I had no intention of getting mixed up with anyone of the male persuasion for a very long time. At the moment, I had a ton of other things on my plate that had nothing to do with Max's smile or the way his dark hair had a tiny wave above his left eyebrow.

Moving back to our conversation, I cleared my throat and my head of inappropriate thoughts. "Okay, so I can't protect myself, but I can buy some time if I can get Waldo to tell me where this money is."

"That's about the gist of it."

"And tell me again why you fought so hard for this assignment?" I crossed my arms over my chest and gave him my best beady-eyed stare. I wanted the real reason.

"I heard through the grapevine something was going down around here. When I found out it involved the girl who used to tag along, hoping her brother would treat her as an equal instead of a sidekick, I thought it would be a good time to cancel my vacation and take a look."

I wanted to believe him despite my skeptical

side. "There has to be more. You could be on some island being served by cabana girls." Did they have cabana girls? Gina and I only ever talked about cabana boys, but I supposed this was an equal-opportunity world.

He sighed and pinched the bridge of his nose: A familiar gesture now for when I exasperated him. "Look, the other part is that your mom and dad treated me like one of their own before I was shipped off to live with my grandmother in D.C. Can we just leave it at that?" He looked up, and I couldn't deny the little tingle that went to my gut and parts further along the road to my toes.

I'd let it go. For now. He might have scared me with his heavy-handed tactics and his scowls, but in the big picture it appeared he was trying to help me. And if he stepped out of line, my parents, who had been nice to him, could be equally vindictive if the case warranted. Hurting their little girl would definitely warrant. My mom might be on me about leaving Waldo, but I'd never told her the whole story and had let her believe that I just was unhappy. Maybe I should have been more honest about the whole thing. At the time, though, I just wanted out and done. Now I was being dragged back in.

"When are you going to let Jeremy know you're in town?"

"He's next on the list. I wanted to talk to you first and see if you wanted me to tell him you're in trouble, or if you'd rather, we could keep it between ourselves."

So the man actually thought I was capable of

making that kind of decision? Would wonders never cease?

I got up to pace. "I'd rather not tell them right now. Long story, but suffice it to say that if they know, they'll take a hammer to Waldo. They'd also make me start working more hours at the funeral home in anticipation of the fall. Not to mention my mother will be crawling all over me about how I either should have divorced Waldo sooner, or should have stayed with him so I would have access to all that money. I'm not sure which would be worse."

He cracked a smile, and I melted just a little, like chocolate in the late-afternoon sun. Not a good sign.

Clearing my throat, I sat down on the chair again. "So how do we go about getting Waldo to tell me where the money is? I guarantee you, he is not going to believe I want to help him after all the animosity between us."

I dug a hand into my pocket so he didn't see it had become a fist. I encountered the crinkled receipt and figured if we were in this together then I should tell him about the piece of evidence I had removed. At least since he was on my side, he wouldn't put me in jail. Or so I hoped.

Walking over to the small dining table, I put it on the polished surface and smoothed it out. The other paper, the one from the Bean, came with it. I'd thought it was my list of houses, but it turned out to be something else entirely.

He was behind me before I could call him, and the feel of his soft breath on the side of my neck sent little spasms to my fingertips. He was my brother's friend, and while he might be here to save me, I was not going to get involved with a bean counter. Maybe next time I'd look for a blue-collar worker with hands that had calluses and a tough exterior with a heart of gold, instead of my usual slick guy who turned out to be more slime than slick. Not that Max was probably slime, but one never knew.

"What do you have here?" he asked at my shoulder. I forced myself to take a step away, circling the table until we were facing each other.

"This one," I said, pointing to the receipt, "is a receipt that I found in Waldo's pants pockets, the ones he was wearing when he was attacked. If you'll notice the order, someone got a baked potato with blue-cheese dressing on it."

"That does not sound appetizing at all."

"I agree, and gagged when she asked for it at our house during a dinner party."

His head snapped up. "And who is *she?*"

"The only person I know who has ever desecrated a spud like that was Darla. But Waldo hated Darla, so I can't fathom why they would have been out to dinner together."

His expression sharpened. "I can think of a few, especially since this was only two nights before she was killed." His gaze moved on to the other paper. "Is this a threat?" He used one long, index finger to turn the paper toward him, and I had no excuse for the flutter that shot through me. Dumb, dumb, dumb.

"That I haven't had a chance to look at since I thought it was my own list, but I'd say *Meet me at eight or you'll regret it. BTDT back* might just be a threat." The writing was in a thick black marker, scrawled across what looked like the bottom of an invoice of some sort. There was a total at the bottom and light blue lines making boxes, yet no address, no account number, no identifying information. But someone had spent over a thousand dollars on something.

"If only we knew who this came from," I grumbled.

"Yeah, that would make things easier and leads me to my next thing. You need to get into Waldo's house and get him talking. Your life might depend on it. I know your livelihood does. I've got your back, I promise. How can I convince you that this might be our best chance?"

I huffed out a sigh. I didn't know the answer to his question, but I did know I was going to have to be nice to Waldo. Which I hated because he always ended up smarmy. The bastard. The bastard with my money and my flimsy financial security in some well-secured place. Yeah, I could do this. Even if I had to make him dinner or clean the house.

In the end, I wound up back at Waldo's, realizing he must be the one at all of Darla's parties who couldn't aim worth a damn. It was oh-so-tempting to yell to him that three inches wasn't too much to keep in his hand, but I was here snooping and didn't want to get thrown out before I found something worthwhile.

I'd walked Max down to Jeremy's office, telling my brother I'd found Max out in the parking lot.

Fortunately, my mom never had called to see what I was doing for so long upstairs, nor had she come to check on me and found a man in my apartment. Not that Mom would have been mad about a man in my apartment. On the contrary, she would have been jumping for joy and trolling the Internet for china patterns. But this way was much easier and avoided all kinds of conflict.

I had walked right into Waldo's, using the key from outside and telling him he needed his sheets changed and his house spruced up before he went to bed that night. Instead, I checked the medicine cabinet but found nothing unusual. Nose-hair trimmer, vats of hair gel, waxing kit for those eyebrows that just wouldn't stop growing. Waldo was a groomer's wet dream and proud of it.

Nothing was hidden in the linen closet and nothing but dust bunnies resided under the bed. He still refused to make the bed, and it was curious to see that, even in a king-size bed, only half had been slept in. My side was perfectly preserved. Part of me wondered if there was something significant about that. The other part didn't give a rat's ass.

His study was down to the left and I trespassed there next, wiping a quick cloth over the surfaces. Not my usual stellar job, but enough that he'd notice, and I'd still have time to look around. As quietly as possible, I opened each desk drawer, looking for some sort of ledger or a checkbook for an account, something that would indicate where the money was. Of course, I hadn't ruled out the possibility that he'd stuffed the cash in his mattress. I'd bounced on the thing before pulling the covers tight, just in case. I'd found nothing.

And I found nothing when I made my way to the bathroom, either. Part of me wanted to take that nose-hair trimmer out into the living room where he was lounging and offer to jam it in his ear if he didn't tell me where the money was. Then again, that was counterproductive to what I was trying to do. *Subtle* was supposed to be my middle name, according to Max.

Standing in the middle of the study, I caught my reflection in the mirror over Waldo's custom bar and saw the faint flush on my cheeks. I would not think about Max and color up at the same time. It was not going to happen. Beyond the fact that I wasn't ready, he lived in D.C. and I was staying here to open my business. If I wasn't leeched by back taxes first.

Thinking of those taxes and the missing gobs of money sent me to check behind the picture of Waldo's mother that hung on the far wall. He had a safe there and had probably been too lazy to change the combination. It was worth trying.

I had my hand on the edge of the frame when I heard the intercom crackle to life.

"Tallie, I need a glass of orange juice to take these pills with. I'll be waiting in the sitting room."

The temptation to yell down the hall was incredible. However, I remembered the money and decided I'd better be on my best behavior. This was the only time I was going to open the refrigerator. If he wanted a meal, he would need a takeout menu.

Glass in hand and snooping eyes still peeled, I

walked it in to him, where he sat in a recliner with his house shoes on and a set of pajamas I'd never seen before. Maybe he'd gone shopping since I'd left him. He'd never shopped for himself in the whole of our marriage, though. Most likely his mother had purchased them. . . .

"If you don't need anything else, I'm probably going to head out. I need to call Darren to see if he needs my help before the funeral."

"Funeral?" Waldo craned around in his chair to rest his blue-eyed gaze on me.

"Oh . . . um . . . yeah, Darla passed away this morning. Didn't anyone tell you?" I'd run earlier before we could have that conversation, I realized.

"No, no one told me," he said almost absently with a small crooking of the corner of his mouth. It wasn't quite a smile, but I'd seen that look before when he'd gotten something he'd wanted for a while and wasn't willing to show how much he'd wanted it. But did it mean he'd paid someone to kill her, or that he was just pleased she was gone?

"You don't seem too upset," I said, fluffing a pillow so as not to face him. I didn't want to seem too curious.

"You and I both know Darla and I have not engaged in a civil conversation in years. She had more money than she knew what to do with and not enough brains to know there was a difference between a left shoe and a right shoe without that maid of hers."

I opened my mouth to ask why he'd taken the woman in question out to dinner, then decided against it. Instead I said, "You're not supposed to speak ill of the dead."

"When have you known me to follow the rules?"

"True, but it's still not nice. She just died this morning. Whether or not you liked her you should at least feel sorry for Darren." The pillow was as fluffed as it was going to get, and I couldn't stay turned from him and read that body language Max had been talking about earlier. The night was incredibly dark outside the bay window. Glancing at the grandfather clock in the corner, I realized it was nine. I wanted dinner and then bed, in that order. This day felt like it had gone on forever.

Max. I needed to remember I was on a mission. Digging subtly had never been my forte, dammit. I was going to have to try, or I'd have to come back and wash his car or something to get more information.

"I'm sure Darren is relieved," Waldo continued with no prompting from me. "He'd come to me about a divorce a few weeks ago. I told him it wasn't worth it when you have to lose half of what you earned to some female who hadn't done more than sit on her ass."

Oh, now that was going way too far. I hadn't taken half of anything, barely walking out with enough to cover moving expense in my haste to get the hell away from this odious man. My hand clenched at my hip, but I held my tongue.

"What? No comeback? That's so unlike you, Tallie. All this cleaning isn't making you slow, is it? Must be all those chemicals."

The fluffy pillow lost some of its oomph when

I grabbed it and aimed it at his head. I yanked it behind my back when he looked up from his paper. Subtle. Subtle. Don't give him a reason to throw me out before I could get anything from him.

"You never were funny and I earned every blessed penny I got." I stuffed the pillow back against the couch, then turned back to him with my arms crossed over my chest. A parting shot here would be completely expected. "Not that there was nearly as much as I thought there would be."

He scowled at me. "I told you I had to put a lot back into the business. Regardless, you were the one who decided to leave. There wasn't a good enough reason, as far as I was concerned. So what if we didn't get along? Plenty of people stay married despite that. You could have just kept your own room and we could have remained as we were." He snapped the paper back up in front of his face as my jaw dropped.

During our marriage, it was obvious he didn't pay attention to me, or really have any clue who I was inside, but that last line was a topper. I would never have stayed in a marriage where I couldn't stand my husband. Quite frankly, I deserved more than that and, even if I thought Waldo was a pissant, he deserved more too. Not that he'd get it, but that wasn't up to me.

"So nice to know you regret me leaving you for nothing more than the money you had to give up." Now, how to cleverly insert a tax question? I had no brilliant ideas. Damn. And being that it was only September, he'd be skeptical if I asked about filing for next year. Double damn. I realized that I didn't even have our tax records from years past. I had never asked about them and figured I would just file my own this year. In fact, I didn't even know who had done our taxes to try to get a copy. How could I have been so stupid?

I was a failure at this whole sleuthing thing, not sure how to even introduce the topic, much less get him to cough up the goods. Maybe I needed to go home and rethink my whole approach before coming back. I would wash his car or even, God forbid, make him dinner if I had to in order to have access to that freaking money. I'd be so far in the hole as to be a resident of China if I got hit with a tax bill for all the money he'd made over the course of our six-year marriage.

He didn't respond, which was probably one of the smartest things he'd ever done.

"I'm finished here," I said, putting the cleaners back under the sink before grabbing my light jacket. "You need anything else, call someone else." I gave him a patently false smile that he returned.

"I won't call you if you don't call me."

"Got it in one, Waldo."

He made to get out of the chair, but wasn't fast enough as I trotted to the front door.

"Bitch!"

"Yep, that too," I said as I yanked open the front door and came face-to-face with Burton, who had his finger poised at the doorbell.

"What are you doing here?" we both asked at the same time.

He raised a bushy, gray brow at me. Sighing, I stuck my hands on my hips. "I had to pick him up from the hospital. No one else would come get him. Then he asked for a prescription to be filled and then I stuck around to clean up a little, since I felt bad that he couldn't do anything." That last part was a lie. I knew Burton knew it when the other brow crept up to join the first.

"I hope you're not sniffing around. I told you to stay out of this. And I have more questions for you." His gruff demeanor set me on edge and gave me pause. I hadn't thought of what I was doing as sniffing around, necessarily. Finding the money was paramount and I'd do what I had to do to get it. Darla's killer was also now my concern. If I could find the money first, then things would go much more smoothly. Besides, it might not pertain to Darla's case at all. Just because Max said Darla and Waldo were in league together didn't make it true.

The receipt for the restaurant dinner with the two of them decided to pop into my head at that moment. I ruthlessly shoved it back down. I would take the rest of the evening to figure out how to hand it over to Burton without having to lie about how I got it.

Instead I smiled. "No sniffing going on here. If you need to talk to His Highness, I'll let you in while I . . . make dinner." Damn, I was going to have to open the refrigerator again after all. I wasn't going anywhere if I could stay to hear what Waldo said to Burton.

* * *

Taking my sweet time, I made a Lebanon bologna and cheese sandwich while I eavesdropped on Waldo and Burton's conversation. I, of course, would never admit I had been eavesdropping. No one but Max needed to know that. Max, who was probably wondering where I was, since I'd been here for almost ninety minutes when I'd told him I wouldn't be more than thirty at most.

"So when was the last time you saw Darla?" Burton asked in the living room. As much as I hated the intercoms, I was thankful for them now. Waldo had made them capable of opening up in a room to listen, not just talk, and though I'd loathed it, it was very handy now.

"I have not had contact with Darla since the night of her party. Even then, it was minimal."

Truth or lie? It had occurred to me that maybe Darla had been the stun-gunner. How would she have managed that, though? Leaving the party and getting back before anyone noticed seemed impossible. With her brash personality and in-your-face hostessing and drinking, someone would have noticed if she were gone for that amount of time.

"We found your car down the block by the hardware store. Did you drive it there after the party?"

"I'd like the car brought to my home. Tallie can drive it if you won't have someone drop it off."

Could I really now? He'd never let me drive the Beemer before.

"There's a matter of evidence, Mr. Phillips. Until I have some answers, I'm not releasing anything to you."

Oh, I would bet my best squeegee Waldo was not taking that well. Was it wrong that the thought filled me with glee? Nah, probably not.

"You will return my car, Burton, or I'll have your job," Waldo growled through the intercom. I backed up because I remembered that voice. It never heralded anything good.

Burton wasn't having the same issue. "You can certainly try, Mr. Phillips, but I assure you that you wouldn't like to be in my seat. I don't think you have the balls for it, as it were."

I choked back a laugh at the last second.

"You may leave now, Burton. I will have my attorney call you regarding the car."

"I'm not ready to go yet, as I have a question or two about Darla's murder that I think you could answer for me. So you either answer now, or your attorney can meet us at the station where we can discuss all this, as well as your car."

Burton was not giving an inch. It made me wonder what exactly they had on Waldo. Especially when Burton had made it clear that I was a suspect in Darla's murder.

"I'm not going anywhere. I'm injured and was told to be on house rest. Beyond that, ask away. I have no idea what happened to Darla. Tallie just told me a moment ago that the woman had died. Surely I can't be your prime suspect."

Burton grumbled something I didn't catch, then said, "We're exploring all avenues at this point."

"Which is cop speak for you have no idea what you're doing and are just fishing around until you snag something. I know how this works, Burton.

Your job isn't as hard as you think it is. But if you're looking at me, you're grasping at straws. I was in the hospital when she was killed. I had nothing to do with it. You might want to look at Darren, her husband, though. He was recently asking me about divorce. This certainly solves his problem without having to give over half his money."

Bastard.

"Can I get a glass of water?" Burton asked.

I had a split second to disconnect, or when Waldo hit the button to ask, it would set off an electric squeal. Then he would know I had heard everything. I rushed to the speaker and hit the button one second before the unit beeped. I sighed in relief as Waldo's voice came over. "Tallie, Burton wants water. You think you can manage that since it has nothing to do with cooking? And where's my sandwich? It can't take you that long to slap the cheese and meat onto bread, unless you think you've gone gourmet and are coming out with some ridiculous concoction."

Fuming, I ran a glass of water and stomped out with his plate and the glass of water. "I'll be going in just a minute, Your Highness. Anything else?"

He peeked under the bread to see what I'd done. Resisting the urge to smack his hand took everything I had.

"No, that'll be all. You know the way out. You've left often enough."

No wonder I'd left him. But as much as I wanted to leave, I also wanted to know what Burton would say about Darren's part in this.

"Thanks, Tallie," Burton said before turning

back to Waldo. "We've already looked at Darren. He has a rock-solid alibi. I guess you do now too." He flipped his notepad closed, then gulped the water down in one swallow. "If you think of anything, let me know. You might not have cared for the woman, but we still need to figure out who killed her."

"So who are you going after now? The maid? The pool boy?"

"Have a nice night, Mr. Phillips. Thanks for your time and the water." He turned toward the front door, winked at me, and left.

I flipped Waldo the bird behind his back where he couldn't see it, then left too, without another word.

Burton caught me outside. "Did you hear every word in there?"

"Nope," I lied.

"I find that hard to believe, but we'll let it go for the moment. Now what else do you know about the scene at Darla's? Did you remember anything since our talk this afternoon?"

I gave him the rundown of where I'd gone and what I'd done, but nothing appeared new to him. I wanted to mention the papers now, but I hadn't had time to formulate a reason as to why I had them, nor did I have them with me. Tomorrow would be soon enough and I'd just fudge when exactly I found them. Not exactly honest, but being honest didn't appear to be getting me anywhere with Burton at the moment, anyway. Scratching his head, he let me go with a warning to stay out of trouble. I promised before hopping into my car. After I turned on the engine, I sat for a moment.

There was something more going on than I was aware of. Tomorrow morning, before I started my cleaning route, I would give over the receipt for dinner and the threat. Though the first might not be proof—perhaps there was one other person in the whole world who ate their potato with blue cheese—it could be a lead for them to follow that I was holding back. The second was definitely something, though I had no idea who had written it. And if I gave them over in a few days, then Burton might be getting in my face in a way he hadn't yet. Decision made, I felt better.

I'd run it by Max to see what he thought. Although why I should do that eluded me. I still didn't totally believe his motivation. Okay, so my parents had been nice. My parents were always nice when my mother wasn't nagging and my father wasn't consumed with dead people. But why would Max come all the way here from Washington D.C. to save someone he hadn't seen or talked to in fifteen years? Unless he really was just that kind of loyal guy. If that was true, then I might be in more trouble than I thought.

Chapter 7

Bodies coming in the back door had never been my favorite part of the business. Fortunately, my father and Jeremy were downstairs to deal with Darla being wheeled in the next day. I would see her at some point, but by then she'd be dressed and coiffed and done up to look as close to her old self as possible.

Instead of thinking about her going down the elevator to the basement, I continued to wrestle with how to tell Burton about the receipt and the threat. It seemed like it should be a given that I hand them over right now, but I still didn't know what I was going to say. Mainly, I didn't know how to hand them over without getting in trouble for withholding evidence. There had to be some kind of law against picking up things that didn't belong to me and taking them.

When the word *stealing* came to mind, I shied away from it. Withholding would be bad enough, especially if it would put them on the trail of Darla's killer, but stealing could just be the cherry

on the top of my idiocy. However, I still didn't
know if the receipt was even proof. The threat, at
least, I knew would be taken seriously.

And I couldn't just leave them in an obvious
place, then hope Burton realized what they were.
I hadn't had a chance to talk with Max since yesterday, when I'd shoved him into Jeremy's office.
I'd heard they'd gone drinking after I'd returned
from Waldo's. Since I had no idea where Max was
staying, or even a phone number for him, I'd
have to wait until he got in touch with me again.
In the meantime, I had nothing to do at the
moment.

Like the shoemaker's children who had no
shoes, I hated cleaning my own house. With nothing else to do and not wanting to go downstairs
just yet, though, I was stuck with cleaning or
watching television. Right now I was too agitated
to sit even to watch my favorite hotties on the
drool box.

Which left me cleaning. I dusted, I spruced,
and I wiped, but none of it took the picture of
Dead Darla out of my mind. How long had she
been in the closet? Who had killed her? What was
that perfume she had been wearing? Who had
done the deed?

Admittedly, Darla had enough people who tolerated her for her social standing and her money,
yet detested her otherwise, but who would have
had the guts to actually kill her? Or even the inclination?

The guy with the shoes popped into my head,
but I had no idea who he even was. I would have
thought I would have seen him at least at one

party if he was invited into her office and felt secure enough to yell at her. And nothing seemed to have come from my mentioning him to Burton.

Which led me back to Darla's circle of friends. It was one thing to covet an invite to one of her parties, yet not like her. But to actually kill someone took a whole lot more than thinking she was a social climber who needed to be set down a peg.

I was never so thankful when my cell phone rang. At this point I might answer it even if it was Waldo, if just to break the monotony.

Instead it was Darren. Was I about to start begging for my job? I was supposed to be there soon due to his request yesterday, so why was he calling me now? If it was to make me beg for my job, as I feared, I could think of other things I'd like to do, including scrubbing my kitchen floor with my toothbrush.

"Darren, I'm so sorry for your loss."

"Right, thanks. You already said that." He cleared his throat. "Look, Tallie, I'll get right to the point. I need you to come pick out something for Darla to wear in the box when you clean the house for the after-the-funeral thing. We have time since your father told me the burial is late next week, but I'd prefer to get this done."

I hesitated. Did I want to be the one to pick out Darla's funeral clothes? That was usually a task for the spouse or another family member. But as far as I knew Darla's parents were both dead and obviously Darren was not interested—even going so far as to call the coffin a box.

From my conversation with Waldo, there had been some tension in the marriage. However, this was more callous than I had thought he'd be. Then again, I could probably look around while I was gathering clothes. Max might appreciate that. Not that I needed his appreciation. Lordy. I just wanted my potentially devastating taxes taken care of and my name cleared.

"I can do that this afternoon if that works for you."

"Fine. Today is Letty's day off and I'll be out golfing, so just let yourself in and do your thing. I'm sure you know where everything is."

I assured him I did, then hung up, feeling almost sorry for Darla. On second thought, if I was still married to Waldo, he wouldn't have flinched if I turned up dead, so what was the difference?

After sneaking out of my apartment, I stopped at the police station, figuring I'd just wade in.

Our police station was small, so I could hear voices down the hall as Suzy tried to get Burton to come up front.

"She can wait," Burton said. "She's not going anywhere and I have paperwork to fill out."

It went back and forth like that for ten minutes until I couldn't stand it anymore. "I have evidence that you're going to want to look at, Burton," I yelled down the hall. "Of course, that's only if you can pull yourself away from all that lovely paperwork."

Funny how fast he came rushing out of his office after that.

"What've you got?"

After carefully placing the receipt and the threat on the counter, I pointed to the first one.

"This is a receipt I found in my car. It must have fallen out of the clothes Waldo had on when he was stun-gunned." I think I covered that well without implicating myself. "See this baked potato, here? The only person I've ever known who orders it with blue-cheese dressing is Darla. This puts them at dinner together two nights before she was killed, even though he hates her."

Burton barked with laughter. "That's not evidence. And you expect me to believe it just fell out in your car? You can't prove that Darla is the only person in the whole of creation who eats her baked potato like that. Sounds kind of delicious, if you ask me. Maybe Waldo just has a new flame who likes things a little different. That bother you, Tallie?"

I was so tired of people assuming I still wanted Waldo. Didn't anyone remember that I was the one who left him?

I huffed out a breath as he shoved the receipt back at me.

"What else you got? Something else to shift the blame off yourself? Something you just happened to have found?"

Well, that put me in a crappy position, but I was going to at least try. If Burton was set on me being the bad guy, I wanted to give him every opportunity to know I wasn't before we got to the jail part of my life.

"This one I found at the Bean. Yes, I know. I found it again," I said when he smirked. "It was on one of the chairs in the back room. I thought it was the list of jobs I keep in my back pocket. But when I looked at it, it was obviously a threat. That serious enough for you, Chief?" I challenged him.

"That one at least has some potential, even though you again conveniently 'found something'. How do I know that you didn't write this? You could have sent it to Waldo anonymously, stun-gunned the poor guy, and then miraculously come across this note to give me like a good little citizen."

"Are you kidding me?"

He shook his head slowly, clasping his hands on the counter in front of him.

A scream built at the back of my throat, but I kept it locked there. "Do you want me to take this one with me too, then?"

"Oh, no, it's mine now. And if I find out you have this kind of paper in your possession or have bought something from whatever store this is, then I have you nailed tight for at least one of these things." He gave me a second to sputter before continuing. "You know the way out. Let me know if you happen to 'find' anything else and I'll certainly give it my full attention." He walked away as visions of jumping over the counter to tackle him whipped through my mind.

I stared at Suzy with my mouth hanging open. She shrugged. "I'd be careful, Tallie. He seems to be gunning for you."

"But I didn't do anything."

"But you have before . . ."

My God. I could go to the pokey for murder and assault because I used to play my music too

loud and didn't pay for going forty-five in a thirty
speed-limit zone. Icing on my crappy plate.

I parked around back at the Hackershams after
I left the police station with the dinner receipt in
my pocket. I didn't want to get yelled at for parking in front. Darla wasn't alive anymore, true, but
I didn't know how Darren felt about the help and
I wasn't taking chances. I'd do everything by the
book, hoping Darren kept me on to continue
cleaning. I really couldn't afford to lose this job,
especially if I couldn't find that money and the
dreaded tax bill really came my way.

The thought made me sick to my stomach, so
I concentrated on finding the hidden key in the
backyard and let myself in.

The house felt different without Darla's presence. As if the structure was breathing a sigh of
relief, although that was ridiculous. The flowers
that had been delivered on the day of her death
were still on the windowsill, wilting in the full-on
sun. I moved them to the top of the piano as I
walked through, purposely avoiding the hallway
with the closet and headed for the second floor.

Of course, I knew where everything was, but
going through someone's closet was different. It
wasn't as if Darla and I had ever been more than
air-kissing buddies. We hadn't shared secrets, or
clothes or even tips on how to get your makeup
right. But now I had to think about Darla as a
woman, not just a nuisance and a reluctant check
signer.

Opening the door of her enormous walk-in
closet gave me pause. How in the world was I

going to choose just one thing for her to wear out of all this mess? Silks flowed next to satins, brocades cozied up with linens and suedes. She had one of everything and in every color imaginable. I stumbled back in the face of the profusion of color and sat on a chair near the window to assess the situation. I'd known Darla had a ton of clothes. In fact, I'd rarely seen her in the same thing twice, but this was astounding.

And I already knew Darren would be no help. Now what was I going to do? Maybe a picture would help: a place and an outfit Darla had looked happy in could point me in the right direction. I'd looked at pictures like that before at the parlor from helpful relatives who brought in twenty-year-old pictures, hoping the Gravers could make Aunt Beatrice look younger for her final viewing.

After entering Darla's office, I sat in the chair at her desk. I had just been in here. It felt like a hundred years and a ton of stress later. Stepping over the threshold had reminded me again of the guy with those shoes. And that made me wonder again if maybe he had been the one who had hurt her. If Burton chose not to use that info, I might have to find the guy myself.

Another bouquet of flowers stood on the top of Darla's desk. If she'd sent these to herself, then it was no wonder she had a huge outstanding bill at Monty's.

There was a card, though. Plucking it from the arrangement, I turned it over in my hand, catching the familiar logo again and wondering who had delivered the flowers. Was it Max? Had he dropped off the flowers, then shoved a knife in Darla before shoving her into the closet? That was ridiculous, though. He'd explained his reasons for being here. I couldn't use him being at every incident as a valid reason to doubt him. Hell, if that were enough, I'd have to consider myself a suspect too.

I'd dug in for a little more research last night after I'd gone to bed and I had finally found Max. He was a part of the IRS Criminal Investigation team and he looked awfully good in a pair of swim trunks at the beach. Apparently, he went by the name Bennett Maxwell on social media. Maybe to keep people from knowing who he was. He probably had people who would be out for him because of his job.

Ten minutes passed with me glancing at the card every few seconds and trying to find a picture in which Darla looked truly happy. The flowers had been signed from one of Waldo's old clients, Mr. Fraller. There could be any number of reasons why he had sent Darla flowers. None that I could think of at the moment, but surely there was some reason he had sent her what I figured was a pretty expensive bouquet. Maybe it was the new rage in the elite set to send flowers all over the place for hostessing.

Leaning back in the chair, I swung back and forth a few times. My whole day stretched out in front of me at this point. With all of my normally scheduled houses cleaned, there was nothing my father would need me to help with at the funeral home, if he knew what was good for him. Even my laundry was caught up.

I kept waiting for inspiration, but it didn't come, so I started poking around the desk. I could have cleaned as I'd promised Darren, but I made note of only a few things that actually had to be straightened as I'd walked around and then upstairs. The police hadn't left the mess Darren had insinuated. I'd get to it soon enough.

The desk yielded nothing worth noticing. It did, however, lead me to begin poking around the room in general. Darla had all the classics stacked on the built-in bookshelves, along with some of the more contemporary bestsellers. Not that she had read any of them. I knew for a fact she hated reading. She kept them for show, just like the rest of her house and her life. All for show and now it was over, the curtain called.

I hadn't exactly hated Darla. I had certainly disliked her, but I'd also tolerated her, and while not devastated at her demise, I was a little sad she was gone. Being honest with myself, though, I admitted I was more curious as to who *had* hated her enough to end her life and so up close and personal. Someone would have to touch the person they were killing to hit that kind of mark, I figured. How had it happened? Where had it happened? I doubted it had been in the closet itself since I hadn't seen blood on the floor. And there would have been blood on the floor, I had no doubt about that.

Running my finger along the spines of the books on the chest-level shelf, I again tried to picture how it could have happened or even where. But my imagination was not that fertile and had never been, according to Waldo. I wasn't creative, according to him, and only good to make his parties sparkle with the help of a professional hostess.

I shook my head and shoved those thoughts out. They weren't doing me any good and had no bearing on what was currently going on. Not to mention Waldo wasn't going to be using that particular equipment anytime soon, regardless.

Leaning against the shelving unit, I enjoyed a moment of pure, unadulterated glee that his second-most prized possession was going to be out of commission for who knew how long.

Something shifted behind me. I nearly stumbled as the wall moved back, then slid into the section beside it. I stood there, stunned. This was way too much like a *Scooby-Doo* episode for me.

That didn't stop me from ducking into the little room, even though I had no idea what I might find.

"Huh." The walls were lined with boxes and boxes. Hatboxes, shoe boxes, boxes with shipping-company labels on them and personal labels. There was no rhyme or reason to the way they were arranged or what was in each of them. It occurred to me that I probably shouldn't move anything. Several times, Burton had very pointedly told me not to touch anything. But honestly, I just couldn't help myself.

Reaching into a shoe box, I pulled out gobs of costume jewelry in every blingy design you could think of. In the next was bow tie after bow tie. In a third, silks scarves ran through my hands like a clown continuing to pull them from his sleeve. What the hell did she need with all this?

A crinkle in the scarf box caught my attention and I pulled out a receipt for over two thousand dollars in merchandise. For a moment, something caught at the back of my mind, though I couldn't figure out what. Until I looked at the bottom of the paper and found the same blue lines and font as the half piece of paper the threat to Waldo had been written on.

I took a step back, because this confirmation only raised more questions, and stumbled into the far wall. Stacks of paperwork fell on my neck and shoulders like mounds of snow dropping from laden tree branches. What the hell was all this?

I used the back of my hand to shuffle papers around so there would no prints. I wasn't dumb. The first pass showed me taxes from years past, paperwork Darren kept on hand per tax guidelines, I guess. But under that was more paperwork, official paperwork to change a person's name with the state seal of Tennessee on it.

I shoved a few things into the top of my baggy shirt. This stealing thing was becoming a habit. But I wanted to read more about Darla and I was hoping the little diary I'd taken, along with the paperwork I'd found, would tell me details to help find her killer.

Holy hell, there was a whole lot more than murder going on here. Darla being dead might only be the tip of the iceberg.

Right now, that might be the least of my problems, though. I tried to move from under the paperwork and found I was stuck. There was no moving the avalanche of paperwork that had come down on me. Every time I tried, another pile would slide in to fill the space I'd created and I was stuck again. I was a half-second away from trying to dig out my cell and call for help when a shadow appeared outside the wall panel.

Should I yell for help or hope the person didn't notice me? Being caught in a compromising position would not be a good thing, but being stuck here all night when I really had to pee wasn't exactly my first choice, either.

"Help me out, please. I feel almost buried alive." I said the words very calmly, but inside I was quaking. I wanted out of here and wanted to honestly scrub my brain and eyes with Clorox. I could have done without this in my already-ridiculous last forty or so hours.

Someone reached down a very masculine hand. Part of me hoped it was Max because that would be the least worrisome choice. It could also be very bad, since he would, yet again, be where he wasn't supposed to be without being asked. Just as I was. I grabbed on gratefully and let him yank me out of the mess I had created. After dusting myself off and taking far longer than I should have, the man cleared his throat.

"Was there something specific you thought you might find in here that you didn't see in Darla's closet?"

Oh, man. Darren. He would have been second-to-last on my list of people I wanted to rescue me, right after the actual killer. How was I going to explain this? "I was looking for . . ." I stopped talking when he just raised an eyebrow. "I was trying to find a picture of Darla happy so I could match it to the mounds of clothes in her closet. I was looking at her books and I leaned against the bookshelf and it opened on its own." I raised my hands in a gesture of surrender, hoping that I wasn't shifting anything I'd stuffed down my shirt. If the book or the paperwork dropped out of the bottom of my top to fall at my feet, I would definitely not have any explanation for that. "I swear to you I did not go looking for anything. I was trying to do as you'd asked and then this." I gestured back behind me as if he wasn't already staring intently at the motley mess of stuff on the floor, spilling out of the hidden room.

"And what is this?" He gestured around. I didn't have to look again to know that there was a ton of stuff. But it did look like maybe Darla had not always been Darla, and that could be sticky, indeed.

"Um, I'm not sure what this is exactly, but if you could step back then maybe I could help clean up?" Not the smartest response, but I really did have to buy time. Did Darren know Darla had once been Marla and that someone was trying to blackmail her? Honestly, I didn't want to know, but I had a sick feeling in my stomach it was going to be a conversation I couldn't avoid.

He took exactly one step back as I wobbled on my feet. If he wasn't blocking the doorway I might have bolted. Instead, he'd crossed his arms and planted his feet. It didn't look like he was going anywhere any time soon.

"Did you find anything interesting?" he asked, an edge to his voice I had never heard before.

Could Darren have actually killed her? Sure, he had an alibi for the murder, but he worked in an office with a back door from what I remembered from my one visit. And he also had a secretary who was more worried about the finish on her nails than she was about where Darren went.

"Define *interesting*?" Still buying time, but the thundercloud that passed over Darren's face told me that the time was almost up. Lordy, I didn't want to be the one to tell him about the Darla/Marla thing. Yet, if he found out and wondered what I knew, then I did not want to be in his crosshairs. Especially if he had killed Darla. This just kept getting worse.

"I'm guessing somehow you stumbled over the fact Darla does not exactly have the lineage she told everyone about."

It wasn't a question. Reckless me, I answered it anyway. "I just saw a sheet that said she had changed her name."

"Changed her name." Darren laughed, but did not sound happy. "Yeah, she changed her name, and her appearance, and her background. I had no idea until last year that she was anyone but a high-society dame from outside Philadelphia."

"I still don't know that she is, and I'd rather you not tell me. That way I won't know anything and can just be blissfully ignorant." I was banking on Darren remembering me as one of his contemporaries instead of just the help. I couldn't afford to be taken out with the trash.

Darren sighed, his posture relaxing while he scratched his five-o'clock shadow. "Tallie, I need you to keep this to yourself."

Great, one more thing I did not want on my plate. That sucker was going to crash to the floor at any moment.

My first thought was to tell Burton, anyway, no matter if I lost my job or not. But then I remembered that he had essentially challenged me to come to him with anything else I happened to 'find' on my own. Damn.

I kept my mouth shut and didn't promise anything. Burton wouldn't be thrilled if it came to light later, but I owed him nothing at the moment and I was going to figure this thing out on my own. He had already made up his mind about my guilt, and anything I tried to give him was more proof in his eyes that I was trying to shove the blame on someone else.

Right now, though, I had more at stake than worrying about making the chief of police happy or not. I had to keep my wits about me because Darren was still blocking the door.

When I didn't say anything, he dragged his hand down his face and reached behind him. My mind went blank and the urge to run made my legs burn. I was not going to die in some secret closet filled with papers and boxes.

But all he did was pull his checkbook out of his back pocket. "What's it going to cost me?"

"Cost you?" I squeaked, then cleared my throat. "Cost you for what?" I asked, trying again to sound more like myself.

"For you to keep your mouth shut. I can't afford too much. I wouldn't be able to explain the amount away, but fortunately you're the cleaning lady. I can just say I gave you a bonus, if my accountant asks during tax time."

Tax time reminded me of the whole Waldo tax-evasion thing, which made me gulp. Darren, having no idea what was going through my head, took it wrong.

"I don't have cash on hand, so we're going to have to make this work this way. Now, how much?"

How much? How much? To keep it together and get out of here in one piece, I had to come up with a number that wasn't too high but not too low. It had to make sense, but not be greedy. I put on my old Mrs. Phillips's thinking cap, no matter how much I now detested that I had been that person. "Let's say five hundred."

He didn't even raise a brow, simply put the checkbook up against the wall and wrote it out, signing it with a flourish.

"You'll keep your mouth shut?" He thrust the check at me without releasing it.

"I have no one to tell and nothing to tell, as far as I'm concerned. If you want people to know, then that's up to you." Of course, I didn't promise to keep from giving Burton a nudge in the right direction if he asked. I just wouldn't be the one to bring it up.

"So, this is where all my money was going." Putting his checkbook back in his pocket, he looked around with a grimace. "I could have sworn she had signed on as someone's sugar mama, but instead I find a bunch of crap I'm going to have to give to the local shelter."

"It looks like most of the receipts are here. You might be able to return most of it."

"I don't have time for that and this way it's a tax write-off. Jesus, what did I ever see in that woman?"

That was my cue to leave. "I'm just going to grab something out of the closet and take it to my dad. I'm sure he's wondering where I am. I can come back later and do the cleaning if you want."

"Yeah, yeah. I have a dinner meeting, so any time after six is fine. If you don't mind going through all this too, I'd appreciate it." He rubbed his hand over his head. "What a mess." And he left without a backward glance.

I was out the door before a body could sing the "Hallelujah Chorus." The diary was digging into my flesh, so I yanked it out of my shirt. Aaron, the pool guy, was standing out at the pool house when I came tearing around the corner. Forcing myself to slow down, I tried not to make eye contact. But then he waved and manners demanded I wave back. Unfortunately, I had the small diary in my hand. I jammed it into my pocket and picked up speed. When I got to my car, I tucked the diary into the glove box and started back to the place I called home.

Heading out of the circular driveway, I was not surprised to see Ellen McKay parking and exiting her car with a casserole. As the chairwoman of the Women's Auxiliary Group, she would be the first of many. Darren had a big freezer. He should be okay, as long as he could fend off the advances of the woman who was famous for her sexual innuendo and trying to get men into compromising positions. Not my problem.

Back at my quiet apartment, I pulled together the things I had and laid them out on the table. Having made a point to sneak back into the apartment, I locked the door firmly behind me. The last thing I needed to do was call attention to myself. I was in far deeper than I had thought and didn't know how to get out. I had not deposited the check on the way home because if I needed to tell someone about Darla/Marla then I couldn't be taken in for accepting a bribe. Besides, I had never really agreed to anything, just given a figure and taken the check.

The three pieces of paper I had used the back of my hand to move had been letters of some sort threatening to tell Darla's secret if she didn't cough up some cash. I had no idea how Darren fit into all this, but I was sincerely happy I would not be at the next round of cocktail parties where this would be discussed to death and Darren would be shunned. If anyone found out, that is . . .

I hoped I was up to this one.

Of course, it wasn't going to be easy. I couldn't trust the police and that was going to make it hard. Burton had solved his share of crimes in the area. Of course, we'd had murders from time to time, but usually it was pretty cut-and-dried. Someone got killed for taking something of someone else's. Or a husband or wife got fed up with their life and shot the other. There was little mystery to that.

This might have been the same. Waldo had said Darren was looking to divorce Darla and I could see why now. Still, a knife to the chest had to be in pretty close contact. Darren didn't strike me as the kind of guy who would want to get his hands dirty. Plus, this room opened a whole other set of complications.

I pulled out my trusty laptop and did a search for Marla, but nothing came up, just like my original search for Max. With the sheer amount of public-domain sites touting that all you had to do was put a name in and know everything you'd ever like to know, I was baffled that I couldn't find a single thing about this woman before she'd become Darla.

A knock on the door forced me to snap down the lid of my laptop. I shoved all the papers into a plastic bag from the grocery store and stowed it under the table. It couldn't be my mom—the door handle hadn't rattled first. And it couldn't be my dad because I could usually hear him tromping up the stairs from one flight down.

It could be either of my brothers, but something—some tightness in my chest I did not even want to acknowledge—told me it was Max.

"I'm not in," I called through the door.

"Tallie, you have to open the door. Your mom knows I came up and had me bring you snicker-doodles."

The curse of the snickerdoodles. I couldn't resist them any more than I could resist whoopee-pie lattes.

"Just hand the plate over," I said as I opened the door a crack.

He put the plate behind his back after snatching a moist cookie and sticking it in his mouth. The odd hums of pleasure coming from his throat made my stomach tighten and my palms sweat.

"Give it over."

"Not until you let me in," he said after he swallowed. "These are definitely awesome. I might just take the whole plate and sit out on the step. I'll knock again when I'm done with them."

"You'll do no such thing. Get in here with my cookies."

He sighed and planted a hand on the door. Bringing his other hand out from behind his back, he presented the cookies. I snatched them, then tried to shove the door closed.

"Not going to happen, cupcake." He was stronger than I had considered and pushed his way in. Though in all fairness, I was going to let him in at some point, anyway. Probably after I'd finished the plate of cookies that I'd now have to share.

"Fine, come in. Make yourself at home." I gestured at the couch and chose the chair under the window.

"Now come on, bring the cookies over here. I have a feeling we're going to have a lot to talk about while we polish them off."

I grumbled even as I did as he asked. Again, his sprawling body on the couch made it nearly impossible not to touch him with some part of me.

"Let's have a cookie while you think about how you want to tell me what you found out today.

You've been busy at Darla's house and the ex's last night while the cop was there, so spill."

How did he know all that? Again it occurred to me he had been at most of the places where bad things were happening when he'd had no need to be there. Was I setting myself up for a big fall simply because he'd bought me candy when I was younger?

But looking at him, relaxed and yet ready to pounce if necessary, I couldn't help thinking my internal radar would have gone off if he really was dangerous. The same radar I had buried deep when it had started chiming that Waldo was not who he presented to the world. I'd chosen not to heed the warning in the interest of living the high life, though. Not a shining moment in my life. I wasn't proud of it, but I had to own it.

"I don't know if I can really say I learned anything," I hedged.

"I can't imagine why you would have bolted out of Darren's house if you didn't have some kind of experience that put that look on your face when the pool guy waved at you."

"Where the hell were you?"

"Well, since my cover as flower guy has been blown, I figure there's no reason to keep the pretense up, so I've taken to following you around."

And I hadn't even known it. Some super-sleuth I was. "Why didn't I see you?"

"Because you weren't looking. You're very single-minded and wear blinders when you have a mission."

I couldn't disagree. I'd often lost sight of a whole forest for marking one tree and going for it. But still, I'd have thought I'd have at least felt someone staring at me.

"Well, you can stop following me. That's more than I bargained for."

"I don't exactly want to do it, but you haven't invited me along and you aren't sharing everything with me, so I'm not sure how else to get the information. I want you safe, Tallie, and you're not. It's going to be more than you bargained for if we don't figure out something soon about this money." He took a cookie and made those noises again. Up close, I almost slid off the couch.

Straightening my spine, I demanded my body knock it the heck off and get back to what we were talking about. Right. Information and what I'd learned.

"Darren has an alibi with work, but I'm not sure I believe it."

"Why not?" He stuffed another cookie in his mouth. By my count, he was up on me by two.

I snatched two more from the plate and a third for good measure. I told him about knowing Darren's secretary and how inattentive she was, much more focused on her manicure than knowing if the boss was actually there. How unmoved Darren had seemed by his wife's death. Along with what Waldo had said about Darren asking for divorce advice.

"Did the cops have anything new that they shared with you?"

"Burton is not going to share anything with me. He only wants info from me or to lock me up. I tried to take him the receipt and the threat and he scoffed at the receipt, then told me the threat had probably come from me and I was trying to pass it off on someone else." The thought of the Marla/Darla twist and the evidence that the threat had been written on the same kind of invoice I'd found in Darla's secret closet had me gulping around the sugar and cinnamon coating my throat. How was I going to convince him of anything when he suspected me of assault and murder? What a mess.

"He didn't believe you?" He took another cookie.

The supply was seriously diminishing. Normally, the plate could have lasted me at least a day. At this rate, they would all be eaten before I even got the whole story out. I grabbed another two.

"Hey now, that's cookie hoarding."

"My cookies, my house, my mom."

"But she had me bring them up."

"That makes you the deliveryman and nothing more." I swiped another one and stacked it on the arm of the couch with the others I hadn't had time to eat yet.

"Back to Burton. Did he straight-out tell you he didn't believe you?"

I ran down what happened at the station. Max sat with the cookie halfway to his mouth, not moving a muscle until I was done.

"Are you kidding me? You handed him both pieces and he told you that you were trying to pass on the blame to someone else?"

I shrugged. "In his defense, I was a menace for over six years. Maybe this is his idea of payback."

"That's bullshit. Tell me you know that's bullshit. There's no way you would have done either of those things. He has to know you're not that kind of person."

That was a lot of faith in me when we hadn't exactly been getting along since he'd re-introduced himself to me. "Why do you believe it?" I asked, truly curious after all our underlying hostility.

"Because I can tell the kind of person you are. You care. You do the things that need to be done. You're loyal. You help even when you don't want to. That speaks to who you are and that person is not a killer and not even a stun-gunner. You might be tempted to do that last one after all Waldo put you through, but you'd never have actually gone through with it."

I handed him a cookie because I just didn't know what to say after that. I knew my family would believe me, but I wasn't ready to bring them into my latest trouble. I knew Gina would believe me because she was my best friend. But this guy was not only trying to help me stay away from financial ruin, he also believed in me. I'd take any allies I could get at this point.

"I didn't say that for a cookie, but I won't turn it down." He grinned at me and I grinned back for the first time in what felt like a long time.

"So what do I do now?" I crammed a whole cookie in my mouth. I was more worried about this whole debacle than I had let myself believe. His belief in me had opened up a floodgate of worries I'd been hiding behind a wall of disbelief and anger.

"We do whatever it takes to clear your name. I don't know how much I can do, but I'll be here for whatever you need. You name it. I'm there. I still have my own investigation, but I believe, even more now, that these two are linked."

And then he reached over and slung an arm around my shoulder. The weight was reassuring. I leaned in, just a little, to his warmth and muscle, inhaling his scent along with the smell of cinnamon and sugar cookies.

"We need to get all the information we can. But first, why do I have a feeling you're not telling me everything?" He moved his arm to stretch it across the back of the couch, and I realized how close we were. I missed the warmth, but it was better this way. I was sure I'd come up with supporting evidence of that in just a moment or two.

"I'm telling you as much as I know." That much was the truth since everything else was speculation. "I'm pretty sure that threat came from Darla, despite the handwriting. I found this room in her house when Darren called me to pick out clothes for her to be buried in." Clothes she was being stuffed into right now. Well, not stuffed, as my father and brother were much more careful than that, but the thought was the same. Damn, I had meant to look for Darla's black pearls to complete the outfit. The woman was never without them, even though she hadn't been wearing them when I had found her body. Had they been stolen? I'd have to ask Burton. When and if I ever talked to Burton again. I didn't know if that next time would involve my arrest, though.

"Darren wouldn't even pick out her clothes himself? That's cold."

"Hey, now. I've done it for other people before. Sometimes the people left behind just can't bear thinking about it. If we can help them, we do."

"Seems strange to me. Why did he want to divorce her all of the sudden? The gossip around town is that they were the perfect set of barracudas."

Was this where I should tell him about the Darla/Marla thing? The problem was I hadn't had a chance to look over the diary, or truly assess the papers I took. Besides, believing this murder might have something to do with her past was all speculation. I shouldn't be spouting off stuff I wasn't sure of. If nothing else, I could be leading us down a completely different path that had nothing at all to do with the money. And the money should be the primary focus.

For that, I'd keep the diary to myself until I could figure out what it all meant. I trusted him to some extent, but I wanted to know what I had before I shared it.

"Have you figured anything out, hotshot?" I asked. He'd taken two more cookies and there were only three left, so I added them to my pile.

"Hey!"

"Just keep talking. I'm sure you could finesse some out of my mom when you leave."

"You're right. I bet I could." He settled in with his arm still across the back of the couch, sinking further into the cushions. "Anyway, I didn't find out much except that Waldo's account is very slim compared to how he's living. Since you left, he hasn't put much more in."

"Really?" That was curious. Unless he was

putting it all into the business. I had not asked for part of that even though my lawyer had told me I should. I hadn't wanted to bankrupt him, just get the hell out with as little debt as possible, and now I had the tax thing hanging over my head.

"Really. I was able to get one of my buddies to look into his accounts. They've been static ever since you cashed your check. The business account is only getting enough to pay the bills and stay above water. I don't know where he's putting it, but it's not in any of his known accounts."

I thought about bouncing on the mattress and the safe I hadn't had time to get into. I might have to go back and see if Waldo was holing it all up in there. Because if he used his low bank balances to say he couldn't pay taxes, I might just finish what that stun gun had started.

"Well, there might be more, but I'm going to wait until I know more before sharing. I'm not sure what to tell you," I said as Max took a small notebook out and flipped the page. It was looking worn on the edges. What else did he use it for?

"Was anyone else in Darla's house when you entered and found her dead?"

"No. I used the key buried in the front garden because Letty had just left to go grocery shopping."

"And who's Letty? I need details. Last name? Age? Height?"

That gave me pause. I had no idea what Letty's last name was. She was as much a fixture of the house as the gaudy cherubs Darla had had painted on the ceiling in the powder room. "Um . . . Letty is the live-in maid. Dark hair, a little shorter than me. She's been here for the last six years, I think. Mid- to late twenties. That's all I know. She ducked out to do errands before I arrived." I shrugged my shoulders, but wondered exactly when Letty had left. Had Darla already been dead?

Max must have been thinking along the same lines, because he drummed his fingers on the pad. "Did they take her in for questioning?"

"I don't know. If they did, I hope they were gentle with her. She's a sweet girl who has the misfortune of working with Darla." I paused. "Had the misfortune." Wow, it was really hitting me now that Darla was gone. I couldn't believe it. I had found a dead body not fourteen hours after I had found my ex sprawled in an alley. What a weird week and I was only three days into it.

Max went over the finer details and I tried to be as succinct and clear as I could be. Some of it had been impressions. I thought my brain had probably blurred a couple of the details just to let me deal with it all, but I couldn't tell for certain.

"So where do we go from here? Do you think Darla's murder definitely has something to do with Waldo? I don't really know how it all connects, unless she had threatened him when she saw him in that alley and stunned him. Then he had someone get back at her?" It didn't make sense. "The timing's too tight for that. Darla had to have been at her party because she is the hostess no one can get away from. And Waldo was in the hospital when she became acquainted with that butcher knife. It just doesn't make sense."

"I agree, but unless you have someone else to add into the mix, that's about the gist of it."

I got up to pace, forgetting my cookies were still on the arm of the couch until he snaked his hand down to grab two.

I stared and glared at him. I could get more too, but that was underhanded.

"I'll replace them. It's just that they're so good, and they're helping me think."

"Right. Make sure you tell that to my mom."

"I'm sure it will make her preen."

I shook my head in mock disgust. "You're playing with fire if you want my mom to preen, but whatever. Look, I don't know what else to do, but I do know I have to go back to Darren's in about two hours to finish cleaning for the after-funeral party. I can try to snoop around then since he won't be there, but I can't promise I'll find anything."

"I don't need promises. Just the fact that you're looking is good."

I almost thought he had said that I was good-looking until I checked my hearing and ran his words through my mind again. There was no need to even go there. He'd help solve this thing, then he'd go back to his life in D.C. The thought of a fling briefly crossed my mind, but honestly, I didn't even need a rebound guy. I just needed to figure out who I was again as a single person—as Tallie Graver—and a guy didn't figure into that right now. I was mighty tempted, though.

Pulling myself back to the moment, I watched as he stealthily tried to sneak another cookie from my pile. I smacked the back of his hand and gave him a frown. "I'll call you later with anything I find. If you want to give me your number I'll put it in my phone in case I need it."

He rattled off the number as I dialed it into my phone. Next, I put in his name and gave him a ringtone that would make me giggle every time I heard *Mission: Impossible.*

"I'll call you," I said as I shooed him out into the hallway. "Go tell my mom you want some more cookies and make her day. Maybe she'll leave me alone if you do."

He went out onto the landing and I closed the door behind him with a sigh. At least that would keep my mom busy for a little while so I could look at the diary to see if there was anything worth sharing, or if it was just a bunch of Darla-isms.

Heading to Darren's felt a little like going back to the dentist for a filling after you'd already had your teeth cleaned.

But I had promised to clean; it had to be today. At least he wouldn't be there to tiptoe around. I'd made a list of the rooms I'd need to clean and put it together as an invoice, then also put together a list of things I'd like to know. That one I would not be leaving behind.

Two roads before my turn, a white hatchback whipped out in front of me from a side street and nearly took my headlight out. I had my hand on the horn to honk at the idiot, when I realized it was Katie. What was she doing out on the hill? Through the windshield I could see her fluffing her hair and applying lipstick in her dropped-down sun visor. Without a turn signal, or a beat of hesitation, the crazy woman squealed into a driveway on the left—my old driveway, to be exact . . .

Now, what on earth could she be doing with Waldo, unless they were . . . I couldn't even put a name to it. Though it would explain why Katie and Waldo were found in the vicinity of each other when neither would admit to knowing each other as more than passing acquaintances.

The evidence that I would have shared with Burton was mounting. But I couldn't share it with him because he'd think I was trying to pass off the blame. I sighed as I realized what it meant. I'd jokingly called myself an amateur sleuth earlier. Apparently, I was now giving truth to those words.

Should I follow Katie? Call Waldo?

Gnawing at my lip did not help me come to a decision. And the devil on my shoulder could not shake the thought that I should call Waldo to see what he had to say about having Katie "I don't know her" Mitchner at his house.

Yanking the steering wheel to the right, I quickly jerked up the e-brake and sat with my phone in my hand for a moment. Should I call Gina first and see if I was doing the right thing, or just go with my gut? I'd meant to call her last night but it had gotten too late. My gut had served me well lately, and I should really trust that. Before I could second-guess myself, I dialed Waldo's cell.

"You didn't clean the stove," he said without a *hello* or a *how are you.* Typical jerk.

"You don't use the stove and neither did I when I made your sandwich. It shouldn't need to be cleaned." But it was the perfect opening. "Do you need something for dinner or is that what Katie brought you?"

"Jealous?"

"Nope, just wondering what the cops would say if they knew that the woman you profess to not know beyond a simple *hello* is at your house a little over twenty-four hours after your non-confession, that's all."

"Are you threatening me?" His voice rose on the end, which was a sure indication he was about to say something that was going to get me riled up. "Because if you're threatening me, you'd better think twice. Your ass could be mine in a matter of moments. And all those cleaning jobs you depend on to make your bills? Those could dry up in a half second with one word from me. Don't forget that even as you *do* forget what you saw. It has nothing to do with you, Tallulah." He severed the connection without another word.

I needed a minute to calm down before driving the short distance to Darren's. Who did Waldo think he was? He could not get me fired simply on his word. He was no one's puppet master and he'd never been the supreme leader of his circle of peers.

Sufficiently unruffled because he had no power over me, I drove around the back of the Hackersham estate and parked. I almost wished Letty would be here today, even though it was her day off. I could work around the other woman, maybe even pump her for information.

But all was quiet on the Hackersham front when I let myself in through the back with the hidden key. I replaced the key as I always did, then started in on the list of rooms. The kitchen would need to be done first since it looked like someone had a hell of a time making pizza sometime in the two hours since I'd last been here. The pizza oven Darla had ensured was custom-made and impressive—due to her Italian heritage—was still warm to the touch, splattered with tomato sauce (I made sure it wasn't blood before touching it by sniffing it), and had pieces of dough stuck to the handle.

Was Darla really Italian, though? I hadn't had a chance to spend more time with the things I'd brought with me after my last trip here. Again I was avoiding the word *stole*. I had to stop doing this and would, once I figured out what they all meant. But really, if I were honest with myself, beyond the need to clear my own name, there was a part of me that was enjoying putting the clues together. And I wanted that money from Waldo.

All good reasons, but another, less stellar reason was that my curiosity was just getting the best of me. Tallie Graver, amateur sleuth, wanted to stay out of jail, get the money, and solve whodunit before anyone else.

With that in mind, I also had to be realistic. So, my plan at this point was to put all the papers and the diary back where I'd found them after I figured out what they had to say.

Toppings were strewn across the 1,300-pound butcher block Darla had demanded be put smack-dab in the middle of the kitchen. I worked around it, bagging up pepperoni, ground beef, and bacon. Someone must have been hankering for the Meat Supreme.

As I stuffed bag after bag of meat, I listened for anyone entering the house. Even though it was Letty's day off, she still lived here. I couldn't believe she would have left all this out. And Darren was at a dinner meeting, so I doubted he had stopped to make a gourmet pizza before heading out.

Soon enough the kitchen was cleaned and I was ready to move on. I studiously avoided the closet where I'd found Darla, not ready to go back there, no matter what it looked like. The bathrooms looked good, so I gave them a quick go-over with my rag and ammonia, then dusted and vacuumed the lower rooms. I really didn't want to go back upstairs, yet I desperately did.

What else was there to find? I was still having a hard time believing Darla's death had anything to do with Waldo's missing money. Yes, stranger things had happened, but this was a small town with few secrets. How was it exploding now?

Although, Darla being Marla in a former life was not exactly a small secret, especially for a small town. I couldn't help being astounded that she'd managed to keep it to herself all those years. Then again, it might just have been important enough to keep her mouth shut. Or was it important enough that someone shut Darla's mouth for her?

Scrubbing at a smudge in the upstairs sunken tub Darla had turned into a garden with calla lilies and hostas, I shivered at the thought that it might actually be Darren who had killed Darla.

His alibi was weak at best, and he had the most to lose if he and Darla divorced. This solved his problems.

But when I moved on to wipe a handprint off the mirror, I remembered the dinner receipt. Waldo threatening me was nothing new, but he had sounded desperate and his moods over the last twenty-four hours had been perplexing. Was he mixed up in something more than just tax fraud? Was he aware someone was coming for him on the embezzlement? And how was Katie involved? And Darla? Did Katie know Darla was involved at all? I wished I had taken the time to call Gina earlier and talk all this over with her. I'd have to make time soon.

My head was spinning with questions when I stepped back into Darla's office. Somehow, I was going to have to face the hidden room again and clean the thing out. Darren and I had not talked about what precisely he meant by cleaning up the space. He could want me to dispose of everything that I couldn't donate to charity as he'd asked, but since he hadn't said exactly, I was going to leave it intact in case Burton needed it here. Though how he'd know about it without me saying something was a mystery to me.

Papers remained a jumbled mess on the floor, and it looked as if Darren had just shoved everything back in the space to cram the door shut. I started picking up papers and scanning them for anything interesting. I couldn't do more than that because if I found something more, I would have no way to say anything to Burton.

Stacking the mountain of papers, I then put the boxes back on their shelves. One would not go back in the right place. I pulled it back out and stuck my hand into the space to see if something was lodged back there. Pulling out a small black case that looked worn and weathered, I stood with it in my hand. I should just put the box back where it belonged and get the heck out of here, I told myself. Unsnapping the button from the small case that looked like it would hold index cards, I saw I wasn't far off. Except that all these note cards—every single one—was a threat of some kind for money. And they were all dated once every week, going back two years.

Before I knew what I was doing, I sat down in Darla's office chair and pulled out all of them. There were exactly 104. Two years to the day since they had started, they stopped on the day Darla was killed. Would there be more? Did the person who had sent them know she was dead so there wouldn't be any more money? Or would they start coming after Darren now that the cash cow was dead? This was more than the piece of paper I had back at my apartment alluding to blackmail. This was absolute proof.

There was no way to tell if more had been delivered. Darla could have had a secret post-office box where they arrived, or they could have been hand delivered. That would've been risky if Darla had wanted to turn them in. Which led to a thought: If Darla had threatened to turn them in, was that why she was dead?

Man, my head hurt and I had barely scratched

the surface. This, combined with the receipt for dinner and the threat, led to a whole new line of questioning. If Waldo had been with Darla two nights before she was killed, then also the night before she was killed because she'd threatened him he would be prime suspect *numero uno*, no matter if he had been in the hospital or not. It looked way too suspicious.

And if Waldo went to jail then I would be up shit's creek without a paddle when it came time to pay the taxman and answer for embezzlement charges if Max found enough evidence to open a case. God, could this get worse?

It was time for some answers and to come clean with Burton. I couldn't keep this info to myself and had no real way of making it all seem innocent that I had these pieces, no matter how hard I tried.

So first I would finish up here, then I'd go see Burton and hope I didn't end up in jail afterward. If he didn't believe me this time then at least I could say I'd tried. Yes, I'd like to solve this all by myself and hand it to him with a bow that featured a certain swear word stamped on it, but I also knew having the police on my side would make this go much easier. If only I could come up with the right words to convince him I wasn't trying to pass off the blame!

I still had a house to clean down the street and had hoped to corner Katie at the house, the only one who might know a thing or three about what was going on. Placing that call to Gina, I gave her a brief rundown of what had been going on, talking over her squawking and finally asking her to tie Katie to a chair again if she had to in order to keep her where I could question her. She also often seemed to be in some place she shouldn't be, doing something she shouldn't be doing.

Much like Max. And, if I were being honest, me.

Chapter 8

I drove away thinking about the room. I had no idea why someone would be blackmailing Darla, and I really didn't need to know. Except that my insatiable curiosity was getting the better of me. I was positively itching to find out why and when and how. Even if it was not connected to Waldo and the money, I wanted to know, not just to clear my name, but to have the knowledge itself.

I could grill Burton to get an update, but first I had to hand over the goods and figure out how to get him to believe me. No easy task.

I saw Katie's car in the Bean There parking lot when I pulled up. I wanted to corner her before she got away. Again.

Gina better have followed my request to tie the woman to a chair, if need be, because I meant it. I wanted Katie to spill, and I knew just how to get her to tell me everything I wanted to know.

Of course, I might have to make that rope into

a lasso first. Katie bolted toward the back door as soon as she caught a glimpse of me.

Now, I was not made for running and she knew that. I had a few pounds here and there that I should probably say good-bye to, but I also had an affinity for whoopee pies I wasn't willing to change. Fortunately, Gina had a head start on Katie and blocked the back door just as I came around the corner, ready to truck my way out to the alley if I had to.

Leaning against the wall with my hand on my heart, I thought perhaps I should consider going back to the gym. Eventually. Right now, I had more important things to do.

"Katie," I sawed out between bellows of heaving breaths, "You are going to talk, and you are going to talk now. I remember how loose those bonds were on your hands and the fact that your slump was a little too practiced. Along with the fact that you are apparently buddy-buddy with my ex-husband, I'm going to say you had a little more going on that night than getting shoved into the coffeehouse as an unwilling prisoner."

Katie stood there mute, frustrating the ever-loving daylights out of me. I didn't know precisely what had happened, but I knew it was something, probably something important. Coming out the gate with my accusations might not have been the best plan, yet it had been the best one I could think of.

Unfortunately, it didn't do anything to move Katie to say anything more.

"So, you're sticking to your story that it was a guy who just randomly shoved you into the coffeehouse and tied you up, duct-taping your mouth for no other reason than he could?"

She stared at me with venom in her eyes. "That's what I told you and that's what I told the police. It's the truth."

As if Katie had told the truth in her whole life. She'd lied about her hair color, her weight, her boyfriend situation. Hell, she'd lied about her shoe size, though I had no idea why that would've mattered to anyone.

Steam was probably streaming out of my ears, but short of stuffing Katie in a chair and torturing answers out of her, there was nothing else I could do.

"Why won't you just tell the truth? I saw your car at Waldo's even after you said the two of you don't know each other. So why were you there?"

Katie's face was immediately covered in a smug smile I wanted to smear off. "Jealous, Tallie? Just because your ex finally saw what a pain in the ass you are doesn't have anything to do with me, other than I showed him the way. He's done with you."

"I'm not jealous. I'm the one who left him, for God's sake. He's a slimeball."

That wiped the smile right off her face. "How dare you?" And she went for the hair, like a typical girl.

I tried to unravel myself from the lock Katie had on my head. Gina pitched in too, but Katie was like a woman gone wild. She gnashed her teeth and gripped my hair tighter. At one point, I felt strands let go of their hold on my head. I'd be bald in no time if we didn't stop her.

And then Max was there. He had the element

of surprise still, despite the noise, and gripped Katie around the middle, pulling her away in a flash. The other woman had a handful of my hair, though, and held it up triumphantly as she spit at me.

"You're going to clean that up," Gina said in a deadly calm voice. "Or you will never come in here again."

Katie's answer was to bare her teeth at Gina while still caught up in Max's arms.

"That's it." Gina pointed at the front door. "Deposit her outside. She's never getting another pumpkin latte." She made eye contact with Katie. "Find another place to guzzle your caffeine. Maybe the diner will take your business, but I don't want another penny of your money."

Max carried the squiggling and squirming Katie to the front of the store while everyone goggled at the spectacle. Honestly, I was trying hard not to laugh, even though my head hurt like I'd gotten my hair caught in the car door. And I still didn't have those answers I needed.

As soon as the front door closed, Katie stomped off down the street, gesticulating wildly. The buzz of conversation increased tenfold at this latest piece of gossip. Not that it would go far toward my trying to keep a low profile. Some things just had to be done.

"You okay?" I asked Gina.

"What are you worrying about me for? You're the one missing hair."

I patted my hair and found most of it still there. I could deal with that later. "I just feel bad for bringing this to your place of business."

"I'm fine, but she's not going to be when my mom calls her mother. If you think my mom can be bad, you should see her sister in full swing." And then we both burst into giggles.

"Oh, man, I was sure I was going to be wearing a wig for a while." I ran a hand over my head again, and felt a slightly bald patch further back than I had expected. I turned my back to Gina. "How bad is it?"

"You're going to have to go see Amanda at the salon and get some cut off, I think. There's no way she's going to be able to blend that in."

I took a moment to grieve for my hair, then figured a shorter cut couldn't hurt. Besides, there wasn't anyone I was trying to impress with long hair, anyway.

Max chose that moment to step back into my line of sight. He had another bouquet of flowers. I swear, if these were from Darla again, I was just going to burst out into laughter, because I really didn't think I could take one more thing at this point.

"These are a real delivery from the shop. I didn't look at the card because Monty said he'd box my ears if I did." He hovered as he handed over the bouquet.

I had no idea who they could be from. Monty must be rolling in the dough right now. "Thanks. I'll look at them later. Right now I have to clean up spit."

The way his mouth turned down and his forehead crinkled made me relent. Now that Psycho Katie had come out to play, I had yet one more person to look out for. He'd saved me from her choke hold and we were partners in this. He wanted to help and there was no reason not to let him. Not to mention, he was growing on me. I wasn't sure how I felt about that. I had just told myself I wasn't out to impress anyone, but when this man walked into the room, all those thoughts flew right out of my head as I remembered the weight of his arms on my shoulders and wondered if his lips were as soft as they looked.

And another ally was never a bad thing with all the trouble going on around here. What had happened to flying under everyone's radar as Tallie Graver, instead of being the spectacle that was Tallulah Phillips III?

Leaving Max to watch over the flowers with my promise to open them as soon as I was done helping Gina, I grabbed a wad of paper towels and did my best to clean up the spit. Gina had gone off to help those who needed to re-wet their whistles, since they were all talking a mile a minute about what had just happened in front of them. Spit was not the worst thing I had ever cleaned up, so I made quick work of it.

Fortunately, Max was still standing guard over the flowers when I was done.

"You ready to open the card?"

He placed a warm hand on my arm. I was shaking a little, fear running through my veins. It could be no one important. It could be my mom, for all I knew. But after everything that had happened, I highly doubted it

"I'm just nervous." I could have just taken the

bouquet across the street and he'd follow me there. But now that my mom probably had ideas about us hooking up, she'd usher him upstairs herself. I didn't know how I felt about him, beyond being thankful for his support. I certainly didn't want my mom getting any big ideas.

With a sigh, I pulled out the card.

It wasn't what it said, so much as who it was from. Darren had sent me flowers with a cryptic message that essentially said I'd better keep my end of the bargain if I wanted to keep my job. Of course, it wasn't that blunt, but he had signed it himself, which meant no one else had seen it. I would have preferred to keep it that way, but Max was hanging over my shoulder.

"Has he ever sent you flowers before for doing a good job and keeping his things clean?"

"Not before now." I thought quickly, but didn't know if I sounded convincing. I still hadn't told him about Marla/Darla and this was not the time or place to do that. "Maybe this is his way of hoping I stay on now that Darla isn't around. I might have to pick up his socks, instead of just seeing them crammed into the hamper." That was my story and I was sticking to it. Much like Katie was sticking to her story. I knew for a fact the other woman was lying, but had no way to prove it.

"Something doesn't feel right."

Yeah, it didn't feel right to me, either, but there was nothing else I could do. A snippet of conversation caught my ear, and I shushed Max with my finger to his warm lips while I listened to the women's-auxiliary lady bitch that Darren had sent me flowers. Not just me, but a *hussy* like me. I didn't know whether to confront her or let it go. I took my own advice, knowing people would think whatever they wanted to think with or without my input.

"Max, this whole thing doesn't feel right to me, but I'm going to have to ask you to let it go. I have to talk to Burton. I need to try to impress upon him that I didn't do it so he looks for the actual killer and stun-gunner."

"But I thought you were leaving that until we could make some connections. He's going to brush you off, and you know it."

"I don't think it matters anymore. I can't keep looking into this myself. What if I find the killer and I don't have a prayer of winning against him? Or evidence only after he takes my life too?"

"I can protect you." He crossed his arms over his impressive chest like a bouncer.

I patted his clenched fist. "Not from Burton, and I don't need you to. I need to come clean in case anything else happens. You saw Katie. I can't take any chances."

"How are you going to get him to take you seriously?"

It was a logical question. And one I'd have to think about when I talked with him and handed over the evidence, since Burton was walking in the door right now.

"Tallie," he said, just as I was getting ready to duck out the back door to think my way through the bluff I needed to hand over with the evidence.

With a sigh, I turned around.

"We need to talk." He narrowed his eyes at me and I knew it was not going to be good.

"I need to run across the street. Can I meet you in the back room of the funeral parlor in ten minutes? I have some stuff for you that I think you'll be interested in seeing."

Narrowed eyes turned to squinty ones, as if gauging the likelihood of my running.

"I know you can find me no matter where I go, so I'm not going anywhere but that room. Ten minutes."

Striding out the back door, I was not surprised to see Max keeping pace with me.

"You might want to be far away when I hand this stuff over, tough guy. I don't think Burton is going to take kindly to you being in town and not announcing your intentions way before now. And this is more than a receipt he won't accept. This is proof that Darla was the one who probably stun-gunned Waldo, or at least had someone do it for her."

He stopped on the sidewalk in front of the funeral home. "You're just telling me this now?" The hurt in his voice was better than censure and I appreciated that, especially after the way we had started off only days ago.

"I haven't even had a chance to go through everything. But I'm not taking the fall if Burton can't find another suspect. Now, I'll give you a chance to run if you want to. I wouldn't blame you, since I want to run myself. You don't have to stay."

"I'll take the risk. If Katie is going to go ballistic,

I plan on being there every step of the way. You should have heard some of the things she was muttering under her breath. I have a feeling she has a thing for your ex and thinks you're all manner of non-flattering names."

I strode down the driveway. When had things gotten so complicated?

"Look, you can stay, but if Burton makes you leave, then you have to do as he asks. I don't want more trouble."

"You're going to be in more trouble than you think when you hand all that over to him."

I wasn't handing it all over, though. No one but me had to know that.

Max was still hot on my heels when I opened the apartment door. "I really don't need a shadow, Max. I'm a big girl."

"I think you do and I'm not going anywhere. Who knows where Katie went?"

"If I was really afraid, I would have had Gina call Burton and report an assault. Katie has always been a little off and yes, she ripped out some of my hair, but we went at it like that in junior high and still manage to talk to each other." Although if Katie wanted my ex, then that might be another story. I didn't care who he ended up with, but Katie's personality would dictate that she make snide comments about her luxury compared to my destitute-ness as often and as loudly as possible.

Then again, at least I wouldn't have to see her

in the coffee shop anymore. Which was kind of nice when I thought about it that way. We made our way to the third floor. The door swung open seamlessly and Mr. Fleefers shot out from behind it as soon as it began its arc inward.

The cat startled Max, almost making him stumble down the stairs. I reached out to grab his arm and we both almost went down. Oops, I hadn't taken into consideration how much bigger Max was.

He caught himself on the banister, then wrapped his other arm around me to keep me upright.

I couldn't deny it felt good to be smack up against him. Parts of me hummed that should no longer have any voice at all. Stepping out of his grasp as quickly as possible seemed the only smart thing to do. And for once I was smart, though I would have preferred being dumb.

"Um, so that's Mr. Fleefers. Sorry about that. He's a runner sometimes when someone comes in. He's not always around, but when he is, he can be skittish."

"Yeah, no problem." Max straightened his shirt where I'd had my hand bunched moments ago and ran a hand over his chest.

I would not lick my lips. Would. Not.

"Paperwork!" I nearly shouted to get myself back on track and away from what could only lead to trouble.

But now came the difficult part: what to hand over and what to keep. I rummaged through the drawer where I'd shoved everything and finally decided to try to give over the receipt again, and my thoughts on how it all fit together. Along with my theories, no matter how weak, regarding Katie's involvement. I'd give him the invoice paper and work on how to tell him about the birth certificate and the legal papers changing Marla to Darla. Perhaps I could lead Burton down the road without actually saying anything. It was as good a plan as any other I'd thought of so far. Taking an invoice was one thing, but taking legal papers felt like it could get me into a whole lot more trouble.

"Let's go back down." I closed the drawer and walked past Max.

He yanked the drawer open before I could stop him.

"There's more in here. What is this?"

"Give me that!"

He had the diary in his hand and flipped through pages with it held over his head, far above my reach.

I thought of stomping on his foot for just a moment before I realized that would be very childish when he was just trying to help. And I needed help, because I was in way over my head.

"Is this why Darren sent you flowers?"

I covered my eyes with my hand. "Probably." That was completely untrue, but I didn't know how to tell Max about the connection without looking like a criminal. How much longer would he believe me about the taxes and the embezzlement if I was willing to steal from Darren's house? "Look, I'm not supposed to tell anyone about any of that. I found it totally by accident. I don't know if Darren killed Darla or not, but I don't really think so. Why do it in such a public way?" I dropped my hand.

"You'd be surprised what people will do to not have to deal with divorce," he said absently as he continued to read the diary over my head. "What exactly is all this? Does Darren know you have this book?"

I didn't really want to answer that since it just stacked more evidence against me being some kind of wild kleptomaniac. When had I stooped so low?

"I took it because I wanted to know more about the glimpse I had gotten. I couldn't take the chance of Darren finding me with it. He doesn't know, but I'll return it once I make sure it has nothing to do with her death." I made another grab for the book when I thought he wasn't paying attention, but I underestimated his agility.

He moved out of my grasp again. "So what's the story behind this? I don't see anything more than a list of all the boring things she did every day. She should have gotten a hobby other than watching some shopping channel. Most of this is about her purchases and what accessories she's going to need to buy to go with them."

Come clean or not? If he was going to help me—and it appeared he was not going to do anything *but* that, no matter how often I protested—then I might want to come clean with him.

"Darla wasn't always Darla."

That got his attention. He put the book down

along his thigh long enough for me to grab it and stick it in my back pocket.

"Explain. You have two minutes before Burton expects you downstairs. If you want me to keep helping you, I need you to fill in the gaps here." He looked completely unmovable as he leaned against my front door.

Blowing out a breath, I launched in. "Marla changed her name after getting out of high school, from what I can tell, and passed herself off as Darla to land Darren. I don't know when or how she managed to get the papers all together, but it looks like she started a new identity. To land Darren, she said her parents had died and left her wealthy. He didn't know anything about it until recently, he said, and now he doesn't want it to get out because it could damage his reputation."

Max stuck his hands in his pockets. "But it could have a significant impact on the investigation into her death, Tallie. The probability of someone from her past having caught up with her is high. This opens up a whole new pool of suspects. You have to tell Burton."

So now he wanted me to tell Burton the one thing I couldn't, while holding back everything else? Men were such fickle creatures.

"I'm going to have a hard enough time explaining where I got the invoice that shows the threat was written on the same kind of paper Darla had in her possession. I can't give him the diary and I can't tell him about the Marla/Darla thing. Darren could be the killer and then he'd come after me. I have to find a way to get Burton to find the information that doesn't include me. As for the diary, it doesn't seem to have anything in it but her ramblings." I wasn't going to mention the check I still hadn't cashed. It was bad enough that I knew as much as I did when I shouldn't.

"But you have to tell him, Tallie. Even if it doesn't completely get you off the hook, it makes your story have legs."

I huffed. "I was trying to come up with a way to lead Burton in the direction of the Marla/Darla thing without having to actually say anything directly to him. That way I can't get in trouble. But I'm coming up empty."

My cell phone played "Tainted Love" before I could get another word out. Great, just what I needed, a Waldo call in the midst of the rest of this crap.

I hit the *answer* button. "What could you possibly want that Katie can't get for you?"

"Jealous, Tallulah?" Waldo asked in his fake-smooth voice.

"I'll tell you the same thing I told your little twit Katie. No—hell no, even. But she's lying about how she got in the coffee shop and you're lying about other things, so quite frankly I don't want to talk to you."

Max was sawing a hand across his neck in the classic *cut it out* gesture. But I was done with the espionage, and half-truths, and playing a part I was never meant to play. No matter how much of a pain I had been when I was Mrs. Phillips III, I hadn't lied this often in my entire life. I couldn't tell what was truth and who I was allowed to tell what anymore, and it was taking a toll on my mental abilities.

"Well, I need to talk to you. I believe you removed something from my house that doesn't belong to you. I'd like it back."

My mind raced with what he could be talking about. The most obvious thing was the receipt, but he had always been stupid about what he did with those. Preferring to send his accountant into epileptic seizures with a stuffed shoe box instead of handing over a neat packet of expenses was Waldo's MO. I wished I could remember the guy's name! But what else could it be? I hadn't touched a thing.

"I have no idea what you're talking about. I didn't take anything of yours."

"You did and if you don't return it, there's going to be hell to pay. Think about that and bring it back. Now." He hung up on me before I could ask any other questions. What the hell was he talking about?

"What does he think you took this time?" Max asked, too close for comfort.

"I have no idea." I shut down the phone. "I have to meet Burton before he sends out a search party for me, or my mother finds out if he has any available, wealthy nephews. Are you coming?"

"Right behind you."

I scooped the receipt and the invoice into my hand, then stuffed the diary back into the drawer at the last second. It wouldn't do to have that on my person and not hand it over.

Trundling down the stairs, I headed for the

kitchen to grab the ever-present plate of cookies my mom would have on the counter. I'd offer Burton tea after he had a fit and needed something to soothe his throat once he'd yelled at me. Another evening of fun. I didn't know how many more I could handle.

Chapter 9

Burton commanded the back room like a general. His demeanor was different and I wondered what had happened in the last fifteen minutes to have put that scowl on his face. He'd taken the best chair and was settled with his hands steepled on the worn table in front of him. When he saw Max, he raised an eyebrow, but didn't say a word about him. Thank heavens I'd asked my mom for cookies—maybe they'd take off whatever new chip was on his shoulder.

"My mom made snickerdoodles. I know how much you like them."

"I do, but they're not going to get you out of trouble. I just want to let you know that up front."

My shoulders slumped as I chose the second most comfortable chair and motioned Max into the last chair. I had a feeling this wasn't going to go well. Especially when he told me I was in trouble before we even got started.

"Let's get this over with, then." I fingered the papers in my pocket, wondering what exactly he wanted to talk to me about. I hadn't had a chance to call for my own meeting yet, so it must be something outside my own evidence. Great.

"I think before we get started you should introduce your friend here."

"Do I have to?"

"Max." He shoved out a hand, then waited for Burton to shake it. "I'm an old family friend of the Gravers, just here starting my life again."

It took all I had to not roll my eyes. That was a horribly lame thing to say to a cop. But Burton seemed to eat it up as he shook his hand.

"Monty said you're down on your luck and here for a fresh start. It's a good town, even if we do have a smidge of trouble now and again."

Understatement of the year. But if Burton bought it, and had already checked up on him and found him okay, then that was one less thing I had to explain. I'd take my blessings where I could get them at this point.

"So what's up?"

Burton lost his smile as he stared at me. "Katie wants to file a restraining order against you for stalking her and assaulting her in Gina's coffeehouse."

I about came out of my chair before Max put a restraining hand on me.

"I wouldn't call Katie nearly making Tallie bald and spitting at her a crime against Katie," Max said. "Gina and I couldn't get her to stop. I had to physically pull her off Tallie." Max kept his hand on my arm.

Burton's trusty little notepad came out. He

licked his finger and turned to a fresh page. "And you were involved how?"

Max cleared his throat. "I was in the coffee-house when I saw Katie go after Tallie. I tried to stop it as quickly and peacefully as possible."

"Katie says you threw her down on the ground after forcibly carrying her from the store. She says she will have bruises tomorrow to show for it."

"Yeah. If she uses that cosmetology degree and paints them on," I mumbled under my breath.

"Care to share with the class, Tallie? Don't be shy now." Burton's bushy gray eyebrow went up, and I bit my lip.

"There's no way she has bruises. You want to put a restraining order on me, then I'd like to return the favor. I don't want her within a hundred feet of me. She's crazy and there's something more going on with her story than she said. Those knots around her wrist were barely tight the night in the coffeehouse. She could have gotten out of them herself. And I'm not even sure she was really knocked out when I came in."

"What do you mean, there's more to her story?" Burton's pen poised over his notebook.

I wasn't sure if I should plunge in now that I'd started. Could this get me into more trouble? Shouldn't I just stick to what I knew?

But Burton was looking intently at me and I couldn't back down now.

"I know I yanked tape off her mouth, but she could have slapped that on herself. And the way those ropes were tied, it's very possible she put them there herself. She could have tied a slip-knot and jerked it tight with her teeth. I don't remember what kind of knot it was since I was trying to get her free, but I do remember thinking she could have gotten free on her own. And she kept saying she didn't know Waldo, but now I've seen her at his house, and both she and Waldo asked if I was jealous of them."

"Are you?" Burton asked.

It took all I had left not to scream. "For the last time, I am not jealous. I left that bastard first, and if he wants to set up with Katie, let him. No skin off my nose." Although that wouldn't be entirely true if the tax thing came true and we owed a lot of money. Then I was sure I'd hear it from Katie about how I was sucking Waldo dry of money.

"And what do you think that has to do with Waldo being out back of the Bean and Katie being inside?"

The opening I was hoping for had just arrived! "See, I did Waldo's laundry after the incident. There were no drag marks on his pants at all. And when I went searching through the pockets to make sure nothing went in the washer that shouldn't have, I found this." I produced the receipt for dinner with Darla from my back pocket. Now if only he'd go for it.

"Isn't that the same receipt you told me you found in your car?" He eyed the slim piece of paper skeptically as he used two fingers to take it from me.

Quick, quick, quick, something brilliant . . . "I was afraid if I told you how I'd really found it, you would be angry. But you're angry and gunning for me anyway, so what do I have to lose? I also figured that if I left it with Waldo he would destroy it, because it's evidence that he was with Darla two days before she was killed."

"The baked potato again? It's not exactly fool-proof evidence, since I can't ask Darla about it." To say the skepticism was thick in the room was an understatement. I turned to Max, but he was no help as he shrugged his shoulders.

"But you could ask the maître d', or ask Waldo, for heaven's sake."

"I'm not asking him anything more than I have to at the minute. He's not only a suspect, he's also a victim. That's a tricky line, Tallie."

I deflated against the back of my chair. Of course, Waldo would stick with the victim line, especially if it would throw off more suspicion on him being Darla's killer. Maybe Darla had known about the secret stash of money the government and I were looking for, and that's why she'd threatened him. Time to bring out the second piece of evidence, though I didn't know if it was going to go as well as the first.

"I also have this, if you're interested." I stood and pulled out the invoice from my pocket, then waited for the yelling to begin.

"What have you been doing?" Burton yelled.

"Let me explain: I was cleaning Darla's house and trying to pick out an outfit for her to be buried in as Darren asked, when I saw this in her closet." That wasn't entirely untrue. I just didn't specify which closet or the fact that it was hidden. Here, I had to be very careful. "I saw this shipping receipt like it and it's the same kind of paper. So I think Darla wrote the threat to Waldo. It might explain how he got out there and was stunned." I sat down again and waited for him to go at me again.

The lecture didn't come. He just dragged a hand from his receding hairline to his chin and shook his head. "You sure you don't just want to do my job for me? Looks like you have more than I do."

I shrugged helplessly. "I'm sorry. I kept meaning to give them to you, but you wouldn't listen and you kept telling me you were going to pin me with this no matter what." There were other reasons, but that one worked as good as any other. Like Darla's secret room and secret identity, but I was not 'fessing up to that. I'd lead him to it somehow if I ever figured out a way to get him to think of it himself.

"I guess I'll have to take this back to the station and perhaps lean on Waldo more than I thought."

"And don't forget Katie. She might have seen Darla and Waldo together and that's why she pretended to be tied up. Darla could have promised her money if she'd keep her mouth shut."

I had been thinking about that since the confrontation in the Bean. Katie had never really looked scared except for when it was apparent I was going to rip the tape off her lips. The more I thought about it, the more it felt like the whole thing had been staged. There had been no lights on in the Bean when I'd entered, so Katie could have watched me approach and been quick to tie herself up, wanting to get caught and knowing Waldo was out in the alleyway. But why would she want to get caught? She could have just left with no one the wiser. And perhaps she would have, if I hadn't come in at that moment.

Honestly, though, this was a matter for the police. Burton could handle it.

"I'll have another talk with her, but again, we have the victim thing. I talked to the others in the shop and they agree with you, but I have to investigate fully before I dismiss her claim. She says you assaulted her and so did your boyfriend here. Not to mention you're already in trouble for enough other things that I just don't have time to list, young lady."

A blush warmed my chest. Max was not my boyfriend and I did not need the reminder.

"She might not be a victim at all, she might just be playing one. And what if she had something to do with Waldo's stunning? Hell, she could have stunned him herself, then run in and tied herself up."

"I highly doubt that."

In the face of Burton's skepticism, I gained steam.

"No, it could make perfect sense. She stuns Waldo because he isn't returning her affection, or something, and then realizes she made a huge mistake in doing it, so pretends to be a victim. What better way to throw suspicion off herself?"

"Have you been watching the Crime Channel again?" Burton stuck his notepad in his pocket and I deflated with the action. He wasn't taking me seriously and probably wouldn't look into Katie at all. I was left holding the bag, yet again.

"Fine, Burton. Don't take me seriously. But I bet when you figure all this out, things are going to come to light that you hadn't realized." I turned to Max, scooping up the plate of cookies. Burton wasn't getting any now. "Let's go, unless you have things you want to say about me being crazy too?"

"Nope, not me." Max raised his hands in the air in surrender, and I stalked out of the parlor.

"Get me that restraining order," I called over my shoulder before stuffing a snickerdoodle into my mouth. I needed thinking food and this was better than nothing.

Max followed. "I think you're smart to get that restraining order now. I wasn't kidding that Katie was saying awful things. What if she killed Darla because she thought she was seeing Waldo? She could come after you next."

Yikes, I hadn't thought of that. Now I really wanted that restraining order. If Katie was a killer and I had pissed her off today, there could be graver consequences than I had considered.

"I'll come with you to the station to fill out the restraining-order paperwork, Burton," I said as I walked back into the room to find the chief of police right where I'd left him. "If you think of any other questions, I can answer them while we're there."

"That's the first agreeable thing you've said this whole time," he said.

Max snickered and I elbowed him. He might have been silent the whole time he'd been sitting there, but I had been far too aware of him. I could use the time at the station to rid myself of those thoughts.

* * *

After leaving the station, I never broke stride, or looked back to see if Max had followed. As I filled out the restraining order, I'd told Burton that maybe he should be also looking into Darla's past. It had been the best I could come up with, but vague enough to not get myself into more trouble. At least not at the moment.

I headed directly for the Bean. Do not pass Go. Do not collect the 200 dollars, which I had a feeling would be a merc atom in the amount of debt I'd be racking up when the tax bill came. Even more if I was tagged with the embezzlement too.

My stomach heaved at the prospect, but I kept it in check as I walked through the front door of the coffeehouse and drew in a deep breath. Someday I would love to own my own tea shop. It wouldn't smell quite like this and would offer less in the way of food, but it would still be mine. And I could run it as I saw fit, with nary a dead body in sight.

"Tallie, I was just going to call you." Gina smiled, but her tone was strained as color streaked her cheeks.

"What's up?"

Gina kept smiling even though it looked like it was about to break her face. "Why don't you come on back? I have something you might want to see."

Strange, but okay. Gina's behavior was totally out of whack, so I hustled along, not wanting my friend's face to actually shatter under the strain of whatever was bugging her.

Once I got within arm's length of Gina, the

woman dragged me into the kitchen, then shoved me onto a stool.

"What on earth is going on and why are you all agitated? What could have happened within the last thirty minutes?"

"You know Ellen, that woman from the auxiliary thing?"

"Yes."

"Well, she was telling some of her friends that maybe you were the one who tried to kill Darla because you'd had enough of working for a living and wanted another man to take care of you. She thinks you want Darren and are seducing him, and that's why he sent you flowers. Because you weren't only cleaning his drawers, but perhaps in them too."

I saw red. I had not actually believed that euphemism was true. But now I knew that if you got angry enough, you really could have red tinge around your vision. "She what?"

"You heard me. Now get yourself calmed down enough to hear the rest."

"I don't think I can handle any more. I have to clean that woman's house tomorrow and now I might want to spit in her shampoo."

Gina snickered.

I held back for about two seconds, but couldn't help myself. I laughed too. "All right—I won't actually do anything like that, but it's tempting."

"The question is why. Why would she say something like that?"

"I have no idea. I always thought we were on perfectly good master-and-servant terms. Especially since she treats me like I'm invisible. So the only thing different here is that I got flowers from Darren and now she's made me a slut." I took a few moments to think about it as Gina stared at me.

"Do you think she's the one who wanted Darren and thinks I'm taking him out from under her?" That would be ridiculous, but what other explanation could there be?

"It would make sense in a weird, rich-people way. I don't get how half of them stay with their husbands."

"Anyway," I continued, "I'm not looking for any more trouble. I think Burton will have a fit if I bring him anything else." I said the words, but inside I was dying to know why Ellen assumed I was cleaning more than Darren's house. And even if I had   not ever going to happen, but worth following the train of thought—why would it be any of Ellen's business? She and Darla had never been friends, ever.

Gina raised an eyebrow as she looked over my shoulder. I didn't have to ask who was striding in behind me. Just the tread of Max's shoes was enough to give him away. And since when did I know a man simply by the way he walked? I needed to slow my roll, or I was going to get into something I might not be able to get back out of. I had enough of that already.

"Can I talk with you for a moment, Tallie?" Max said in his deep voice, which did things it shouldn't, like awaken parts of me that shouldn't just be dormant but dead like roadkill.

I put on my best fake smile and turned to him. "Sure." I turned back to Gina and dropped the smile to plead with my eyes for her to get me out of this. Gina just smiled back, the brat.

"I'll bring you two some lattes. It's quiet in here so you can take the booth over there if you want."

Max was already heading in the direction of Gina's nod, so I had little choice but to follow.

"So who's this society dame who thinks you're sleeping with the dead woman's husband?" he asked as he slid into one side of the booth.

"How long were you standing in the shop before your shoes announced you?"

"I wasn't standing there at all. Monty got the call from Ellen about Darren's flowers when I was standing at his counter. I could hear her from across the room berating him for allowing his business to cater to home wreckers."

My God, what had I done in a previous life to deserve all this crap at once? And if that woman lusted over Darren, I couldn't imagine what she would think about the prime specimen sitting across from her.

I immediately bit the inside of my cheek at that thought. It would only get me into more trouble.

"It's just Ellen. She doesn't know what she's talking about. Apparently, the bouquet you brought me this morning from Darren set her off. I don't know why."

"She might be someone to look at then. If she knew Waldo went to dinner with Darla and she had interest in Darla's husband, there could be a very strange love square there we shouldn't dismiss."

"Ellen's alibi for that morning is her husband. I can't imagine she'd kill Darla for her husband when she already has one of her own. What would she have gained?"

"People do a lot of stuff in the name of passion, Tallie."

Why did he have to say my name in a way that made me think of hot drinks and hot nights? I hadn't thought of those things in almost three years.

"And how would that connect with Waldo and the money?" I asked, wanting to get back on topic and out of my thoughts.

"It doesn't have to all be connected, you know."

"We haven't had many unexplained deaths, especially by mysterious and violent means, in the last few years that I know of, so this is different enough that maybe it was someone else. Someone Burton doesn't know." Which immediately led my thoughts back to how I'd come up with a way to get Burton to think of the Darla/Marla thing on his own.

"Or maybe Katie wanted Waldo and Ellen wanted Darren and they were working together."

Like I needed one more person to worry about.

Gina joined us after a moment. I gave her the rundown from the station.

"And then he kept asking if I knew anything else." I stirred a pumpkin-flavored straw in my mocha. Of course I did know more, I just wasn't telling.

Hopefully, I'd led Burton down the right path when I mentioned that perhaps he should take a look into Darla's past. I had been very convincing, if I did say so myself, when I said I didn't remember Darla coming onto the scene until after Waldo and I had married. I also mentioned she seemed to have no family, but had supposedly gone to one of the best schools in the area.

Hopefully, it was enough to get Burton looking in the right direction. If it wasn't, then at least I had tried.

There was a bit of a lull in the Bean There with it being two in the afternoon. The early birds had left and the after-work crowd hadn't yet shown up, so Gina and I sat in the main part of the Bean, talking. Max had gone out to take a call from Monty, but I knew he was watching through the front window because I hadn't taken my eyes off him the whole time.

"Why do I get the feeling you're not telling me *or* Burton everything you know?" Gina got up to wipe down the counter with a purple rag.

"Can you keep a secret?" I asked, leaning in close and looking away from Max.

Gina leaned in closer until we were nose to nose. "Of course I can."

"So can I," a deep voice said from the front door.

I sat back in my chair and crossed my arms. When had his phone call ended? Shouldn't he be out playing Spreadsheets and Numbers? It was an irrational thought, but I was feeling irrational with the shitstorm that was swirling around in my previously boring life.

"What's the secret, Tallie?" he asked as he sidled up to the counter with a vase of flowers.

And where did he get those flowers? "Why are you still delivering those?"

He snuck a glance at Gina before saying, "Monty dropped them off out front. It's my job while

I'm here trying to figure out things." He slid the flowers to Gina. "These are for you this time."

While Gina preened and yanked the card out of the bouquet so hard she almost ripped out the pansies, Max and I had a stare-down. I was not budging and, it seemed, neither was he.

"You need to go away," I whispered out of the corner of my mouth while Gina was distracted with her posies.

"I'm not going anywhere until we know what is going on, or I find that money for you."

"I don't need your help." In fact, I did, but honestly, I was getting in way over my head. I needed to just settle back and think about things for a little while. Now that I knew there was money, I needed time and space to think about where it might be, or where Waldo would have hidden it. He had certain hidey-holes, but I doubted any of them were big enough to stash the amount of cash he might have. And I had no clue on how to start looking. But now that the police part was done, having Max around was distracting me and not making things easier. Especially when he seemed to turn up everywhere he shouldn't, exactly when he shouldn't. Like in my dreams, wearing nothing but a smile.

"I think we should try to go to Waldo again and see if he'll tell you anything," he whispered.

"Perhaps I wasn't clear on what a mess my marriage was. Waldo hates me and will only do anything that will embarrass me or make me feel less. He is not going to blurt out where the money is if he's never shared before."

Our whispered conversation had finally gained

Gina's attention. I tried to distract her. "Who're the flowers from?"

"Just some guy I met last weekend. Nothing special."

"That's a good-sized bouquet for nothing special."

"Meh, so what are we whispering about?" Gina fixed her gaze on me as I squirmed in my chair. What was I going to say?

"Game night!" I nearly yelled, then calmed down. "I was inviting Max to game night at your house and wanted to make sure he could come before I asked if it was okay with you." Lame, lame, lame!

"Sure." Gina looked baffled, but there was nothing I could do about it. She kept trying to catch my eye, but I was looking at everything but her. "Um, I hope you like nachos and Parcheesi. Nine okay?"

"Sounds good," Max said with a smile in his voice.

What had I just signed myself up for? I had less than an hour to convince him not to go.

Chapter 10

Game night usually consisted of more than just games, but it wasn't like Gina and I could compare our failures in the love department with Max sitting right there.

Instead, we played several board games and tromped Max until I was laughing so hard I feared I might fall off the couch. Or at least I was laughing hard until Gina brought up Waldo.

"So did your ex-bastard ask for anything more? He doesn't want you to come clean his house, does he?" she asked as she picked up the card I had just put in the discard pile. Gina was fierce at Skip-Bo, so I would have to keep an eye on her.

I cleared my throat. "I already did that, so no, not again." I reached into the plastic flowerpot Max had brought as a thank-you-for-the-invite gift. He'd said not to tell Monty, since it was from the grocery store and not the flower shop. I didn't think Monty would have sold this particular arrangement anyway. Max had filled the bottom with Tootsie Rolls to mimic dirt, then bought a truly awful bunch of plastic flowers, probably from the dollar store, and "planted" them in the Tootsie Rolls. He'd also said that he thought I needed a real flower delivery, not from someone out to scare me. I admit it touched my heart, even though I wasn't sure I wanted it to.

Unwrapping a candy, I tuned back to hear Gina snort in disgust. "You shouldn't even have done that much." She turned to Max. "You haven't had the displeasure of meeting the ex, have you?"

"Ah, no." He took an inordinate amount of interest in the cards in his hand. I could see he had an eleven that would go nicely on the top of the ten in the pile in front of him. Then I could use my twelve and the rest of the run in my hand to finish off the game.

He discarded instead, causing me to gust out a sigh. We'd be here all night.

"Well, I think that stun-gunning might have something to do with Darla's death. The timing and the fact that they were done to two very nasty people makes me believe there has to be a connection." Gina nodded to punctuate her point.

That's what I thought too, but I wasn't going to share it. It would only open up more conversation in this direction. I cast around in my mind for something else to talk about. Unfortunately, Gina was on a roll. With my apartment right across the street, I glanced over for inspiration and caught Mr. Fleefers's shadow pass along the window blind in the bathroom as he strolled on the windowsill. I had left the light on in there for him in case he needed to do his business. He liked to stalk around the apartment when I was gone. A light bulb went off in my head.

"Are you going to still get a kitten?" I asked as casually as I could. Apparently not casually enough.

"Probably, but that isn't what we were talking about, Tallie. Get your mind here in the room. I heard they were at some out-of-town restaurant together. Now Burton's looking into why two people who hated each other were having dinner." She looked at me. "You don't think they were having an affair, do you? I don't even want to imagine the two of them together."

"Me neither, but I don't think so. Can we talk about something else? Burton won't leave me alone about the whole thing because I found her. I was just hoping for a night off." I promised myself I would spill everything to Gina tomorrow when I had it all straight in my head. There were too many players in the pool right now for me to keep everyone straight. And I didn't want Gina to know anything at this moment that could get her hurt. Max could take care of himself. Gina probably could too, but there was a part of me that wanted to protect her to make up for the time I'd been away and snotty.

From the corner of my eye, I caught the way Max lifted an eyebrow. I wasn't playing his game when I had a real one in front of me. I drew a card, got the eleven Max wouldn't put down, and ran the table with the rest of my cards.

Sitting back, I took the final sip of wine in my glass and was ready to call it a night. But Gina wasn't ready to let go yet.

"I heard through my uncle someone might be

after the money we always thought Waldo had hidden. Someone from the state tax bureau came sniffing around town the other day, and Uncle Fred, being the county tax collector, was put on the hot spot for a few unanswered questions."

Well, that was not good. I turned wide eyes on Max. They weren't supposed to be making noise yet. That was the whole reason Max had come, to gather his own information before an actual case was opened. But we weren't any closer to finding the money. This could go from bad to horrendous in a short time.

"Have they questioned Waldo?" I asked cautiously. I didn't think Waldo would bolt with the money, but couldn't be sure. With someone being brave enough to kill Darla, and someone else brave enough to stun Waldo and tie up Katie, our town was approaching something more than it had ever been before. Gone was the quaint, little, safe town. Now almost anything was possible.

"Not that I know of, but it might not be long before they do."

This was in no way good. The timetable to get to the money just got shorter.

"You did not have to walk me home." I cradled my potted "plant" of candy and garish flowers in my arms. Gina had insisted I take it with me and I hadn't argued with her. I was nearly certain I would never throw this thing away, not matter how gaudy it was. It had been super-sweet of Max to put it together. I might not tell him that, since my feelings were completely confusing to me, but that didn't stop me from thinking it.

"You don't know if it's safe out here anymore." Max walked alongside me without actually touching me.

His words echoed my earlier thoughts enough that it made me shiver in the cool night. "I'm sure it's fine, and really, it's right across the street." Gina lived above her shop too. Our small town boasted many three-story buildings where apartments took up the top two floors. Gina had taken advantage of that and had essentially made herself a two-story house above the Bean. It was a heck of a lot nicer than my own studio apartment, but then Gina owned hers and I did not.

I tried to leave Max at the back door. He made that impossible by insisting on walking me up the two flights of stairs to make sure everything was okay. I was not, however, going to invite him into the apartment. And because of his insistence, now I was going to have to walk him back down to lock the door behind him, and then back up by myself. Well, at least that would be my exercise for the day.

I turned the key in my lock, and it gave with much less resistance than before. My brother must have finally changed the mechanism like I'd asked him to. It sucked to have the door stick when I had my hands full of groceries and couldn't get it to budge.

I stood on the threshold, sure I was not going to invite Max in. He tried to invite himself in, but I pushed him out. "It's all good, now let's trudge back down the stairs so I can lock up behind you and then I get to climb the stairs again."

"You're so good at it, though."

Had he been watching my butt while I took the stairs at a steady pace that wouldn't leave me out of breath? A flush started at my neck and I ignored it. I was not going to even think about that. This time I could watch him walk down and then I could walk back up alone.

The view was not bad on the way down. Not at all. I assigned my shortness of breath at the bottom of the stairs to all those steps.

"I'll talk to you later, then." I shooed him out the door, then stood in the doorway while he was one step below me on the veranda that wrapped around the old house.

"We're going to need to formulate a plan on how to get Waldo to talk. If we can't find that money, I can't guarantee they won't take it all and demand more."

"They'd do that?"

"I won't say definitely, but I can't make any promises if we don't get to it first."

The thought of that made my stomach churn. I had to put more effort into getting the location of the money out of my ex-husband. I had cast enough doubt on my part in either crime to hopefully lead Burton in the right direction and get him to stop sniffing around me. It was time to concentrate on Waldo.

"I'll see what I can think up, and you do the

same thing. I have houses to clean tomorrow, but I'll get in touch with you at some point in the day."

He raised that eyebrow again, this time radiating skepticism. There was nothing I could do to alleviate it. So I didn't try. Instead, I shut the door in his face and ran back up to the apartment. There had been something in Darla's diary that struck me just now and I wanted to see if I'd remembered it correctly.

Treading the stairs again, I noticed the carpets needed a good cleaning and several of the brass bars that kept the runner in place needed a good polish. They were dulled with a scuff my mother would not be happy to see. I'd do it tomorrow. Tonight, I was weighed down with everything going on.

I let myself into my dark apartment, flipped on the lights, and started yelling like the dead had come to my place for a party.

"I told you that you should have let me walk you in." Max paced back and forth as Burton and two other men went through the apartment, turning tables back over and righting chairs.

Someone had come in and trashed my apartment and I wasn't sure yet which feeling took precedence—being pissed that someone dared, or fear that someone had been in my place. I certainly did not need to be taken to task by Mr. Tax Ninja.

"I don't need a scolding, Max. If that's all you're

going to do, then I made a mistake calling you and you can head right on back out. You can see the door from here."

He stood with his arms crossed and his feet spread. "I'm not going anywhere."

Something inside of me sighed in relief, but I was not going to share that with him.

"Fine. Make yourself useful and make some coffee then."

He gave a narrow-eyed stare before he went off and did as asked. Picking carefully over the littered floor, I made a beeline for the drawer in the kitchen. I should have looked there first to see if someone had taken Darla's diary. Because my house had been ransacked, I hadn't thought of anything but the destruction.

Now that I did, I was happy to find the diary was still taped to the underside of the counter above the drawer. I patted it before leaving it in its place. Taking it out now would be a disaster, as it would call attention I did not want. For the last ten minutes I had been trying to come up with a way to ask Burton if he'd followed my trail of bread crumbs to finding out who Darla had previously been. Despite racking my brain, I still hadn't come up with a good way to do it.

Maybe later. Now I had to see if anything else was missing. On a quick pass, the answer was no, but I couldn't be sure. With the destruction, there was no way Mr. Fleefers would be anywhere in the vicinity, so I could be assured he was prowling somewhere else. I had seen him walk across the window about thirty minutes ago during our card game, so that made me feel better. He was probably just roaming one of the many corridors or playing in his favorite corner of the attic.

"You see anything not here, Tallie?" Burton sidled up to me, hitching his pants above his waistline.

"I don't see anything missing. I don't have a lot to begin with. It looks like whoever it was just tossed the place."

"Any idea what they might have been looking for?"

I deliberately made myself not look at the kitchen drawer and lied through my teeth. "Not that I know of. And I don't exactly have anything valuable after the divorce." Which reminded me of Waldo. Did someone think I might know where the money was? Who else would know about the money? Darren? Did he also notice the diary was gone and hoped to come and find both? Maybe he shouldn't be given the pass I had given him.

"Well, you be careful. We're going to head out, but I don't like this. There's nothing else I can do right now, though, and we're too small of a department to focus on this when we have Darla's murder to figure out still." He scratched his head and peered at me. "You haven't been asking more questions that you aren't supposed to be, have you, girl?"

"No, no, of course not." Just taking things I shouldn't. And keeping secrets I shouldn't. I would flush in about two seconds if I kept thinking about it and give myself away. Instead, I focused in on Max making coffee and how right he looked standing in my kitchen. That wasn't any better for my mental stability.

"What's the guy doing here, again?" Burton said in a low voice only I could hear.

"I called him to come back because he'd walked me home. I didn't know my home looked like this when he left. I don't know why he was the one who popped into my head."

Thankfully, my parents lived a few blocks away and so did both of my brothers. I'd be swarmed right now if they knew this place had been broken into.

And then I groaned because I heard my mom coming up the stairs, yelling. Yeah, I probably should have called them. If someone had gotten into my apartment, it meant they could have entered any other part of funeral home. I was in for a long night.

I hadn't been wrong to anticipate a long evening. I just hadn't calculated exactly how long it could be until three a.m. showed up and Max told my mother and father he would be sleeping on the couch in case anything else happened.

My father had given Max a long look that made me want to tell him that of course I wasn't a virgin. I'd been married for six years and I could take care of myself. Fortunately, I said neither and the whole family left after my brother had a short chat with Max involving furious whispering and a few dour looks from Jeremy. Good God, did none of them trust my own judgment and my inability

to attract men anyway, except for the slimy ones
who hid money and caused a ruckus?

And then I was left with Max, who grabbed me
into a hug before I could walk away from him.

"I was scared for you," he said into my hair.
Without another word, he took the sheets in my
hands, made the couch, and promptly started
snoring as soon as he lay down.

I pulled the Murphy bed out of the wall and
laid there for another hour listening to his deep
breathing before I finally drifted off myself. Tomorrow I had things to do and people to talk to.
I wanted that money and I wanted to know what
the hell was going on before one more crazy
thing happened.

Carrying my vacuum cleaner into the infamous
Ellen's house, I planned on using the time with
my earbuds in and the magic wonder-vacuum
in my hand to sort out the parts and pieces I had
at my disposal. I needed to see if I could make
any connections. Part of me was still sure Darla's
death had to do with her not really being Darla.
How had the woman kept that a secret in a town
with more gossips than a high tea?

One more thing to add to my list to ponder. I
got to work on the first floor, picking up after
Ellen and her husband. Would it kill them to
straighten up the house themselves before I got
there? Why did I have to find socks stuffed in the
couch and cups on every available surface?
Yeah, I was a maid, but I was really only hired to
do the deeper cleaning. However, I couldn't do

that if the whole place was also a mess on the surface.

Halfway through the house, I heard a shrill whistle. Popping an earbud out, I turned to find Mr. Ellen behind me. Actually, it was Mr. McKay but I thought of him as an extension of his busy wife, not the other way around.

"Hey, Winthrop."

"Hello there, Tallie. I just wanted to let you know I was here in case we bumped into each other. I didn't want to scare you."

"No worries." Although I did look down and saw that he had no socks on, which might mean there were yet another pair shoved in the couch.

"I'll be in the office if you need me."

"Thanks."

So much for the thinking time. Now, I'd be aware he was here and just want to get the heck out. I finished up in record time and was out the door with a quick wave. He'd mail me a check once I invoiced him; he always did.

With some extra time on my hands, I decided to take care of one of the things on my list. A call to Darren was in order. I had to tell him I wasn't cashing his check. I just couldn't take the money.

"Tell me you don't need more," he said when he answered the phone.

I pulled my cell away from my ear and gaped at it for a moment as I turned on the car. Now I was thinking about cashing the damn check just because. But I wouldn't. "No, I'm no longer part of your inner circle, so that's not how I operate."

"You aren't above it, Tallie. I hear there might be tax trouble coming your way. Now, how much?"

That check was about to burn a hole in my gut. I clenched my teeth. "I was calling to tell you I'm not going to cash it, you jerk, though I should just on principle."

"I don't believe that. I told you it's part of your bonus. Just cash it for future cleanings."

I might never clean for him again. Then again, the tax issues he alluded to were one of the reasons I would not be able to tell him *no*. "Fine, but it's not a bribe. I'll put it on the books as paying forward."

"Good." He cleared his throat. "Will you be out to clean this week? I don't know what days Darla had you come. Then I think I need you tomorrow for deep cleaning. That closet isn't as empty as I wanted it to be." Censure was in his voice and I cringed. "The day after tomorrow, I'd like you to come back for the funeral because the house will need to be spiffed up. You did a good job earlier, but I'd feel better if you went over it again. From next week on, we'll do Thursdays. Is that possible?"

Did he want to keep me busy or close? I'd never cleaned their house so many times in one week. Then again, I'd never needed so much access either, so who was I to complain?

I felt a little like we were back to business as usual, even though his wife was dead. Then again perhaps that was how he ran his life. Death could do things to your norm. "Is Letty still on staff?"

"Yes." He sounded baffled that I would ask.

"What about the pool boy?"

That one got a snort out of him. "Yes, for the moment, until I can figure out how to get rid of him. I don't know why Darla wanted him in the first place. He has no idea what he's doing, but he's paid through the month so I can't fire him until then. I checked in his contract."

They had a contract with the pool boy? Then again, he did live there, which was different than most people. Why did Darla need a live-in pool boy, anyway? We lived in a state that had pool use for about four months out of the year. It was a question I had wondered before, but had never asked.

"Are you sure no one else knows about Darla's past? You don't think Letty might have found out some way, do you?"

"No," he said flatly. "I only found out myself by accident and confronted her about it. She was furious. I can't imagine she would have told anyone. And Letty's no angel. If she thought she knew something to hold over Darla, I'm sure she would have used it ruthlessly."

How could he employ people he didn't trust?

"I told Darla I wanted a divorce when I found out her little secret, but then I talked to a lawyer who told me what her cut of my money would be. Needless to say, I didn't go through with it. It wouldn't have been as cut-and-dried as your divorce. There was too much at stake."

So Darla knew he wanted her gone. Had she blackmailed Waldo to make money if Darren really did get rid of her? Or was she trying to set up someone else who would take care of her and let her live in the luxury she was accustomed to? If she'd chosen Waldo, she wasn't a very good picker, because he was no prize.

"I'll be there day after tomorrow. Will you?"

"No, I have things to do in the office and want out of this house. It should be all yours since Letty won't be here, either, and apparently the pool boy has let me know he has a day off coming up."

Interesting. That meant I would truly be alone in the house again. Maybe there was more to find . . .

Really, I shouldn't be thinking like that. Now that someone had broken into my house, I might want to worry about myself instead of the death of someone who had hated me when she was alive.

Unless everything was related, and it wasn't a coincidence everything crappy was happening at the same time.

It was time to cash the check, since Darren had said it was advance pay and I had written it down in my ledger as such. No way would he be able to say it was a bribe if Burton followed my trail and came to the Darla/Marla info all on his own.

But first I needed to stop down in the funeral parlor to see how my brother and father were doing. It hadn't been easy to have my space violated, but my dad was more shaken than even I was. This place was his lifeblood. To have someone walk in when they shouldn't have had shaken him up.

After a quick pit stop up at my apartment, I came back downstairs. I heard raised voices before I made it to the second-floor landing and tripped down the next set of stairs to see what the heck was going on.

From the curve halfway down the stairs, I could

see a man with light brown hair and a nose as hooked as a parrot standing in the foyer, flanked by two other men with the same nose. If I had to guess I would have to say they were related, probably brothers, but I'd never seen them before.

"Look, I ain't telling you again, I want to see my sister and I want to see her now. You can't keep us from her. She has to be identified, you old coot."

Oh man, I hoped he wasn't calling my father that. But it appeared he was, as I came trundling around the corner from the final descent and stopped behind the wall that was my brother and father. Another thought hit me as I stood behind them: My God, these were Darla/Marla's brothers! They had to be. I tried to struggle through the human wall, but my brother and dad blocked me.

"Sir, we don't need you to identify her. She is here for her final resting. The police would be the ones to take this matter to. I'd be happy to call them if you'd like." My father held out his hand and Jeremy handed him a cell phone. "Now, would you like to go to the police yourself, or shall I call them for you?"

The three brutes took a collective step back, then turned as one and left. Their ability to synchronize like that was pretty impressive, but nothing compared to the swearing my father was doing in his perfectly pressed suit. He pulled his handkerchief from his breast pocket to dab his balding head.

"I want you to hire security until this funeral is

over," my dad said to Jeremy as he continued to stare after the trio. "We'll add it to the bill at this point, because all I want to do is get this broad into the ground and out of my hair."

I gave myself away by snickering. It was rare that my dad slipped into a less formal speech pattern. For the perfectly proper Bud Graver, it was vocabulary less than stellar. Calling a woman a "broad" was a big jump.

"What do you need, Tallie?" Dad asked, most likely onto the next topic in his own head after taking a moment to acknowledge me.

"I just wanted to see what the raised voices were. Is there anything I can do to help?" I asked, but I already knew what I was going to do. I'd call Burton in just a moment and tell him to question the goons very closely about how they knew the deceased.

"No, just keep your eye out and the door locked. I don't trust those ruffians. I'll call Burton now to let him know they should be on their way."

My phone buzzed in my pocket. The readout said *Burton*. I'd programmed him in when this all started. Shaking the phone in the air, I said, "He's right here. I'll let him know."

"Are you coming to the station to fill out the report, Tallie?" he asked. "I don't have time to follow you around."

"Yes, sorry. You were my next stop." Cashing the check would have to wait now. Maybe I could get some more of the scoop on the three brothers Grimm if I was actually at the station. "Hey, heads up: There are three goons coming your way saying they want to identify their sister. Since we only have Darla here, I'm not sure who they're talking about, since she had no family that I knew of." A thought struck me and I almost slapped my own head. How had they known she was dead or where to find her?

Chapter 11

The trip was short since the police station was less than a block away. I made it in record time even without running. Whisking through the front door, I ground to a halt.

"Tallie, Burton isn't going to have time for you now." Suzy sat behind her desk, her cotton-ball white hair poofed above her head in a cloud. The woman hadn't changed in all the years I had known her.

"I need to fill out that paperwork."

"Yeah, well, the second he hung up with you he had a trio of big, mean-looking guys come in demanding to see him. I can let you talk to Matt if you want."

Matt's office was right next to Burton's. That would work as well as anything else. The walls were not exactly thick and, with how loud the leader was in the funeral hall, I doubted he'd keep it down with Burton.

"Sure. I'll just show myself back."

I was back through the half door before Suzy

could stop me. Making my way through the
hallways, I kept an ear out for any yelling in other
conference rooms. I heard nothing, so chances
were Burton had taken the three men into his
office. I barely kept myself from rubbing my hands
together. If these guys were legitimate, then I
wouldn't have to tell Burton that Darla had for-
merly been Marla at all, and Darren couldn't
blame me for the info getting out. Win-win for me.

Matt sat at his desk with his feet up on the
scarred wood. He dropped them quickly when I
headed for him. Most likely he was thinking of
the times he'd been a victim of me knocking his
feet off a table when we were kids. One time he
had almost lost a tooth. He used his tongue to
probe his right front tooth, and I knew he was
thinking about that time too.

"What's up, Tallie?"

Shouting started up on the other side of the
wall and he cocked an ear for it, his gaze sliding
to the right.

"We want to see her, you bastard. She was our
sister."

Clear as day, which made me as happy as if I'd
gotten a new squeegee.

"If you're here to fill out the report on the
break-in, we should go to the room down the hall
for privacy."

I glared at Matt. "No way. These guys were just
at Dad's. I'm here to make sure they aren't going
to come back."

"That's not your job. Burton will handle this."

At that moment Burton raised his own voice
and it shook through the halls. "Sit your ass down

and listen to reason, or I'm going to lock you in a damn cell."

I raised an eyebrow at Matt. "You really want to miss this?"

"No." He settled back in his chair. We listened to the volley of voices as the leader of the trio demanded to see Marla and Burton continued to shout that there was no Marla here. Well, that answered one question. The other burning one was: How had they known where to find her?

Burton's door crashed open and the three stepped out in tandem. Burton followed along behind like a sheepherder with errant lambs, though the thunderclouds on the three similar faces did not lead one to truly think of lambs, but maybe velociraptors.

"I'll fill out the paperwork later," I whispered to Matt, preparing to follow along behind the men to see where they went next and who they harassed. My plan was thwarted when Burton caught my arm on his way back to his office.

"You have some explaining to do and I don't want any more runaround. I don't have time for this, Tallie. You're going to tell me everything you know, or you're going to be the one sitting in a cell. I don't think your clients or your dad would be too thrilled about that." He didn't even look back at me as he dragged me through the room. When I made pleading eyes at Matt, he merely shrugged and raised his hands in a gesture of surrender. Yeah, that didn't help at all.

"Sit." He let me go as he passed his visitor's chair. I plunked down and he took his own chair across the desk from me. "Now, we're going to do this again and I don't want vague, nor do I want pat answers. I want to know what the hell you know. Now." He placed a piece of paper in front of him, took out a pen and stared me down.

At least I wouldn't be telling him anything he didn't already know. "I gave you the receipt and the invoice. I told you to look into Darla's past."

"You said it might be a good idea to see where she came from to see what might have been in her past. That's not exactly telling me Darla had changed her appearance and name."

"I wasn't entirely sure about the appearance thing."

He grunted. "Don't. Just don't. Did you, or did you not, know Darla had once been Marla?"

"I heard that might be true." I had not been able to find a picture of Marla on the Internet no matter what combination of words I used. It was if she had erased herself previous to her transformation.

"And you didn't think it was significant enough to tell me?"

"I was trying to tell you without telling you," I said.

Another grunt. This was not going to go well.

"I don't know whether to just shake my head or take you in for obstruction of justice. At least then you wouldn't be in the middle of my investigation every freaking time I turn around."

"I don't mean to be." I crossed my arms and jerked back in my chair.

"Yeah, you're like a bad penny." He sighed. "Look, be honest with me. Are you looking for stuff? Or do you really just keeping happening upon it?"

Honesty was not going to earn me points right now, but I was going to try anyway. "I'm looking, Burton. You gave me no choice when you made it clear I was your number-one suspect." At least now maybe I could stop. I would go clean Darren's house and leave the secret room alone after replacing the birth certificate and the papers changing her identity. The entrance of Darla's previously unknown family was not something I wanted to delve into.

"Well, I'm looking elsewhere now. Stay out of it from now on, or I'm going to have to take it up with your father."

Christ, I was almost thirty years old—this had nothing to do with my father. I was a grown woman. But I didn't say that because I did not want to get into an argument with Burton, or send him immediately to my dad. That would not go well. Because, though I knew I was an adult, my father did not yet get it when it came to matters of scolding, much like my brothers. Max, though, he got me and that frightened me more than I was willing to examine.

Thoughts of Max followed me out of Burton's office and across the way to the funeral home once again. I needed to change and get to Darren's to supposedly clean again. I'd told him I wasn't quite done, but really I wanted to get the documents back where they belonged and not in my apartment. With luck, the trio wouldn't be there. I could be in and out before anyone came home or saw me.

The coast was clear when I got to Darren's. No cars were in the driveway and no one was in the house. I'd get in, do the closet and a few other rooms, and get on with things. There was no need for me to be involved anymore.

I was in the middle of cleaning the dreaded downstairs toilet, sure now that it was Darren instead of Waldo—or maybe both of them—who had the aim of a blind elephant, when the front door opened, then slammed, and someone started banging on it. I couldn't tell if the banging was from this side or outside and sat frozen on my haunches in the tiny powder room, not sure what to do, or how to get out without being noticed.

"Tallie, are you here?" Darren yelled from the front foyer.

It wasn't like I could say no, since he had to have seen my car around back. "Just finishing up."

"Don't go yet. There're madmen out front. I need you to stay in case they break the door down." The pleading in his eyes wasn't enough to make me stay, but the very real possibility of being assaulted by the people banging on the front door was not something I wanted to face.

I didn't want to say it, but I had to. "Maybe you should call Burton."

"Good idea." He yanked his cell phone out of his pocket, along with his keys and a handful of receipts. Everything fell to the floor and he ignored it to dial the police station.

I didn't want to touch another receipt to save my life since they always seemed to get me into trouble. But I couldn't just leave them on my clean floor. Scooping them up, I made a point not to look at them. Unfortunately, one caught my eye, anyway. It was a receipt for a hotel that was notorious for renting out rooms by the hour, and it was for this morning.

Against my better judgment, I shoved it in my pocket and put the rest on the front hallway table while Darren spoke with Burton. Within minutes I heard sirens and running feet as the guys took off for whatever they were driving. I saw the tail end of a truck fishtailing out of the front drive and knocking over Darla's prized Aphrodite statue in the process.

Darren ran a rough hand over his head. "Jesus."

"Yeah, well, I'd better go. I don't think there's anything more to do here, and quite honestly I've seen enough of Burton over the last few days to last me for a lifetime."

I ducked out the door before Darren could protest. I didn't need to wait for a check this time. And I did not want Burton to see my face—again—and blame me for being—yet again—in the wrong place at the wrong time.

Something hot and yummy was in order after my morning of chaos—and no, I didn't mean Max of the dreamy biceps. I was putting him permanently out of my mind. I'd gotten into more trouble than I had in my entire life since he'd shown up, trying to get me to find the money. I was done now. The taxmen were going to just have to do their worst. I'd work until I was ninety-seven years old if I had to. My dream of my own shop floated away down the river of shit that was currently my life.

Just as I was taking my first sip of pumpkin spice, though, guess who walked through the door? I wanted to run and hide, but couldn't make myself do it.

"I hear there's some commotion in town." Max straddled a chair across from me and crossed those fantastic arms over the back, making the biceps I'd been thinking about bulge.

I had to remember that first and foremost this was my brother's old friend. Second, I was recently divorced. Both huge strikes against doing anything with the man. I couldn't come up with a third strike on the fly, but I was sure there was one out there if I thought hard enough.

"I wouldn't know anything about that."

He smirked at me. "Yeah, I don't believe that for a second."

I bristled. He was so tempting and I should not be tempted. That word shouldn't even be in my vocabulary right now. It didn't escape my notice that I was arguing with myself about something that might not even be on his mind. So I went on the defensive instead of facing my own confusing emotions. "Why are you here again, Max? You decide to come out and help an old friend's sister? I'm still having a hard time believing that. Are you sure you're not after the money itself and you'll leave me in the dust when we find it, with a fat tax bill in my hands and nothing to pay it?"

He reeled back as if I'd slapped him and I felt terrible. "Is that what you think, Tallie? That I have nothing better to do? Yeah, I wanted to help. Your mother and father showed me more kindness than I ever have had before or after. I lived with a grandmother who I could not please to save my life and the memory of your parents welcoming me, showing up for plays and awards ceremonies and including me in your dinners and your celebrations, kept me afloat all those years until I was old enough to leave the old battle-ax. They even came to my college graduation. That meant something to me. I was trying to repay it in a small portion by saving their precious daughter." He glared at me. "Not anymore."

Well, I felt about two inches tall in three-inch heels. How did that go so wrong? Oh, right—because I was scared and taking it out on him.

Gina shot me a disapproving frown from behind the counter as Max stalked out the front door.

"Yeah, yeah, I'm going." The only question was how was I going to get him to accept my very humble apology?

I caught him outside the bank down the street. Fortunately, he was not in a car or I would not have caught him at all. I still didn't even know where he was staying.

I had been so focused on myself and how this would all come tumbling down around my head that I hadn't even taken the time to think about his part in helping. His monologue about my parents had hit me harder than I was willing to admit. I had no idea what it would be like to grow up without the support of the people who were supposed to love you. Their care must have really impacted him in a way that helping was giving back. And I'd taken that from him in one fell swoop.

"Max!" He didn't even turn around. I was so blind to getting to him that I didn't see someone coming my way. I was knocked hard in the shoulder and went down on my hands and knees. A paper fluttered down and I picked it up, looking after the person who had bumped into me. All I caught was a glimpse of black-and-white fancy shoes rounding the corner.

I was momentarily stunned. I knew those shoes. They'd come a hairbreadth from stepping on my face, and whoever it was had been fighting with Darla the day before she was killed. No matter if I was supposed to be staying out of this or not, I couldn't leave that lead alone. Burton be damned.

The squeal of tires had me up, swearing at the pavement for cutting into the palms of my hands. By the time I got to my feet and rounded the corner myself, whoever it had been was gone from the street. I couldn't be sure he had been in the car with the squealing tires and as I looked up to the buildings above me, all three-story monstrosities with shops and apartments and private homes, I realized he could be lost forever. There was no way I would be able to find him if he'd hidden in one of these buildings, not even if I took all day to knock on every single door.

I called Uncle Sherman, not sure what else to do.

I'd catch up with Max later. This took precedence, even if that wasn't the way it should be.

"What you got, girly?" Sherman said as he answered my call.

"I just saw a pair of shoes that belong to the guy who was fighting with Darla before the day she died. Should I call the cops?"

He snorted out a laugh. "What are they supposed to do with a pair of shoes? Did you see a face?"

I sighed in defeat. "No."

"You might want to hang up your deerstalker, honey, and let Burton do his job. Though I doubt he really knows what he's doing."

"Uncle Sherman, what is it between you two?"

"Nothing for you to worry about, honey. Just go clean your houses and keep your nose clean too. I'm sure this will all settle down soon." He disconnected the call.

Yeah, that didn't help at all.

I'd lost Max when I'd gone after the shoes, but at the bank I found Letty.

"Hey, Letty. I'm glad to hear Darren is keeping you on."

But Letty didn't even look at me. In fact, she went so far as to turn her head away and hustle down the street.

All in front of Katie the Barracuda. Could things please maybe stop spiraling down the toilet? Just for today?

"I don't think you're making friends anymore, Tallie, what a pity." Katie smirked. It was all I could do not to haul off and whack her in her recently duct-tape waxed lips.

"You know, the cops don't believe your story at all. And the next time you want a free lip wax, tear your own duct tape off."

Katie scurried away with her hand over her mouth. Probably off to see Waldo. What did I care? Not a whit, but it was irritating on top of a day of irritations.

The culmination of it all was my phone ringing with Waldo's tone. Good grief!

"What? What do you want? I have no patience right now and no time for more crap."

"My, we're in a mood. Is your monthly craziness coming on? I remember when I wanted to lock you in a room for that week and only let you back out when your eyes weren't wild."

"Waldo, I do not need to reminisce about my periods. It was the only time I was truly happy, since you wouldn't try to put your paws on me. The one time a month I wouldn't have to pretend that three inches did something for me other than make me yawn. Now, what the hell do you want?"

"We need to talk."

"We are talking and it's giving me a headache."

"You need to come over. There are some things we need to discuss."

"I don't have time, and I certainly don't have the inclination to be anywhere near you. Just say what you have to say right now."

"I'm not having this conversation on the phone. It has to do with money, enough money that you'll be cleaning houses twenty-four hours a day for a very long time if you don't get over here."

He must have heard about the tax thing. I still

wasn't going there. I wanted nothing to do with the twit. If I had to make a payment plan, then I would. Perhaps I could get Max to intercede on my behalf. Of course, I'd have to apologize to him first.

"I also want the jewelry you took from my house back."

"I told you I didn't take anything. What jewelry are you talking about? The only things I have are the ones you gave me when I left."

He ignored that. "Oh, and there's something else you'll want that you can't have unless you come here bearing my possessions." A pause was followed by Mr. Fleefers howling. I'd know that sound anywhere.

My rage knew no heights. I hadn't seen the cat since my home had been broken into. I'd just thought it was his way of showing displeasure at his environment being disrupted. The bastard had him! That led my mind to other things I would probably have no way of proving.

"I took him when I tossed your house. Now come get him before I toss him too."

"You bastard!"

"Come now, my mother would take exception to that, just as she did to me marrying you in the first place." Another pause, another yowl. "Better come quick, Tallie. I don't have any cat food. I think the poor thing might starve to death."

He hung up before I could yell at him again.

I couldn't walk to his house, so I had to go back to the funeral parlor to pick up my car. Time wasted when who knew what the jerk was doing to my poor kitty cat.

Hoofing it back to the house, I prayed no one would waylay me or need anything from me. I'd made up my mind to ignore everyone and anyone when Max stepped into my path.

"I'll apologize to you as soon as I get done at Waldo's. I promise. Right now I have a cat who needs me and no time for anything but that." I darted around him and was in my car and out of the tunneled driveway fast enough to whip his hair around his head as I blew past him.

Zooming out of the garage was the only speed I got on what should have been a ten-minute drive to Waldo's. Traffic was slow as hell and then there was an accident that I had to wait to get around. It was only a fender bender, but it took precious time to clear from the road, precious time that kept my cat waiting for me.

I zipped up the driveway to my former home, slammed my car door, and headed for the front door like I was leading a charge into war. I leaned on the doorbell three times, becoming more and more inventive with my language with every stab at the button. Thirty minutes had passed since Waldo had called me with the yowling Mr. Fleefers. It felt like thirty years.

It was just like the bastard to demand my presence, then not answer the damn door. Next, I tried knocking, I rang the doorbell again at the same time, then I pounded my fists on the door and even kicked the freaking thing, but still no answer. He was going to pay for that.

I took out my old key, because he still hadn't

changed the locks. That would require effort on his part.

Unlocking the door, I called out his name in various forms, even resorting to saying his real name in case he was being obstinate. Nothing. I was halfway through the downstairs and hadn't seen my cat or my ex-husband. When I entered the formal dining room, I had an answer to at least one of those questions. Waldo hadn't answered the door or my calling for him because he was sprawled out on the dining-room table with his eyes wide open and the chandelier covering his whole body.

Another freaking body! And, oh Lord, money that would never, ever be found now . . .

I was so screwed, especially since Burton was going to want my head for this. Talk about wrong place and wrong time. I could explain why I was here, but I was going to have to go through so much more interrogation this time. I had no idea who would want Waldo dead, but I had a feeling that being the first on the scene might not be in my best interest this time.

I couldn't walk away, though, no matter how much I wanted to.

Chapter 12

"Really? You have got to be kidding me!" Burton's disbelief came over the phone loud and clear in the laundry room where I had hidden myself. I'd look for Mr. Fleefers in a moment. Since he hadn't come running when I yelled, he must be locked in a room. He'd have to wait. I didn't want the cat trying to claw Waldo like he had when we'd lived here and making the crime scene worse.

"I'm not kidding you. Believe me, I would not kid about this. Please get over here. I'm not sure what happened, but it looks like something horrendous happened, maybe an accident, but I just can't believe that anymore with everything that's happened in the last few days. All I know is I don't want to touch anything."

"Sit tight."

I hit the *off* button on my phone and tucked my legs up under me on the washing machine. I was not moving.

The scene, however, kept running through my

mind: Waldo on the dining-room table, a gun next to him like he'd dropped it after he'd pulled the trigger? I didn't know. There had also been a hole in the wall across from him. Had he tried out the gun before he'd missed and hit the chandelier, rocking it from the ceiling to fall and pierce him? It had been a design I wasn't entirely comfortable with, the huge spire at the bottom a hazard in my eyes. And now it had proved true. He must have hit it at exactly the right angle. How, though? I'd reinforced those brackets, knowing something horrible might happen if it ever let go at the wrong moment.

I leaned over the side of the washing machine and puked into the utility sink to my left. I flicked on the tap and looked away as the water took the mess down the drain.

Well, I'd asked how it could get worse. Apparently, this was my definitive answer. Of course, I was shocked he was dead, another life cut short. Sadness was overwhelmed by panic, though.

The tax bill would be mine totally, and I had no idea where the rest of the money was. That felt like such a horribly self-centered thought, but maybe it was just my poor mind trying to shield itself.

I was seriously on overload here.

Digging my phone out of my pocket, I hit the speed dial for Max's mobile and climbed down off the washer. I needed to touch base with the one person who knew everything going on and would hopefully be levelheaded in this moment when I was freaking out. I also needed to hear someone's voice that would make me feel like I wasn't all alone.

Mr. Fleefers needed to be found. Burton would just have to take my word that I'd found Waldo dead or finally charge me.

Exiting the laundry room, I was fueled by anger and fear. I had taken no more than two steps when I ran straight into a wall that had not been there before. The wall didn't have any give, but it did breathe and clamped a hand on my arm. I opened my mouth to scream, lifting my face at the same time.

Coming face-to-face with Max was much preferable to finding a murderer manhandling me, but what the hell was he doing here and how did he get in? I tried to back away from his grip, but he wasn't letting go.

"Tallie, you need to be calm."

Add that to my list of other needs.

"I am calm and I'm calling you. My cat is around here somewhere and I want him before something else freaking happens in my vicinity!"

Bolting away from him, I shoved the phone in my back pocket and didn't look to see if Max followed. I ran up the stairs to check the five bedrooms on the second floor, coming up empty at each.

If I knew anything about Waldo, it was that he would never willingly leave the cat to roam on its own. He'd always shut the poor thing in the laundry room anytime I'd left, even if it was for hours. But Mr. Fleefers couldn't be in the laundry room because I had just been in there, puking, after finding Waldo. God, my head hurt.

Making the rounds of the bathrooms next, I found my poor kitty cowering in the corner of the bathtub, soaking wet and shaking. Dammit! If Waldo hadn't already been dead, I would have killed the son of a bitch!

Grabbing a towel from the linen closet, I wrapped up Mr. Fleefers and went to head back downstairs, only to find Max in the master bedroom, going through drawers.

I was so stressed that I gave free reign to my bitch on wheels. I didn't care at that moment who deserved my angst; Max was getting it. "What the hell are you doing?"

He turned just his head and looked at me with his hand in what used to be my underwear drawer. "Tallie, I know the scene downstairs is hard to see, but there is not going to be a better time to go through things before the police get here."

"Are you sure you're in this for the right reasons?" At this point I did not care if he got mad at me. Here he was, contaminating a crime scene, and somehow he always seemed to be right where he shouldn't, at exactly the time he shouldn't be there. Had I been an idiot for trusting him and right all along when thoughts intruded that maybe he wasn't here for the reasons he said?

"Yes, for the last time. I just want to be able to find this money for you." He straightened to his full height and took a step toward me.

Mr. Fleefers howled as I took a step back. Max took another step forward, reaching out his hand this time.

"Seriously. I'm in over my head now. I want resolution for you."

I placed my free hand in his and he pulled me up tight against him, laying a kiss on me that made me see double.

Immediately after, Max backed up. "Sorry."

"No, don't apologize," I said absently, walking forward. What little attention I had left after that kiss focused on the mirror I'd never seen before. I was still recovering from that kiss, but my mind was also whirling with this new addition to a house Waldo hadn't changed since I'd decorated it.

Waldo had never bought his own furniture. Hell, he didn't even buy his own clothes. So where had this mirror come from and who had bought it?

Running my fingers over the gilt-edged frame, the flesh of my pointer finger snagged on something sticking out the back. Max had come up behind me, so I stuck him with Mr. Fleefers in order to be able to use both hands to feel around the edges. Something was there. I wanted to know what it was before anyone else could discover it.

The mirror itself wasn't heavy. I lifted just the edge from the wall to find a folder taped to the back. I ripped it off with a feral sound deep in my throat. I did not need one more secret unless it was finally the answer to the question of where the money was.

Yanking open the folder, I found page after page of figures. At the top of every page was the name the Book Nook, a small used bookstore I'd tried to run at the beginning of my marriage that I'd given up on because it was too much work.

This deserved a closer look. I needed to study what exactly the numbers were. Then Max was over my shoulder. All I wanted was a private moment to figure out what I was looking at before I did anything else.

"Why don't you take Mr. Fleefers downstairs and put him in my car? Open the window so no Good Samaritan breaks it in to save him. He likes to curl up in there. I have some food in the glove compartment. Come right back after you're done, though, because I have to face Burton, and I am not doing this alone since you were in here too."

He peered into my face just a little too long, but I wasn't budging. "Take the cat and go, Max. I'm not going to leave. I want you here when Burton arrives."

We had a brief stare-down that I won. I held in my sigh of relief until I heard the front door close and then I got to work.

The pages contained entries of sales for a store that no longer existed—or at least I had thought so. I put those aside for the moment because I didn't know what all I could process in the short amount of time I had. Sifting through the remaining pages, I came to a full stop on the last page: A listing of all the times he'd been with Katie and Darla. I had no idea if these dates were sexual in nature or if they were for other nefarious reasons, but I wouldn't have put either past Waldo.

On the back of that last page I found a sticky

with a series of numbers and the name Grafton, and almost crowed. There was only one Grafton I knew and it was a bank. Could I have found the hiding place of the elusive money? Removing the last page, I almost choked when I felt the weight of something still in the folder. There was a small pocket on the folder that had blended in because it was black like the rest of the thick material. But the pocket was plastic and in it was a freaking key. A small key that looked like the one we used to have when Waldo had insisted my jewels go in a safety-deposit box.

I almost swooned, but kept myself upright long enough to shove the key in my bra. Walking back downstairs, I studiously avoided the dining room. I'd probably have to go see Waldo again soon enough, but I wanted to put that moment off for as long as possible.

The last hour had been hell. If I'd been scared with the amount of questions I'd had to answer when I'd found Darla dead, it was nothing compared to the barrage I was showered with over Waldo. And *scared* didn't even begin to describe the pounding of my heart as I sat on my old couch for an interrogation—there was no other word for it.

They wanted to know where I was and how I came to be here. Why did I think Waldo had taken my cat? When had I gotten there and how had I gotten in? Had I moved anything?

I answered as best I could, but I was getting a headache. And the damn key was burning a hole in my boob. I wanted out of here. Away from my ex-husband's dead body. I might not have loved him anymore, but being in the same house with his corpse was making me ill.

I'd take Mr. Fleefers home, put him away with some much-needed food, and then distract myself by sneaking off to the bank. I needed to get this over with. Time felt short and we were so close to answers. Finding the money became the one positive thing I could do in this time of horror. I was almost positive that the money was now the answer to all my questions, one way or another. I had to get it first before the person responsible for all this carnage got away with murder *and* got a big payday for it.

"So, what time did you say you found him?" Burton asked for the hundredth time.

"Seriously, Burton, do you really think the answer is going to change? Why are we doing this here? Can't I meet you down at the station in a few hours and tell you everything I do and don't know?"

Burton squinted at me. "You got somewhere you have to be, girly?"

"Ah, no." I cleared my throat. "I just . . . uh . . . don't like being in the house with my dead ex-husband, if you must know. And I have to get Mr. Fleefers home."

He harrumphed and went back to questioning Max in the same relentless tone. He had already told the officers who he really was and had tried to get buddied up with them over a common goal, but Burton was having none of it.

"And you say the door was unlocked even though Tallie here swears she locked it behind her?"

"Yes, sir."

"And what are you doing here again?"

Max sighed even as he valiantly answered the question. "I'm here trying to help a family friend stay out of trouble." He'd come clean with Burton at the beginning of the question-and-answer session, because he couldn't keep hiding behind being a flower guy when he always seemed to know more than he should.

"And are you helping her stay out trouble, or making it worse with this money thing?"

I inwardly cringed at the mention of the money. That damn key was going to sear my skin in 2.4 minutes if they didn't let me the hell out of here so I could beat the bad guy and clear this all up. I needed to find out if my hunch was wrong. Of course, I'd rather it be right, but if that wasn't the way it was going to work, then so be it. It would be a start and a start meant an end in sight. I wanted that more than anything.

"I'm trying to make it better with the money thing, as you call it. If we can find the money, then perhaps we can keep Tallie out of financial ruin. Isn't that what you want for her too?"

Burton harrumphed again and tapped his pencil on his notepad. "Don't be throwing stuff like that at me. That's not my business here, but I'm not even sure there's really trouble to be had."

I couldn't do it anymore. I'd actually taken to sitting on my hands to keep myself from showing Burton the folder, but I couldn't do it anymore. Plus, it might have something to do with why

Waldo was dead. I'd already withheld evidence once. I couldn't do it again. I had to trust that Burton would do the right thing, no matter how he felt about me.

I left the room, intending to come right back from the kitchen, but instead everyone followed me. "Burton, I was going to show you this." I slid the folder off the top of the fridge with a blush. He was not going to be happy.

That was an understatement.

"I can't keep giving you the slide, Tallie!"

I handed it right over to him, then backed up against the counter, waiting for the rest of the explosion.

He visibly pulled himself together. After a few deep breaths, he stuck one hand on his waist and thrust the other into his graying hair. He paced back and forth in front of me and stopped a few times, shaking his head, then resumed pacing. I didn't open my mouth the entire time, waiting for him to calm down. It was a long wait.

Finally, he shook his head one last time and scowled. Opening the folder, he stared at the list of numbers for a moment, then looked me dead in the eye as he waved his hand at the papers. "Care to explain what exactly I'm looking at?"

I twisted my fingers together. I wasn't entirely positive I knew the answer to that, but with him looking expectantly at me, I had a feeling telling him "I don't know" would not fly.

"I think Waldo might have kept my old bookstore open and used it to filter all his tax money and embezzled money through."

The hand went to the hip again. He really needed to come up with a new gesture.

"So you think Walden Phillips the Third was pretending to sell romance novels to hide his money?"

"I've never seen that folder before. In fact, it was attached to the back of a gaudy mirror upstairs, which I'd also never seen before." Maybe the new mirror had something to do with the jewelry Waldo had thought I'd taken from him. Was it a hiding place after he thought I uncovered his secrets when I'd been here the other day? "When I felt the edge of it under the mirror, I flipped it up and there it was. It was minutes before you arrived, so I'm not sure what it is exactly. But if you look at the last page, you'll see a detailed list of all the times he's met Darla and Katie too. There's a series of numbers back there also, but I'm not sure what they mean any more than I'm sure of what the first list is." The key was now causing a raging inferno in my bra. Burton would kill me if I kept the key back. I was not, however, going to pull it out in front of everyone in the kitchen. My cousin was in the room, for heaven's sake. And, as much as I was stunned and seriously interested in that kiss Max had given me, I did not want him to watch me fish around with my hand down the front of my shirt.

"Can I got to the bathroom?" I asked, laying my hand on my stomach.

Burton raised his eyebrows. "Don't go finding anything while you're in there."

Well, shit, what was I going to do now? Be

cheeky. "I make no promises. If I stumble across something, I'm not going to keep it from you."

I could have sworn he mumbled, "Well, that will be a first" under his breath, but I was ignoring him. I'd tried in the beginning to give him everything I'd found and he'd ignored me. He shared in making that situation worse.

Hustling to the first-floor guest bath, I paced the small room, trying to think of a plausible reason to have the key. Burton was not going to buy that I just happened to find it in the powder room. I no longer wanted to do this by myself, though, so I was going to have to come clean. I just wished there was some way to do it without having to show my hand—or bra, as the case may be.

Brilliance struck me. I palmed the key out of my cleavage and held it between my fingers. I'd simply get my hand back on the folder, then slip the key back into the pocket.

For once something actually worked for me as I asked to see the numbers again, and casually slipped the key back in. After a few more minutes of showing Burton where I thought the money might be, I removed the papers, spread them out over the counter, then moved the folder.

Now it would be important to not overplay this. I sent the folder over the edge of the counter. It landed with a very satisfying *clunk* on the ground. Just enough to make people stop and notice.

"What was that?" Burton asked as if on cue.

"I have no idea." I was not going to be the one

to pick up the folder. I wanted this to all be Burton's discovery from here on out.

He bent over to pick up the folder and then examined it, finally finding the little pocket and holding up the key. "That's a safety-deposit key."

I bit my tongue because I wanted to say that of course it was, and make him let me go right now to get the box. But I didn't want to push him.

"I'm going to have to get some sort of court order to have this used."

"Or . . ." I started and Burton cut his eyes to me.

"Or?"

"Or you can let me have it, and I'll go down and see if that's the same box Waldo and I had when we were married. Because if it is, then Waldo would've been too lazy to take my name off of it. We could see if we can finally find this money. There might also be more clues in there about why all this is happening."

"That might be skating the line of legality. You and I both know that he might have been lazy, but if he was alive he would not want you in that box. I go by the book, Tallie."

Dammit, I should have kept the freaking key and then just handed everything over to him when it was all done. But I'd shown my hand, so there was nothing more to do. "He's not alive, though."

Matt stepped in right behind me. "You know, Burton. I could take Tallie down to at least see if the old box is still there. Maybe ask about if anyone has come in to retrieve it, do some investigative work. And if we had the key, and it happens that she does have access to the box, then there's nothing illegal about that."

I beamed at my cousin, then turned to beam at Burton. The wattage went down a little when I saw his scowl. He wasn't going to go for this. I'd have to take my cat home and sit like a good girl while Burton mucked his way through forty-million feet of red tape. It could have been so simple.

Max had been quiet through most of the proceedings. Whether because he wanted to stay out of the chief of police's way, or had nothing to offer, I didn't know, but he stepped forward now. "Burton, there's a possibility we could shut this whole thing down now. Don't get all that tape involved if you don't have to. If Tallie can't open the box, then we'll regroup and find the box another way. But don't give it up until we know for certain she can't get in."

So now it was three against one. I could almost see Burton conceding, but then he stood up straight. "We're going to do this right," he said, and I couldn't contain my groan. "You didn't let me finish, girly. We're going to do this right in that we aren't going to involve ourselves at all."

The second groan was about to surface when he handed me the key. "We're both right. He wouldn't let you in that box if he was alive, but he's not, so I'm going to pretend I never saw that thing. You go to the bank and try to use it. If they won't let you, then you bring it right back to me as if you discovered it like everything else in this blasted case."

I could barely contain my glee. I only did because it would make him rethink his decision if I did a little jig right in the middle of the kitchen, not to mention that dancing was not one of my many talents.

Chapter 13

After I dropped Mr. Fleefers off and fed him, Max demanded to come with me. It didn't occur to me to refuse. I was in deeper than I had ever been and there were bad guys around. I welcomed his help.

I'd take a little time and space from him later to process that kiss. I hadn't been kissed in years, literally. Perhaps it was the novelty of it all, but I doubted it. I was pretty confident Max knew how to use his lips to devastation, and he'd chosen me to devastate. I looked over at him in the passenger seat of the Lexus to find that he was looking at me as if he wanted to eat me up. Or at least I thought that might be what the curve of his mouth and the hunger in his eyes meant. I'd never been the recipient of a look like that, but I'd seen it on TV.

Fortunately, at that moment, we arrived at the bank, and I could yet again think about the money, instead of all the humming going on throughout my body.

Sitting for a moment with my hands gripped tightly on the steering wheel, I let the anticipation rush through me. This might be the end. I was done with spying and stealing and trying to keep myself safe. I wanted my boring old life back. Maybe it would be a little less boring if Max decided to stick around, but at least I would be physically safe, even if he threatened the emotional drought I'd been in for years. To be honest, that might not be a bad thing for me.

Apparently, I waited too long, because Max had already exited the car and stood at my door, popping the handle, then standing in the V he'd made in the open door.

In this position, I was practically nose-to-crotch with him. It wasn't exactly a bad view. Mentally rolling my eyes at myself, I tried to get out of the car, but he refused to budge. I was not going to get in his space like that.

"Can you back up?"

"I want to get a few things straight first," he said, leaning an arm on the door and ducking down to come eye level with me. "I'm here to keep you safe and make sure this all goes smoothly. I want you safe, Tallie. I need you to be safe."

"I don't know what to do with that, Max, not right now. Let's find the money before we go making any declarations, okay?"

I forced myself up and out of the car, cramming my chest against his to move him out of the way. He still wasn't budging. He wrapped his arms around me and I sunk in just for a second. "Let's go get the deed done."

I strolled into the bank as if I belonged there.

The three goons who'd been at my father's place earlier were the first thing I saw. Darla's family was in the corner, loudly arguing with a teller about wanting access to Darla's bank account as her only living relatives. I mentally wished them good luck. Darren was the only holder of the money. They would have no access while he was still alive.

Approaching the one teller I didn't know in the bank, I quietly asked to be shown to safety-deposit box number 769. The woman, whose nametag said CANDY, did as she was asked after she took my identification and I showed her the key.

We went through the whole rigmarole of getting into the vault and then going down the aisles for the safety-deposit box. Whenever I was in here I always wondered what other people had in the boxes. You could have jewels, cash, documents of adoptions, any number of things that could change a person's life, and no one would ever know.

Finally Candy showed us to the box, we did the key insertion, and then she brought out the box and handed it over to me. It felt light as a feather. That couldn't be good.

"I'll be at the counter if you need anything," Candy said as she edged away.

What the hell was in here and why was she edging away like a demented clown might pop out?

But that wasn't a question easily answered. I'd just have to open it up and see. I wanted this to end now.

Craning open the box, I nearly screamed. Not because there was a severed head or even a spider, but because there was a complete and total absence of anything. Whatever had been in there was long gone. Not a single thing remained.

Max leaned over my shoulder. "Damn," he said quietly when I wanted to scream the whole bank down.

"Candy, has anyone else come in looking for this box?" I turned to the woman who was trying to obviously not pay attention to us when it was plain she was taking in every word.

She hesitated, gnawing on her perfectly manicured thumbnail.

"Come on, Candy. I really need to know. My ex-husband told me there would be something in here I needed to find. We're trying to reconcile, and now that I'm here, there's nothing at all." It was a lie, but if it helped me get the info I needed, then I didn't give a care.

"Your ex-husband?" She moved closer to us, hovering just out of reach.

"Yes, my ex-husband. He wants to reconcile. He told me that if I came here for this box there would be something to give me a clue to my next adventure in bringing our love back." Now I was laying it on thick enough to almost gag myself, but Candy seemed to be eating it up.

"That's so sweet. And it makes more sense than the reason the guy this morning gave. He said he was here to pick something up out of the box, had a slip of paper with all the info and a signed note from the owner allowing the removal of the contents. He was not very happy when we told him his paper was not enough to get him into the box legally. The owner would have to be here for that."

"There was a man here for this?" I asked.

Max and I looked at each other. Maybe Waldo had come and picked the contents up earlier before he was killed. That meant whatever was here was probably back in the house.

"Yeah, this guy came in, dressed to the nines with a letter of instruction. We don't do that kind of thing. It's illegal. The branch manager said it looked all official-like, but if Mr. Phillips wanted the contents released then he'd have to come down himself to do it. The guy was beyond angry, but then got himself under control and said he'd bring the owner back here."

Fat chance he, whoever he was, could do that now since the owner was dead.

I nearly vibrated to get out of there and go see if Burton would let me truly ransack the house.

Max had other ideas. "Could you describe the guy, Candy?"

"Well . . ."

"Please, it would be a big help. I'm trying to help my sister here get back together with her husband." I could hear him almost choke on the last word and kept a snicker to myself. "Maybe the guy was the clue, sis. Maybe you were supposed to come for the box, find out the guy had left here empty, and that would clue you in to something."

I nodded my head, because, really, what else

could I do? "Is there anything you remember about him? Hair color, eye color?"

"Brown and brown."

That could describe over a third of the population around here.

"Anything else specific? Something to identify someone with?" Max added.

"Well," Candy cracked the knuckles on one hand. "He did have these expensive-looking black and white shoes."

I almost fainted where I stood. My phantom shoe guy was back again. We needed to find him and figure out how he was involved and who the hell he was. Someone was one step ahead of me at all times, and I wanted to know why. And what the hell this game was that I seemed to be involved in, but hadn't gotten a formal invitation for.

After that, it was just a matter of getting Max out the door and catching my breath.

"This black-and-white shoe bastard has to go." I stalked back and forth along the sidewalk in front of the bank with my arms crossed at my chest.

"Who is it?" Max leaned against the hood of the car, not interfering with my movements, but watching me like someone would a tennis match.

"The day before Darla died, she was fighting with some guy in her office when I went to go get my check from her. I fell onto the carpet." I wasn't going to explain that one despite his grin. "And all I saw were black and white shoes moving past my head, almost stepping on me, if you must know, as the man strolled out. Then Darla dismissed me by putting my check on the floor next to my face before telling me to see myself out."

"So you have no idea who he is?"

"No, I don't even know if his hair really is brown, or his eyes, but this is the first description I've been given. And the only other person I know who saw him is dead."

Max crossed his arms too, and looked like one of those centerfolds on the hood of some fancy old car. I had to get that image out of my head if we were going to be able to get anything else done today.

"So, this guy had on the shoes and has brown hair and eyes. That's not going to help a lot unless he still has the shoes on when we see him again."

I groaned, "I know and this sucks. But who is he? If I could hear his voice again, I'd know him And he smelled of some cologne that tickled my brain, but not my nostrils." I grabbed the ends of my hair, trying to rack my brain for what the smell could be.

"Describe it to me."

"I don't know. I'm not good with smells. It was like something from summer."

"Cut grass?"

"No. Not sun tanning lotion, either. Something harsher."

"Wood burning?"

"No, that's going the wrong way." I kept stalking around and was starting to get noticed. I waved to a few people who hurried along.

"Harsh, as in chemical smelling?" Max asked, continuing to watch me like a hawk.

"Yes, something chemically, like . . . I don't know, but not pesticides."

"Chlorine?"

I stopped in my tracks. "Chlorine." The smell of the pool mixed with Darla's blood rose in my nose. I nearly gagged, but suddenly my mind was clear. The pool boy at Darla's, Aaron, had brown hair and brown eyes. He'd asked me out a few times, but I had not been interested. He had been nice enough, even waving to me that one day as I left Darren's, but looks could be deceiving. Had I waved to a killer that day? I got shivers just thinking about it.

"Isn't there a pool boy you and Gina were talking about that one day?"

"Yes, yes there was."

"Do you think that's our guy?" His voice had gotten deeper as he'd straightened from the hood of the car.

"It might be."

"Because I have to tell you: I saw someone walking down the street who fits that description right before I entered Waldo's house and found you. I didn't notice his shoes, but a guy with brown hair walked by Waldo's house as I was coming up to the front door. What if he was still in the house when you entered and snuck out, leaving the door unlocked?"

It was a convenient way for Max to not be involved, but I had a feeling that was far more plausible, especially since I knew in my heart there was no way Max had been the killer. "I guess that's possible."

"Did you hear anyone leave?"

There had been a moment when I'd thought I'd heard something, but then I also had been screaming that I'd found my ex dead, and there was not a good way to tell if I'd actually heard something. However, if the killer had been in the house and Max had seen someone on the street, maybe he'd be able to give a better description.

"Tell me what he looked like."

"Kind of wavy hair, scruff on the face, tall, a walk that was a little more macho than most."

"Aaron." Shit, now we knew who it could be, but how to go about proving it was a whole different matter.

Our plan wasn't brilliant. I, however, only needed it to be effective. I started at the Bean There, Done That with Mama Shirley after calling Burton to let him know there had been nothing to find in the safety-deposit box. I did mention seeing the shoes again, even though I didn't see the guy, but hung up on Burton before he could tell me to stay out of it again. Time was of the essence and I was going to solve this on my own. I wanted my name cleared and I did not want to wait for a full-blown investigation to do that. Aaron had already shown that he was perfectly willing to kill for what he wanted. There was no guarantee that I wouldn't be next.

"Hi!" I said, taking a seat at the counter after making sure there was a pretty big crowd around. "Can I get a latte and can you let Gina know I'm here? I need to talk to her."

"I heard about the scumbag and, while I'm sorry someone else is dead in our little town, I can't be too sad it was him. He was taking up the air." Shirley patted my hand. "You okay?"

"I am. It shocked and saddened me to see another life cut short. He wasn't my favorite person by any means, but he was still a person and didn't deserve that."

"Well, you keep your chin up."

"Will do."

"Your dad going to take care of him?" Shirley asked as she wiped down the counter.

"Um, I would think so." Holy hell, that might need supervision, especially if this tax thing actually happened now. Waldo might end up being buried facedown with his bare ass in the air and a clown wig to cover his bald spot.

"Well, I hope he keeps the quality of his work, or hands him off to somewhere else. No need to ruin years of reputation by letting that sleaze in."

"I'll make sure I tell him that. Can you please go get Gina? I really need to talk to her soon."

"Make sure you do. I'll get her for you." Shirley squinted at me, but went to do as I'd asked. I had a feeling I'd get a talking-to later, but at this point it would all be worth it if we could flush out Aaron.

Max was doing a background check on the pool boy as I set our plan into motion. He'd report in as soon as he found some kind of connection, if there was one. This way, we didn't have to lose face with the police department if I was totally and completely wrong in my assumptions. Wasn't Burton going to be pissed if I figured it all out myself? Well, he'd just have to deal. Or maybe I'd study to be an investigator and really get out of cleaning rich people's houses. Too much went on there that I didn't need anyway.

Gina came out of the back and swooped in. "What's up? Did you find it?"

She'd kept her voice down, but that didn't play into what I needed. I hadn't had time to explain the plan to her, so I'd just have to hope she'd follow my lead.

"Make that latte a double, Shirley! I have good news." I beamed at Gina and winked.

Gina looked baffled for a moment, but communicated with her eyes that she'd play along as long as she got the full story later. I nodded.

"And what are we celebrating?" Gina said, a little too loud. I wanted people talking, not clapping after the performance.

I gestured for her to cut down the noise just a little. "I won't be cleaning houses anymore. I think I might actually be able to open that teahouse next door in a few months."

That caught Gina off-guard, but she rallied with very little pause. "Wow, that's awesome, Tallie. Did your dad give you a raise?"

I laughed, hoping it sounded natural. "No, it turns out when we got divorced, Waldo never changed his will, so I'm the sole beneficiary of everything he owns. Remember when we were talking about the money that seemed to be missing?" I nudged Gina's hand and gave a slow nod.

"Of course I do. You're going to use it to open up next door?"

"I sure am. I found it all in a safe in the wall at the house. Apparently it's all mine. Can you believe it?"

"I can't."

There was a scurry of chairs scraping back

behind me. I made a point not to turn around as some of the most virulent gossips went forth to spread the word that I was a rich woman again.

Shirley came back with the latte with a lid on it. "Better go tell the same story at the diner if you want it spread everywhere," she said with a wink.

"Bless you. Can you do a little phone-tree work too? I want this over and I want it over soon. You know everyone who is everyone."

"Did you think you even needed to ask? I already sent out a text blast to all my friends and hit them all at the same time. The story will be all over the place within an hour."

Which gave me sixty minutes to get back to the apartment and see what Max had found out, and how we might be able to get Aaron to confess to the cops. I'd have to make phone calls later in the day to assure my cleaning clients I really wasn't going to quit on them, or I'd be out more than just a job.

I didn't know what the rules were on the tax thing now that Waldo was dead, but it would have to be saved for another day. I wasn't banking on Waldo not having actually changed his will. If he was smart, I was pretty sure that was what he would have done the day after I left, but it was as good a story as any. Hopefully, it would flush out Aaron if he, indeed, had been the one at the bank trying to get into the safety-deposit box.

Now I'd just have to wait and see. In the meantime, I had an appointment I couldn't put off and perhaps another avenue for my story to make the rounds and hit as many people as possible, including Katie.

Because I wasn't letting that woman off the hook just yet. I had a feeling Gina's cousin was far more involved in this than I had previously thought. Time would tell. If I had enough left . . .

The Cuttery was hopping when I went in under the pretense of getting my bangs trimmed. I paused a moment at the threshold, knowing that I had to bring Katie down. Gina had seemed okay with it, and I couldn't let who she was related to keep me from seeking justice.

I hadn't been to the salon in quite some time. After my fall from grace I just couldn't afford it, but before that I'd come here at least weekly when I'd been Mrs. Phillips III.

Max was paying for this little jaunt, however, and had given me cash to use for the fringe cut and brow wax. It felt good to sit in the comfortable chair and be pampered. Lately I had just gone into whichever walk-in haircutting place was closest to my last job to get a quick trim, but this place was an experience.

"Tallulah, how wonderful to see you again." Mimi Granger was in her mid-fifties and had always been a fixture at the Cuttery. She was the owner and had taken the enterprise from a one-bowl setup in her garage to what amounted to a spa for the rich and well-heeled.

I had made a point to dress to the nines before I came. I'd run back to the apartment to do a quick change after digging into a box I still had in my apartment to find some of my old clothes, those I hadn't consigned as soon as I'd left Waldo.

I had to play up the fact that I was about to be rich again, and would be able to afford all the luxuries I'd had to cut out after the divorce. Not that I'd missed many of them, but this one I had definitely missed.

"Mimi." We air-kissed and she stood back with her hands locked on my wrist.

"The hair needs a complete overhaul and your hands, my darling, we must set you up with a paraffin wax immediately." She turned the hands in question over and tsked.

"I know, I know. One of the hazards of the jobs I've had to do to keep afloat until this windfall." I put one of my hands over my mouth and giggled like a stupid idiot girl, the one who I used to be, and made eye contact with the only woman who was a bigger gossip than Shirley. "Sorry, that's inappropriate when Walden just died." I made sure to use his correct name because Mimi would be giving a report to everyone who was anyone. It had to sound like I was as vapid as ever.

"Oh, darling, we all grieve in our individual ways. Nothing is inappropriate when an ex dies."

"Thank you, Mimi. And while I'd love to do a manicure, I have a few other things to do today before a dinner date. Can we trim my bangs and wax my eyebrows now? I'll come back another day for the rest."

"Of course, you're always more than welcome."

Yeah, now that I supposedly had money again. "Wonderful. Who do you have me set up with?" I listened with half an ear for the answer. I'd just caught sight of Katie being removed from the washing bowl and led to a chair in an alcove I knew held two chairs and would be far more private than being out in the middle of the floor.

"I have Penelope."

Yes! I wanted to jump for joy. Penelope had always had the chair in the back, right around the blind corner from where Katie was sitting, currently having foils put in her hair.

"I'm sure she'll do a tremendous job as she always has. Shall I sit and wait for her?"

"Absolutely not. I'll wash you out myself and then take you back to her. She should be ready by then."

"Great!"

And with that I was treated to a five-minute hair wash that felt like heaven and left my scalp tingling in a super-pleasant way. Mimi even waxed my eyebrows before sitting me in the chair around the corner from Katie. Katie, who I could hear, but couldn't see. And the "couldn't see" part was awesome because it meant Katie was blind to my presence. Hopefully, she thought of her hairdresser as her mother-confessor, the keeper of all her secrets, and would speak loud enough to be heard near and far. Maybe not too far, just around the corner to my chair.

Penelope came up behind me and I was quick to tell her about wanting the bangs trimmed so I could get on to listening as intently as possible. I had a short amount of time to get back to the apartment and see what Max had come up with in case this didn't work.

Penelope stepped away to go get a new set of shears, apparently thinking the ones she had weren't sharp enough for the forest that was my bangs. I sat forward with my drape nearly touching the floor and my ear cocked to the right.

"And that bitch, Tallie, walked in," Katie was saying. "You remember her; used to think she was all high and mighty and then didn't even have the brains to make sure she got half of everything Walden had. Well, I wasn't so stupid, I'll tell you that. He might be dead and I'm sad because my gravy train is gone, but it's not the end of the gravy. I've still got quite a bit coming to me."

Penelope returned and I sat back in the chair, still listening.

"You should have seen the look on her face when she caught us together. She was so jealous."

That almost made me jump out of my chair to throttle the woman. Penelope cursed as her scissors slid up instead of straight across.

"Please sit back or you're going to be completely hairless up front."

"Right, sorry," I said quietly. I did not want Katie to know I was here and make her stop talking.

Katie had been talking about some kind of ring, but I missed that part.

The hairdresser chimed in. "Did he give you the ring before he died? That would give weight to your claim."

"No," Katie grumbled. "But I have a plan to get it before they shut down the house. I had a necklace we were going to turn into a ring. Or at least I was going to have a ring made, then show it to him. But then he was gone." She sighed. "It doesn't matter. I'm sure he had one for me. He told me he did, and I know right where he would have hidden it. Once I get it on my finger, no one will be able to say he hadn't intended to marry me. Which should give me leverage if anyone tries to go against me."

I asked to use the restroom and, though Penelope sighed, she waved me toward the bathroom over to the left. I had my phone in my hand before I even fully closed the door and was calling Max before I locked myself in.

"You have to go to the police and let them know Katie is planning on breaking into Waldo's and taking something. I think it's a ring. And she might have a really expensive necklace that belonged to me." Was that what Waldo thought I had taken? If it was one of his mother's necklaces, it was worth a shit ton of money. He would have been ballistic to get it back.

"Jealous?"

"Don't start that with me, again. You know I'm not. But this whole ruse isn't going to work if she gets some court to believe he had intended to marry her. I don't know if he changed his will, but we can't expect anyone to believe he left me his money if she's wearing his ring."

"Fine. I hope you're coming back soon. I've found out some info that you're going to want."

"I want it now, but I don't have time. Hold on to it. I should be home in about thirty minutes."

True to my word, I was cut and ready to leave twenty-nine minutes later. Katie had gone under the dryer to have her foils set, so there was no more talk about me being a bitch, or how Waldo had intended to marry her. Somehow, I had a hard time believing that was true. Although, from what Katie had said, she was just going to take a different piece of jewelry from Waldo's place, stick it on her finger, and make up some romantic dream about the way he had proposed to her.

I ran up the two flights of stairs to find Max right where I had left him. He swiveled in his chair, revealing a batch of snickerdoodles at his elbow and Mr. Fleefers in his lap.

"Really? My two favorite things and you have to steal them?"

"Hey, now. Your mom brought me the cookies without my even asking, and the cat jumped up here about ten minutes ago. I think he's still overwrought about the kidnapping. He's been eating and using the cat pan almost constantly since you left."

"Aw, poor kitty." I bent down to rub a hand down his back and came dangerously close to forbidden territory. I was eye level with Max now too, who leaned forward and stole a kiss that made me want to sit, somewhere, anywhere. Maybe shoo Mr. Fleefers off and cozy up in Max's lap myself.

I straightened before I could do something inherently stupid. "So what is this info I need to know?"

"Well, first I found definite proof that Marla and Darla are the same person." He turned to the laptop he'd set up at the kitchen table and hit a few keys. A yearbook picture of a definitely less stylish Darla came up, but it was assuredly her.

"Why couldn't I find it before? I tried everything I could."

"You don't have hacker friends who can get

behind firewalls that are so tight I wouldn't even know where to start. That's why I called my guy in D.C."

"Wow, look at those bangs. And that nose!" Yeah, those men who had confronted Darren earlier were definitely her brothers, and she had absolutely gotten a nose job at some point.

"And it seems Marla left town quite suddenly when she was brought up on charges for grand theft auto."

"They didn't chase her down?"

"They didn't have to, because someone else took the fall for her, or at least that's the way I read the report and the testimony."

"What?"

"Yeah."

"Are you kidding me?"

"Nope. Marla was caught almost red-handed with a car that most definitely was not hers. They had all the evidence, but then a boy named Arlin Freedman stepped forward and told the cops he was the one who stole it, then let Marla borrow it to impress her. He had all the details about when and where and how. Valiantly, he told them they needed to arrest him and leave her alone. They didn't have any evidence he didn't have an answer for."

"So do you think Arlin is Aaron?"

He tapped a few more keys. A younger version of the pool boy popped up, but it was definitely the pool boy.

"Should we just go out and get him at Darren's?" I asked as I walked three steps closer, almost landing myself in his lap as I kept looking at the picture.

In this picture he also had on short shorts. Had the man not learned?

"No, we still don't have evidence, but maybe we now have a name to give Burton to look more closely at. Evidence, proof—to take that will make him move fast if he's smart."

"That is excellent!" The relief was huge as the weight of who the hell was doing all this slid off my shoulders. We still needed to know why, though I had a feeling it had something to do with the money that was hidden. At least we knew who to watch out for. Now all I needed was to find out where the actual money was. I didn't have any leads on that and Max hadn't had any new thoughts either, but it was enough for today. If it was the pool boy, I had a feeling Burton was going to catch him. My plan to flush out the murderer had not been fully formed in the first place. I doubted Aaron/Arlin would hear from any of my gossips, being that he was further out of the loop than me.

Now I just had to wait to see what happened next. Burton should be calling soon because I'd left him a message about there being nothing in the safety-deposit box. I needed to hand the key and the folder back over to him. And now I could also give him the person I thought had started this whole thing.

In the meantime, I had a man in my apartment who kissed like electric. What the hell was I going to do about that?

I gave him a closer look, taking in his dark hair and the way it brushed over his collar. Taking in the way his dimple showed directly outside the left corner of his mouth, and the way his long fingers stroked the keyboard of his laptop. Could I? Should I? Had I remembered to shave my legs?

"Hey, why don't you go grab some dinner from Gina and we can watch a movie or something tonight before you have to head back to wherever you're staying?" I would have just enough time to shave my legs and see if I still had anything in my cabinet that screamed *you can take me if you really want to.*

He looked up from the laptop and smiled, melting the rest of my legs into something resembling pudding. Fortunately, there was a chair right behind me for me to sit gracefully in without looking quite like that pudding.

"Sure. Write down what you want. I'll grab it and a couple of drinks. We deserve a celebration. I have a feeling we might already have the money close by; we just need to figure out where it is. If that guy had a note and the access, then Waldo couldn't have moved the money too much earlier, or the bank would have immediately alerted the man there was nothing in the box he wanted." He shut the lid on the laptop.

"True. And if Waldo had gone there earlier, before the guy arrived, then it would have seemed okay to have the man come in and expect to find something."

"Instead of *the man*, I think we should call him Aaron. I'm sure that's who it is."

"Guilty until proven innocent?"

"Nah, I just don't believe in this many coincidences." He gave me a look that I thought might have meant more than just Aaron was a coincidence, and that there could be more here than just some harmless flirting and kissing.

But I was trying not to read too much into it beyond the physical, so I shooed him out the door and got out the razor.

The door reopened as I was rummaging around in the bureau. Max put his hand over my mouth and bumped up against the back of me. Maybe I had sent out stronger signals than I had thought. Not a bad thing to have a take-charge guy, but this wasn't quite like him. It wasn't me either, since I'd never been into the control thing. We could talk about that once he removed his hand.

If I had been asked what kind of lover Max would be, I would have thought softer, a little more gentle, a little suaver, a little more sophisticated. However, I could probably stomach this if I looked into his eyes again, and saw their brilliance and the hunger there.

And then when I turned around, I realized why my nose seemed to have called up the smell of the pool again. Because it wasn't Max.

It was Aaron.

Chapter 14

My first instinct was to scream, but his other hand clamped around my neck, choking my breath out. Without a second's hesitation I brought my knee up as if my old band teacher was telling me to get those knees higher.

The blow landed with all the ferocity I felt in my body, in my soul, for all the crap he had put me through. For all the people he had hurt, and for all the underhanded, sneaky stuff he was doing. I might not have called Darla my best friend, but she had been a human who did not deserve to be knifed in the chest and stuffed in a closet. And I might not have loved Waldo anymore, but he hadn't deserved to be spread over the dining-room table like a stuffed turkey.

While Aaron was doubled over, I tried to karate chop him in the back of the neck As Seen On TV, but he went down before I could get the swift chop done. Instead, I booked it out the apartment before he could get back up.

He made a grab for my ankle and I kicked out

at him, heard his hand smack the end table. He deserved that too.

Scrabbling at the door to the apartment, I couldn't seem to get the damn thing opened. I looked to the left to make sure he was still on the ground and saw my closet door hanging open. Jesus, had he been in there the whole time Max and I had been talking about him and what he'd done for Marla/Darla? He was going to kill me, not just force the location of the money out of me, but actually kill me.

And what the hell was it with him and closets?

Finally, the latch unhooked and I ran down the first flight of stairs. He must not have been as disabled as I thought, because he was only about a flight of stairs behind me when I reached the first landing and closing in with his long stride, jumping down the stairs.

"You can't run," he said. "I got the rest and you're all that's left. You should have dated me. All those times I asked you and you thought you were too snooty for the pool boy when you were just the cleaning lady."

Really? I shuddered and refocused.

Good Lord. Where was I going to go? No one else was here, and who knew how long it would be before Max came back? Once Gina got talking, she could last all night. My parents were out for the evening for their anniversary and my brothers had houses across town. My cell phone was on the nightstand upstairs.

Damn!

All these thought kept running through my

heard as I ran down the stairs. How many of these freaking things were there?

I rounded the corner on the first landing and tried to think the opposite of the heroines in those stupid horror movies. I knew that all exits had several locks on them and I didn't have the time to unlock them all and escape before Aaron caught up with me. I'd just have to find a safe place in the funeral home. I kept going down the next set of steps and tried to think of what was below.

Dead people. Dead people were below. Darla was below. Maybe seeing the woman he'd taken a fall for would be enough to make him pause. It would leave me time to get out the basement door. Who knew if it would work, but it would be better than being stuck on the first floor. The front door had too many complicated latches to get out and the back door had four separate locks. Damn my dad and his complete security. Too bad it hadn't worked to keep this psycho out.

I started jumping down the stairs too, and prayed I wouldn't break my leg in the process. We had an elevator to move the corpses down on their trolleys, but there was no way I could wait for that to arrive.

He yelled and it shot down my spine. He was not pleased. Too bad. I was not going to give up now and lay down like some shrinking violet.

"Don't make this harder than it has to be," he taunted, sounding much too close.

Yeah, right. I planned on making it damn near impossible, thank you very much.

Flying down the stairs, I dashed through the swinging doors into my father's domain. Formaldehyde was the prevailing scent down here. The shelves were lined with rows and rows of bandages and sutures and makeup and combs and superglue. I shot past it all, but stumbled on a wheel of the gurney where Darla was laid out.

With a sickening feeling, I watched her body start to roll off the table. I shot out a hand to keep her from doing a face-plant on the floor and threw up a little in my mouth. I did not like touching the dead, especially if they weren't done and ready to go in the casket.

Aaron whished through the swinging door and was mere steps behind me. Shit!

Picking myself up off the floor, I ran into the back room, where I had some hope of hiding out while I circled back to the rear door.

As I hoped, he stopped for a moment at Darla's body and seemed to turn a little green. Well, at least if he didn't have a conscience about killing, he at least had a weak stomach when he saw the aftermath.

I bolted into the next room. Immediately, he was there too. How did he move so fast?

I had one chance. On its prize stand was a coffin from the 1800s. It was my very last hope at this point of getting away from him.

I jerked the latches out of place on the bottom before jumping in. I waited to hear him lumber over to the coffin. When he did, I released the latch to open the bottom from the inside the way they used to for pauper burials, then sealed the doors back together. Springing out from under the coffin, I flipped the coffin lid open and finally got the chance to try out my real karate chop. I delivered the blow to the back of his neck as hard as I could. He fell, face-first, into the coffin and I rolled him in the rest of the way.

I locked the latches on the side, double-checked the lock on the bottom, and then went to the phone on the wall in the next room. There was no way he was leaving that thing and quite honestly, if he died from lack of oxygen, I was not going to cry.

Burton was both impressed and exasperated. The crime of the decade and I'd figured it out for him. But at least it was figured out now and we could go on with our lives. He'd tried yelling at me at first, but I simply pointed to the coffin again and he rubbed his hand down his face and sighed.

That part was at least done. Now, there was just the issue of the money. If only I knew where Waldo had hidden it, the bastard. Burton had let me back into Waldo's house to search for it after they'd gone over the place with a fine-tooth comb, but it was a no-go.

I had, however, gotten a call from our old attorney. It turned out Waldo really had been too lazy to change the will. To Katie's absolute screaming fit, she got not a single penny. Of course, she'd been picked up when she'd tried to break into Waldo's house to get the elusive ring he'd promised her and had spent the night in jail, wailing about how unfair it was that I was out

walking around when I was demon spawn. That
had me yawning like I was back at one of her
horrible high school monologues. Burton had
known what he was doing and was able to pin her
with changing the original meet time behind
the Bean on the threat from five by changing the
number into an eight. Turns out, Darla had put
five on the note, but Waldo had never shown up
because Katie had changed it to an eight, then
stun-gunned Waldo for coming to meet Darla in
the first place. She really had stuck that tape on
her own mouth. So the lip wax was all her own
fault. Served her right. It also served her right
that I'd been able to figure out that the things
Waldo thought I stole was a necklace of his
mother's worth almost a million dollars. I gave the
info to Burton as soon as I'd determined which
one it was and they searched Katie's house for it
after they'd arrested her for the breaking and
entering. She was going to be doing some serious
time, since as the beneficiary of the estate, I pressed
charges on Waldo's behalf.

Aaron wasn't too pleased, either. Besides being
in jail, he had none of the money Darla had promised. Apparently, Waldo had spilled his money
secret to Darla on one drunken afternoon. She,
in turn, wanted a piece and had promised Aaron
money when he'd come to find her after being
let out of jail. When she couldn't produce the
money, or wheedle it out of Waldo, Aaron had
killer her in a rage and ripped her pearl necklace
off her throat, thinking he could sell it. Waldo's
murder was more deliberate when he wouldn't talk
and give up his secrets. As for that unidentifiable

accent, apparently when he forgot himself he was from the Deep South and his words were all hick. I wouldn't have believed it if I hadn't heard it for myself from the other side of the one-way mirror in the station.

Someone knocked on my door and I primped my hair just a bit in case it was Max. He was leaving today. There wasn't anything more he could really do, and his time to find the money and help me had run out. But he'd promised to stop by to say good-bye. He made good on his promises.

I was surprised when I pulled open the door and there stood Letty.

"Hey, Tallie. Your mom sent me up. I hope that's okay."

Letty had bags on top of the carry-on bags under her eyes. Her shoulders were slumped in a way they hadn't been the other day when she'd refused to even look me in the eye.

"What's up?"

"Are you really going to give up all your cleaning jobs?"

Well, that wasn't exactly what I had thought was going to come out of her mouth. "Um, probably." As soon as I found that money.

"If you do, could you recommend me to them?" She rushed on before I could say anything. "I will totally understand if you don't want to, but I'm really going to need something more, and I just thought—if you don't mind—I could take them over. Or even—if you want me to—I could work under you, clean some of the houses and give you a percentage. I could do that too."

The desperation in her voice was almost more

than I could stand. Normally, Letty had always been standoffish. I had thought she had the world at her feet. What had happened? "Is Darren firing you?"

Her shoulders shook and she held herself tight like she was going to break apart at any moment. "He's thinking about it. And I just found out my mom has cancer, so I have to go home to live with her. He wasn't willing to let me just be a day maid. I'm going to have to help with the bills for my mom. I would really appreciate it if you'd at least think about it." She turned to leave and I put a hand on her shoulder.

"Are you going to be okay?"

"I'm not sure, but I'm going to have to be. Darren doesn't think he wants to let me go, because he's so used to me being around I'm like that automatic vacuum cleaner—useful, quiet, and a tool."

"The help." I knew all about that feeling from both sides. "Did he ever say anything in front of you that he shouldn't have?"

"I'm sure he said a lot of stuff he shouldn't have, and that's the other reason he doesn't want to let me go. He doesn't want his secrets out there. I could tell you all about Darla being Marla, and how that happened, and about a secret closet she has."

"I know about the Darla and Marla and the secret closet. What I want to know is if you know anything about the pool boy that could help Burton."

"Yes. I was going to go there next."

"Let me think about what I can give up. Call me tomorrow. I'm sorry you're going through this. I wasn't sure what I had done to make you stop talking to me, but I guess it was nothing to do with me. Sorry for not seeing the signs." I dropped my hand from Letty's shoulder

"You saw them, you just gave me space, and I appreciate that too. I'll talk to you tomorrow. I promise I'll make you proud. I needed to get out of that house, anyway. There was too much discord in it. Now that Darren is alone, I really don't want another Darla telling me I'm a piece of shit every day and then having to make her toast without spitting in it."

She was letting me off the hook too easily, but I let her. I laughed for the first time in twenty-four hours. I showed Letty to the door with the promise to talk to her tomorrow. Now, if only I could find that damn money!

Mr. Fleefers tossed something around on the floor with abandon. He liked pieces of paper balled up so he could bat them around and this was just that.

Or at least I thought it was, until I got a good look at what kind of paper it was, and saw the crumpled face of Benjamin Franklin.

My heart stopped as I considered the fact that I had no cash money in the house. I made a point of not keeping it around with all the people coming in and out downstairs. So if I didn't have money in the house, then where had the cat . . .

I was on the phone to Max in the next breath. "Get over here right now. We're going on a treasure hunt."

* * *

"Where does he normally hang out?" Max was crawling around my floor with a flashlight. I was not going to complain about the view from up here.

"Everywhere, anywhere. The only place you'll never find him is the body room in the basement." My dad had given me a stern talking-to about using his prize antique coffin to trap the bad guy. Aaron had made a ton of claw marks on the underside of the lid before Burton had made it down to handcuff him. But I'd told dear old dad it was more authentic now, as if someone had been trapped and the little bell and cord they used to put in with the deceased hadn't worked.

He hadn't found that as amusing as I had hoped he would, but he had puffed out his chest and walked off with only grumbling instead of another lecture. I considered that a score.

"And you don't know where he'd been when you were talking with Letty?" His butt moved around some more. It was all I could do not to at least reach down and touch it. I could pretend I had accidentally brushed against him. Couldn't I?

He turned his head in my direction. "Are you thinking, or are you ogling?"

I cleared my throat. "Thinking, of course." About his butt, but that was still thinking.

"Fine, so you have no idea where he was?"

"Well, he came in from the closet, so unless he's had the money for a while, he might have found something back there." But where and what?

I had no idea and I really didn't want to go into the closet one more time. In fact, I was thinking about some kind of hanging tree for my hangable stuff and only using a bureau from now on. Seriously. I was done with closets.

Max's arms flexed when he hoisted himself off the floor. I didn't hesitate in taking in the view. He would be gone this afternoon. The interlude and kissing would be over. He lived in Washington, D.C., working for the government in an important job, and I wasn't willing to go anywhere. Things had to be taken care of here, and while the tax bill wasn't as whopping as I had originally thought it was going to be, it was still big and would drain all of what Waldo had unexpectedly left me, as well as leaving me with a payment plan that would conceivably last until my retirement at eighty-five. The embezzlement was still an issue for the people he'd taken money from, but I would not be held liable for something I knew nothing about.

Max pointed to the double doors on the far wall. "Walk-in closet?"

"Uh, no, Murphy bed, remember?" And wouldn't it be nice to pull it down right now and stretch out? I had, after all, shaved my legs when I would be wearing pants for the fall and winter months to come. They should be seen by someone besides Mr. Fleefers when he prowled the edge of my bathtub.

A wicked little smile curved Max's mouth, and I wanted to lick it. Down, girl!

"It's . . . um . . . the next door."

Max opened the door and shone the light on the floor and around the side of the walls. Then he used his flashlight to separate my black pencil skirts from my jewel-toned shirts. I had a moment where I was embarrassed by the sheer amount of shoes lining the left side, but it couldn't be helped and it didn't matter. He would be leaving.

He stepped into the closet and used his hand to keep the clothes separated. I might never again wash the peach shirt.

"Did you know you have a door back here?" he asked, his voice muffled by the clothes.

I almost smacked myself in the head. I had forgotten all about that door. It almost never even registered anymore. Most times, I opened the closet, grabbed the closest skirt and shirt, then closed the door again. "Where does it go?"

"You don't know?"

I had a vague recollection of being up here and playing with the boys long ago, but not any real remembrance of where it led, or what was on the other side, at all. Trying to lay out the top floor of the house in my mind, I couldn't imagine what was beyond the door. The attic took up the other side of the house.

"I don't. The attic, I think, but I don't know which part."

"Well, let's find out, then."

The door opened on soundless hinges and swung out to a small room with a window. It was the garret at the front of the building, one of the features that made the building unique. Long ago, when I was a small girl, I'd thought of being a painter and suffering for my art up in that garret, but hadn't given it a thought since.

"Do you see anything in there?" The anticipation was killing me.

He took another moment to sweep the light around and then I heard a shooshing of something across the floor.

"Do you want to open it?"

It was a huge carry-on case, one of those bags that looked like something a trendy man would wear over his shoulder as he swiftly walked to get on a plane to jet off to a business meeting. And I'd bought it for Waldo four years ago. My heart didn't stop this time—it almost did a hula in my chest.

"Oh, my."

"That's right. Oh, yours."

I dropped to my knees and unzipped it so fast it could have been Max's fly. But instead, bunches of money, enough to lie down and roll around in, spilled out of the case. Mr. Fleefers chose that moment to crawl through a hole that probably led to the attic on the other side and attack one of the many bills. I crumpled it and let him have it.

Maybe I'd be opening that store next to Gina after all.

Before I had a chance to cry, Max lifted me to my feet by my elbows. "We did it."

"Oh holy wow, we did!"

"And I'm sure with this much cash we'll be able to better settle on an offer to pay the taxes all at once. They want it off the books as badly as you do."

"Oh." Before I could start to bawl like a baby, he kissed me square on the mouth, making my toes curl.

I enjoyed the time in his arms, now that I was out of danger and could not only pay the taxes, but also try to give at least a percentage back to those who Waldo had stolen from.

Then all thoughts of money and restitution flew out of my head when Max coaxed my mouth open and delved in deeper.

When we came up for air some time later, my hands were shaking. Was that what kissing was supposed to be like? What it was supposed to do? Jesus, I'd been doing that wrong for years.

"Will I see you again?" I asked as I toyed with the ends of his hair.

"Oh, I have a feeling you're going to be seeing more of me than even you can imagine."

"I don't know. I have a pretty good imagination when it comes to this kind of stuff."

"We'll have to put it to use." He pulled me into his lap. "For the moment, though, we should call my office and Burton and let them know it's all wrapped up with a shiny bow. You were brave, Tallie."

"Thanks." I was pretty proud of myself, to be honest. I'd caught a killer, found the money, and saved the day. Not that I ever wanted to go through this being a suspect thing again, but at least I knew now that sometimes things were worth fighting for. I'd take that lesson with me when next I thought of doing the easy thing, instead of the things that were right for me.

I reached up for another kiss, which Max gave me in spades.

We were interrupted by a knock on the door right before the thing swung open and my mom walked in with a plate of cookies.

"Oh, look at you two! So cute! I love it!"

She'd just used up her quota of exclamation points for the day.

Gina came trucking in behind her, yammering on about how pissed she was that I'd left her out of all this when she could have been a big help.

Perhaps following Max at a later point might be something worth thinking about. D.C. wasn't so far away after all. I could always come back here to visit.

But then I'd miss my family, my friends, and my community, and I wasn't ready for that. With the taxes cleared up and the charges about to be dropped, I felt like I had a new lease on life.

Things were good and they'd stay that way.

Or so I hoped.

Keep an eye out
For Tallie's next adventure

GROUNDS FOR REMORSE

Coming soon from

Misty Simon
And
Kensington Books